# Spies on Safari

**A novel by**
**Oliver Dowson**

This is a work of fiction. All the names, characters, businesses, other organisations, events and incidents in this book are either the product of the author's imagination or used in a fictitious manner. Any resemblance to actual persons, living or dead, or actual events is purely coincidental.

Published by BKssss Publishing
https://bkssss.com
info@bkssss.com

ISBN: 978-1-7392988-1-4
eBook ISBN: 978-1-7392988-4-5

British Library Cataloguing in Publication Data

A catalogue record for this book is available from the British Library

# Contents

# Prologue

Gideon Caesar reclined in his chair and perused the business card he'd been proffered. "CASCADA Achievement Travel? Funny name for investigators." Something of an American drawl in his voice. The Asian-looking lady sitting in front of him replied in what she imagined to be a posh English accent.

"No, Mr Caesar. It's appropriate. We travel to places and achieve things. And a travel agency dedicated to business incentive travel is an excellent cover for our more discreet activities." She opened her bag and removed a tablet computer. "Let me show you our team." She clicked on 'play.'

"They don't look much like secret agents," observed Caesar. "More like hippies or university dropouts, if you ask me." The total opposite of the power-dresser sitting opposite him, though he kept that thought to himself.

"Surely you'd agree that's the whole point? The operation needs to be above suspicion. I've told you they work in espionage. If you don't think they look the part, nobody else is going to think that either, are they, Mr Caesar?" The woman fixed him with an accusing stare.

"You have a point. And call me Gideon, please." He returned his gaze to the screen. "What are they doing, anyway?"

"This is their reading group. They convene once a week to read a book together. And to receive new instructions."

"Hmmm. They're all spies?"

She bristled at the term. "The correct term is 'covert researchers.'"

"Whatever. They all work for you?"

"The two without beards aren't my operatives."

"There are three without beards!" Gideon chortled.

"The two men, of course."

Dealing with this customer was proving to be an exercise in stress management. How did men like Caesar get to be put in charge of multi-billion-dollar corporations, she wondered. Not only stupid and facetious, but with unkempt curly ginger hair? Dressed in jeans and a plaid shirt? In Mayfair? And more importantly, deficient in his personal hygiene. She suppressed an urge to delve into her handbag to retrieve the interdental brush she carried so she could remove what looked like a black seed trapped between his two upper front canines.

"Are you always this tetchy with your customers?"

"I am sorry if I give you that impression. I am just being serious. Professional. This is a serious subject, is it not?"

"True." Then, looking back at the screen, he said, "They appear too old to be whatever-you-call-them. Don't they need to be fit? I was thinking James Bond or Matthew Bourne, not geriatrics."

"They're younger and fitter than they seem. Long beards disguise age as well as faces."

"What about the woman? She's one of yours too?"

"Indeed she is. And before you ask, she is not merely a covert researcher. She was in the Olympics judo team. And she trained as a professional makeup artist. How is that for diversity?"

"Not the sort of training I would have expected in a — what do you call it, covert researcher?"

"Espionage requires a varied and comprehensive skill set."

"I'm sure, but I was thinking along military lines."

"Every one of my team has been professionally trained by a state service."

"Hmmm. If you say so. You seriously believe those guys can pull off our project?"

"Without any doubt. They are perfectly suited to it. It will be a pleasure doing business with you."

"Speaking of business. How much are we talking about here?"

"Three million up front, including expenses."

Caesar gulped. "That's ridiculous. Four people for a project you told me could be wrapped up in two weeks? These guys get paid more than football stars?"

"Plus another three million success fee." Seeing Gideon raising his eyebrows and opening his mouth to register another objection, the Asian woman continued. "We call it value pricing. You know that the result is worth a hundred times that to your company." Gideon said nothing and looked pensive, so the woman continued. "Paid to a numbered account in Grand Cayman. I will send you the details. I recommend you use one of your offshore companies to make the transfer."

"It's extortionate. Especially since we've never done business before and your team may fail in the mission. A hundred thousand up front and three million success fee if your team find the mine."

"That's not acceptable, and you know it. We will incur very substantial costs in setting up the project, and our team will be risking their lives, Mr Caesar. Two million up front then, and four million success fee."

"Totally unrealistic. Tell you what, my final offer, one million up front and three million success fee. Do we have a deal?"

"How certain are you that this mine exists, Gideon?"

"Ninety-nine percent."

"Very well. I will accept your offer."

"Well, I'll still have to consult colleagues before we can shake on it. I'll call you. On which point, what do I call you? Your office didn't tell me your name. And it's not on your card."

"You don't call me anything. Surely you expect a project like this to be handled with the utmost discretion? The number on the card is my direct, secure line."

"You must have a name, though?"

"For security, we never use our real names. In my business, I'm simply called Laoban."

"Laoban? What's that?"

"It's Mandarin. Laoban. It means 'the boss.'"

Gideon laughed. "I wish my staff would call me that. Anyway, you should be right at home then searching for Chinese miners."

"What makes you imagine I am Chinese?" Laoban adopted her fiercest stare.

"Sorry, no offence meant."

"Hmmm. I need your direct mobile number and private email address."

"I expect all communications to go through my office."

"Do all your staff know about this project, then? Do you have total trust in every single one of them? Are you sure none of them might be compromised by your competitors? By your alleged Chinese miners?"

Gideon reclined and sucked on his teeth. "Of course, I do trust them all. But, again, you have a point." He tore a sheet from a notebook on his desk and scrawled a number and email address on it. "For your eyes only." Then, as a realisation appeared to dawn, he grinned. "Hey, that was a great James Bond film. Guess your agents won't be in that league."

"We're not making a movie, Mr Caesar. I understood your requirement to be serious."

"Oh, it is, Madam Laoban, it is."

# Background Checks

Leaving Gideon's office, after first glancing up and down the street to make sure she wasn't being watched, Laoban walked the fifty metres to the hotel just around the corner that she had scouted out before the meeting. She approved of big five-star hotel lobbies. Not of the furnishings and fittings, mind. Faux Victorian in a new build skyscraper? What idiot dreamed that up? No, she liked the size, the space, the sense of calm that prevailed regardless of the dozens of people passing through every minute of the day. Like a luxury airport terminal with no planes. And without a fried chicken counter emitting noxious odours. Importantly, even if she didn't appear anonymous enough already, any passer-by who noticed her would see that she fitted right in, and simply dismiss her as just another guest. A business visitor from Asia? Probably. Always thousands of them in London, several hundred of them in this hotel alone. One could always find a quiet spot to efface oneself.

Settling into the furthest armchair in the bar area, she waved away the approaching waiter. Next, she delved inside her Hermes bag for her phone, unlocked it, and selected a number.

"Toshio."

"Yes, Laoban. You have something for me?"

"I'm texting you two email addresses and one cell phone number. On Telegram. The usual, as soon as you can. Please." The pragmatics of the English language irritated her. Having to say 'please' and 'thank you' all the time. She's the one paying; surely she shouldn't have to ask nicely? Neither necessary nor expected in her native language.

"Can I use Guangzhou to help? The guy in Belgrade took too long the last time I used him."

"Better this one isn't done in China. Offer your Belgrade guy double if he gets what we need in thirty minutes."

"OK. He can do the emails. I'll work on the phone number myself."

"Quick as you can. Send everything to the Project Coordinator as soon as you have it. She knows what to do."

Well, she would soon, once she'd talked to her. She placed her next call.

Latviana was curious. "I can't imagine that emails about mining are going to be very interesting. What should I keep an eye out for?"

"Anything that might affect the project or prevent our team from completing it. Oh, and anything that might put our people in danger, of course."

"As long as he pays, what do we care?"

"I've no doubt he will pay. But I'm not sure I trust him about the African mine. In fact, I'm sure I don't. We need this project to complete. There's a big success fee riding on it."

"Why would he pay us so much to send our assets to look for something that's not there?"

"Oh, I am sure there is something there. But maybe not what he is telling us. This appears to be a very unusual mining company."

"Why do you say that? How many other mining companies have you visited?"

"None. But surely one would expect to see posters, maps, something about mining? At least a mounted rock on the boss's desk? Their office is just a posh house in Mayfair. Red flock wallpaper. Minimal furnishings. Looks like something out of Vanity Fair. Gold-framed paintings on the wall. Hunting scenes, not mining maps."

"Smith's office was in Mayfair, too, but that was just to be able to put an impressive address on his cards. It was horrible. A grotty apartment on the fifth floor."

"I forgot you visited him there. I never saw it, of course."

"Lucky for you. I didn't see all of it. Smith wanted me to focus on the bed. I think there was a room with a desk and chair, but I'm not sure any proper work ever got done there."

"Anyway, Caesar's offices look the part of an expensive consultancy. The sort of offices we might aspire to. A management consultancy. A financial advisor. But they just don't seem right for a mining company."

"So, back to my first question. Emails. What should I be looking for?"

"Use your skill and judgement. That's what you're paid for."

Calls made, and making certain that nobody was watching her, Laoban went to the disabled toilet. Three minutes later, the door reopened, and a cleaner emerged clutching a garbage bag, the only resemblance to the woman who had entered being her vaguely Asian face. No observer would have made the connection in the instant it took before she floated out through a door marked 'Staff Only.'

# The Reading Group

"Am I in the right place? For the reading group, I mean?"

It didn't look like a reading group to Brian, not that he knew what a reading group was supposed to look like. Three men seated on fold-up plastic chairs around an old wooden table, five more chairs currently unoccupied. All three men wearing winter coats. Two cocooned in thick woolly scarves. One sporting an olive-green beret. All with hands folded on laps and heads bowed, contemplating the vinyl-tiled floor, an unattractive shade of blue, faded and scuffed. All three had beards. Different colours, one neatly trimmed, the others left to grow freely, but all beards. He wondered if that's what all people who join reading groups look like. Though this assembly looked more like a prayer meeting. He stroked his stubble. Maybe he should let it grow properly, then.

Long black beard, seated at the end of the table, raised his head.

"You are indeed. Will you be joining us?"

"Yes, if that's alright? I saw it advertised on the noticeboard at the entrance. I enjoy reading."

"What genres of book do you prefer?"

"Oh. Anything really. Well, anything with a good plot and well written."

"That's fine. We are currently reading *Our Kind of Traitor* by Le Carré. You might find a copy on the library shelves. We start at six."

Ten minutes to kick-off, then. Back to the library proper on the other side of the stairwell. Fiction shelves. J, K, L. Nothing by Le Carré. Not one book. That was surprising. On a whim of inspiration, he checked the shelves for C. There it was. Obviously not a very clued-up librarian. Brian checked out the book at the electronic machine with his card, and clutching it as if it were a prize, returned to the reading room. Choosing the chair furthest away from the others, he removed his coat, noted the temperature and, then registering that all the others were dressed for arctic conditions, promptly put it back on again.

He broke the silence. "It's freezing in here."

Silverbeard lifted his head. "They turn off the boiler at five, and the windows don't close properly." Thus spoken, he dropped his head again and resumed contemplation of the floor.

Brian would have expected the council to care for their library better than this but kept the thought to himself. He followed the example of the others in floor-gazing, as if some hidden inspiration for readers might reveal itself there.

Somewhere outside, a clock chimed. Six o'clock. The signal for a flurry of activity. Heads lifted, as if controlled robotically. A man of Asian appearance wandered in. No beard. The others all nodded a cautious welcome to the newcomer. Brian revised his initial analysis. Facial hair was not an essential qualification. Confirmed by the next arrival, a woman. Now they were six.

Blackbeard addressed the assembly. He spoke quickly and, in Brian's opinion, neither clearly nor loudly. "For the benefit of our new arrival and to remind everyone, I am Humphry, and I chair this group." Humphry! Seriously? Brian hadn't heard that name since he was a child. It definitely wasn't a name that fitted Blackbeard's face, anyway. "Everyone reads aloud one chapter from the book. All of us will then offer our thoughts. We are all gathered here in a spirit of helping each other become better readers and deeper thinkers."

Humphry paused and looked around to confirm everyone was listening. He hadn't finished his introduction.

"All of us must adhere to the rules. No one is to say anything of a violent, sexual, or political nature or use crude language that may cause offence. Unless it is part of the text of the book, of course. No one is allowed to enquire any personal details of the other members of the group. Anyone may leave or return at any time without comment either way. Is that all understood?"

He looked around to confirm that everyone had nodded. Brian hadn't caught all the details but nodded along anyway.

"Let's go round the table and introduce ourselves and say what each of us is reading at the moment. I'll start. I'm reading *The Perfect Placement* by Francesca Absolom. It's a romance set in a Job Centre. I am finding it very moving."

While Brian was digesting the credibility of this, Silverbeard started to speak. Brian noted that, fortunately, the direction of travel around the circle meant his turn would come last.

"My name is Richard. I read rather slowly, but finally succeeded in finishing another chapter of *A Blessed Release* by Johannes Ezekial." He had a low, mumbling voice, just about intelligible, belying the bulk of his frame. Brian recalled his mother telling him not to talk into his beard when he had experimented with growing one as a young man; maybe this was an example of what she meant. "Those of you who were here last time will remember me telling you that it's a science fiction thriller set in a space-time continuum where the religion and modality of the travellers, an LGBTQ+ couple, changes as they are teleported in time and migrate between planets. I find the underlying message highly appropriate to the times we live in."

Brian racked his brains to think of any personal circumstances of the times he lived in which matched up with any of those plot attributes. Nothing. He wouldn't have minded moving to another planet, though, if it was warmer than this library.

Next, Brownbeard. A thin face and a thin neck. Possibly a thin body too, though impossible to ascertain since it was hidden behind a bulky puffer jacket that might have been yellow once. Indeterminate age too. In his thirties, perhaps. Or forties? "Hello, I'm Rob. I mostly read poetry. Haven't got around to reading anything new this week, though. I've been too depressed with the weather. I didn't have any work on, so I spent most of my time rearranging my shelves in alphabetical order. Just not sure how much space to leave for each letter of the alphabet for future purchases. Is that something we can discuss later?"

He'd come to a reading group to talk about bookshelves and cataloguing? Seriously? Nobody answered the question, anyway, and Rob didn't seem to expect that they would.

Watching the company, Brian realised that after speaking, each cast member dropped their head again, so at any time all except the current speaker were firmly focused on the floor. If that held no secrets, perhaps the intention was to clear the mind and better appreciate the insight of the speakers. Brian followed their example. For the first time, he saw dark flecks in the vinyl tiles. Not dirt or dust. Embedded. Sprinkled randomly or arranged in a pattern? Did the specks actually spell out messages, the importance of which explained why they were all concentrating their gaze downwards?

Blackbeard — Humphry — lifted his head, nodded sagely, and uttered a deep *sotto voce* "Well done." Resumed his contemplation of the floor. Brian realised he had actually made the same movements and said the same words after each of the preceding introductions. Perhaps his intention was simply to show that someone had been listening.

"Most of you know me. I'm Chetwan." Proving by his accent to be a first-generation immigrant from the Indian subcontinent. "I'm working my way through first time novelists from my home country. I'm struggling a little with *In Pursuit of the Holy Cow* by Satrajit Poonawalla. His style is complex. It's a thriller about cattle rustlers in agricultural villages in the foothills of the Satpura mountains. A sort of Hindu western. Or should I say eastern?"

Was he joking? Brian wondered and stole a glance to see if Chetwan was smiling at his witticism. No. He looked serious. Well, at least it was an original line.

Seated next to Chetwan was the sole female of the group. "I'm Beatrix, but everyone calls me Bea," she began. What a big smile! The only cheerful one. "I've had a really busy week, so I haven't done a lot of reading. I managed to finish the first three chapters of *She Fell for His Eyes* by Rebecca Lovelace. It's a new romantic comedy. The publishers sent me an advance proof copy and are pushing me to review it in the TLS." Times Literary Supplement, eh? The first one of the group who gave Brian the impression of being a serious reader, like reading as a job. If romantic comedy counted as serious literature, that is.

Finally, it was his turn. "Hello, I'm Brian." Much to his surprise, everyone looked up and at him. Because he was the new boy? Possibly they thought he had been sent by a higher power to deliver new wisdom and understanding to the group? "I've just finished a novel about industrial espionage in South America."

All eyes swivelled towards Humphry, who lifted his head to the ceiling and, one long moment later, lowered it again. All were waiting for his pronouncement. Humphry gathered his thoughts.

"That is not a popular genre. Is it any good? Is the romantic aspect of it powerful?"

"There isn't anything romantic about it, I'm afraid," replied Brian. "But I found it excellent. Great plot twist at the end."

"Perhaps it has an element of fantasy, then? Or one of the characters could be working with the paranormal?"

Brian was at a loss as to how to respond. In just a few words, and knowing nothing about the book he had been reading, Humphry had essentially rubbished it entirely. Brian had never seen or heard of any law that said that books had to fall into certain popular genres. Surely there were many famous works of fiction that were not romantic, fantastical or paranormal?

Brownbeard — Richard, was it? — proffered his wisdom, or at least his opinion. "I find I best like stories that weave a little of everything into them," he said. "Those have the widest appeal and are best for reading groups. Mark my words," he added, nodding sagely to himself.

"Surely Le Carré doesn't fit all those parameters?" asked Brian.

Humphry butted in. "When I was setting out the rules earlier, I forgot to say that questions about which books we choose to read are prohibited."

At which point, the door opened to a new arrival. A young woman, appearing more prepared for a job interview in the City than a reading group in Leytonstone. Chinese? Japanese? A long dark blue coat, made of angora wool, guessed Brian. He'd had a girlfriend a few years back who was a fashion student and talked about little else. A matching beret. Glittering earrings. Surely not all diamonds? Clutched under one arm, and now placed on the table in front of her, a glossy black Hermes bag that was more like a briefcase, out of which she drew a few sheets of white paper and a well-thumbed copy of *Our Kind of Traitor* with sticky notes in a rainbow of colours poking out from its pages.

The regulars in the group were clearly not surprised to see her, but offered no greeting. She obviously didn't expect one. Nor did she make an apology for lateness. She stood at the head of the table, as if addressing a meeting.

"I will not be able to stay tonight," she announced. "It is an interesting book. I have written up my notes." She distributed the sheets of paper to the group, minus Brian. "I see there is a new member. I am sorry, I did not print enough copies."

"No problem. I saw a copier in the library next door. I can go and make another copy," said Brian, thinking he was being helpful. The others in the group transfixed him with stares. OK, not a good idea then.

"Humphry, use my copy to help explain my notes to the others. I will take yours." And without further ado, she pushed her book over the table to Humphry and retrieved his copy, putting it straight into her bag.

"Yes, ma'am," intoned Humphry. Ma'am? Why? Who was this woman? Brian had no opportunity to ask his question as Humphry lost no more time in starting to read his chapter, whilst the Asian woman disappeared as unobtrusively as she had arrived. The others, as if following an established procedure, folded the sheets of paper she had given them and tucked them away in the back of their books.

Brian was glad he had acquired a copy of the book to follow the passages as the others read aloud, as none of them would have rated as public speakers. Their dull delivery persuaded him that they were only reading their allotted chapter aloud because that was one rule that had to be adhered to. Their delivery ranged from mumbled-and-too-quiet-to-hear at one extreme, to rushed-to-the-point-of-incomprehensible at the other. Brian had once spent an enjoyable week on a public speaking course — booked for him by his employer — and, when it was his turn, gave it his all. A wasted effort, as within a minute of him starting to read, the others all packed away their books, wrapped their coats more tightly around them, and got up to leave. Humphry, the last to move, at least stopped briefly to speak to him. "We have to vacate the room by eight," he explained. "You can be the first to read next time. We meet every Tuesday." He held the door open, clearly waiting for Brian to get up and go.

# The Pub Quiz

Bea didn't like pubs as a rule. In her younger years, she'd gone along with her colleagues from work on a Friday evening and enjoyed a few glasses of wine, which she always drank too quickly. Inevitably, by the time she'd finished her third, the other girls had all been picked up or had gone off somewhere, and she found herself forced to wander home on her own, the worse for wear. Waking up hung over on Saturday mornings, she always attributed the blame to the pub, never thinking for one minute that it might have been, at least partly, her own responsibility.

Now her visits were limited to once a week with her associates — she would never consider them friends — from the reading group. An obligatory debrief of sorts. As a cover story for four unlikely individuals (and Laoban, their boss, when she deigned to join them), she had to admit it worked well. They all enjoyed reading, and the official group gave them an excuse to meet in public. Nobody would think their going on for a drink afterwards unusual behaviour.

At least the pub was quiet on a more than usually freezing November Tuesday night. Empty, in fact. That said, this establishment was probably quiet every night and day of the week, having been deserted even by the drug gangs that posted their people around most of the watering holes in Leytonstone. Destined for closure, like so many others. Whilst it remained open, however, it provided exactly what the small group sought: peace and discretion.

Bea didn't mind going to this pub because she never had a hangover the following day. Despite being a mistress of subterfuge, it never occurred to her that the vodka and orange that Richard always bought her might actually have no vodka in it. "Tastes so much better with a tiny drop of Angostura Bitters," he always remarked as he set the glass down in front of her. Bea was surprised that this run-down pub stocked such an exotic ingredient.

The four of them — they'd never needed to face the embarrassment of saying Chetwan wasn't welcome, as he was religiously opposed to alcohol — gathered around a corner table, putting their heads close together to avoid any possible risk of the invisible phantoms in the pub's ether overhearing. Such phantoms may have speculated that the four were having a séance, using their glasses full of beer (and vodka-free orange juice) to move around an invisible Ouija board. They would have been mistaken and disappointed. In the centre of the table lay the annotated book that Laoban had exchanged for Humphry's clean one.

"Good to have a new mission," said Robert. "I hope to hell it's not following jilted lovers' exes around the back streets of London like last time. I started reading a bestseller that reminded me so much of that project that I gave up after fifty pages. Too depressing. Thank goodness we get more interesting stuff than that author gives her hero to do."

Richard interrupted. "I'm sure we all agree that we're not here to discuss Robert Galbraith's book. Or should it be J.K. Rowling's? Reading group is over. Mission group starts here."

"We can fully interpret our instruction sheets later, at home," said Humphry. "But we should jointly review the headlines now. Today's the eleventh, correct?" He looked around the table. Bea pulled out her phone, glanced at the screen, and nodded along with the rest. "So, blue tags," said Humphry, leafing through the book.

First blue-tagged page. Line sixteen, word three. 'December.'

Second blue-tagged page. Line four, word seven. 'Sixteen.'

Third blue-tagged page. Line twenty-one, word one. 'Victoria'.

"Shit!" Robert exploded. "The week before Christmas standing in an effing railway station? And looking for what?

"Hold on," said Richard. "There must be more blue tags."

"Can't see any," said Humphry, riffling through the pages.

Bea proved more observant. “Look, stuck to the back of a green one.”

Line one, word two. ‘Falls.’ “So, what does that mean?” asked Humphry.

“Victoria Falls!” Robert was excited again now. “Africa! Kenya, I think.” Richard looked straight at him, finger on his lips. Don’t want to get those phantoms excited, too.

“Zimbabwe,” corrected Bea. “But that makes no sense. Quite unbelievable. Laoban is seriously going to send us to Africa?”

“Our first foreign project together,” smiled Robert. “Christmas somewhere warm and sunny!”

Humphry had found another blue tag. Two words on that page. ‘Diamond’ and ‘Mine.’ “Sounds exciting. If it’s true.”

“Sounds to me like it calls for another round,” said Richard, rising from his seat and heading for the bar.

# A Year Previously...

"We will be landing in twenty minutes."

Jane Smith gazed out of the window at the island beneath them, then turned her attention back to the young, handsome man dozing in the seat beside her. "Wake up, lazybones, the holiday starts here."

It had taken Jane little more than a month to transform her life following her husband's arrest and incarceration. Not that he'd actually been convicted. Yet. Justice moves slowly. Jane would be quite content if it was paralysed. Barry had been transferred from Belmarsh prison to Wandsworth, the authorities deeming it easier for visiting while he was still on remand. Not that she felt much in the mood for visiting him.

However, for the first three weeks she had deigned to join the flotsam and jetsam, the wives of all the other cons. Keeping up appearances. Wifely duty and all that. To listen to all his excuses, all his lies. Well, probably lies. She no longer knew what to believe. It was easier to disbelieve everything he said. "It was all Arbuthnot's doing," he kept repeating. "I never did anything wrong. I didn't even know what he was doing. I should never have agreed to invest in his operation."

Ignoring Jane's scepticism, he would continue, always saying the same things. "He even stole my name as a disguise. Called himself Smith. Called his business Smith and Smith or something like that. Pretended I was an equal partner in his enterprise. Now the PC Plods of this world can't work out which Smith is which. As far as they're concerned, if Arbuthnot is a Smith, am I a real Smith or something else? And if it's a Smith who did wrong, then they're saying it must be me, not him, because I really am a Smith. He's just a fake Smith. It's like being accused of using one's own name illegally."

Even though Jane had stopped listening, he carried on with his tirade. "The police are also tied in knots because they can't find the associates he claimed. Can't get their heads around the idea that when one man sets up as a consultant, he tags 'and associates' on the end to make it look like there is more than one of him. Or, in this case, more than two. I was the only associate. But all I did was invest money. He told me it was going to be a professional business consultancy. Not espionage. When it gets to court, I'll be vindicated. You'll see, Jane." She didn't look like she would. "We are both Smiths, real Smiths," he'd howl. "You need to tell journalists, tell the world, get me out of this place. Why do they think I'm a flight risk? Get me bailed."

Jane had no intention of doing any such thing. If anyone was going to fly, it was her. If her husband hadn't been helping Arbuthnot-alias-Smith with his odious business, some other illicit activities must have been occupying his time. He certainly hadn't been at home very often, and the credit card statements she had discovered showed that whatever it was he was doing, he was doing it in high style. A rich trophy husband was no longer an asset to her, even less so now that he was in jail. He was not needed for her to go on enjoying the good life too. She had her own big inheritance, after all, enough to afford a lavish lifestyle. A nice mansion in Richmond. A Mercedes cabriolet on the gravel drive. All in her own maiden name, safe from whatever fate might befall her husband. Both of them Smiths, indeed? She would ditch her married name as soon as she could.

Jason leaned over her, kissed her forehead, and looked down. "Looks like desert to me. Why are we going here?"

"Five-star all-inclusive hotels, pools, beaches, bars, warm sunshine every day. What's not to like, baby?"

"We could have got all that in Portugal, or the Canaries. Much nearer. No need to fly for six hours." Then, looking around at their fellow passengers and back towards Jane, "No need to mix with package holidaymakers, either. You told me you liked to be exclusive?"

"Yes, but this is the only direct flight. It doesn't have a business class. And I have another reason for coming here."

A week earlier, taking advantage of her husband's absence, she had raided his study, or 'man cave,' as he preferred to call it, and immersed herself for several hours sorting through mounds of paperwork that he had simply piled up. Papers that he kept away from his proper office in a local business centre, where no doubt his PA would have filed them properly. Mostly junk mail — why hadn't he just thrown that out? — but some of it personal. Or secret. Credit card statements that revealed his profligate lifestyle. Legal documents for investments she knew nothing about. An expired membership card for the Randy Rabbit Club.

Much more interesting, a solicitor's letter attached to a wad of papers in Portuguese. Dated 2017. Nearly five years ago. The covering letter confirmed the completion of her husband's purchase of a house. In joint names, his and hers. On an off-plan development in a place called Murdeira. Misspelt? Madeira? No, surely not. The name was repeated on several pages of the documents. Searching maps on her phone, she found it on the island of Sal in Cape Verde. Another thing that Barry hadn't told her about. Presumably, he wasn't ever going to do so. Even so, why had he left this paperwork buried within a pile of miscellaneous junk?

The police had helpfully given her a bag with some of Barry's personal effects, taken off him when he was arrested. Within it was a passport. He obviously must have had two, as the one he used when he travelled with her was in the home safe. Interesting to look at the stamps. Places she would quite like to have gone to herself. Cancun. Bali. Bangkok. She wondered who his plus one was. Not his PA for sure; she was older than Jane and holidayed in Blackpool. Anyway, back to the stamps. Just one for Cabo Verde back in 2017. Presumably when he bought this mysterious house. Nothing since. Had he forgotten all about it? That wouldn't be a surprise.

She called the solicitor named on the documents. After making a transfer of five hundred pounds to his firm's account ("we always require a deposit"), he deigned to talk to her, though making a lot of noise about client confidentiality, but under the circumstances and since her name was on the deeds, he supposed… yada… yada. Yes, it was all legal. The property had been bought in 2017, but building works were only finished in 2019, when the solicitor had been sent the completion documents and keys. Barry had instructed him to forward those to an office address in Mayfair. Where

Arbuthnot masqueraded as Smith. No hope of getting in there now. Probably had crime scene tape over the door.

Spending a little time on some online research, Jane learnt Sal was an up-and-coming tourist destination — although it obviously still had quite a lot of coming up to do, as there was just one flight a week from London — with just a handful of five-star resorts. Not much else, but three hundred and sixty sunny days a year. Her personal trainer, who in perfect mid-life cliché had subsequently become her lover, needed little encouragement to agree to perform his lessons in a sunnier and warmer climate than Richmond offered in November. In the next five minutes she had booked flights and a week's stay in the Hilton for both of them, paying with a card in Barry's name that she had found amongst the papers, and which hadn't been stopped by the provider.

"If you've got a house there, why are we staying in a hotel?" Jason wasn't just a pretty face.

"A, I don't have keys, and B, I don't know what state it's in."

"How are we going to get in, then?"

"I suppose there'll be an estate agent or manager or someone about. Somebody must have the keys. I've got all the legal papers with me. We'll go and explore tomorrow. Meanwhile, it's been a long flight, as you say, so I'm already panting for you to give me one of your special massages. And lobster for dinner afterwards, I thought?"

**

Whilst it was a posh hotel, the concierge obviously wasn't used to having rich guests giving generous tips. The taxi Jane had asked him to arrange arrived the next morning in the form of a long black limousine. As Jason observed, probably the most ostentatious car on the island. Definitely the only car parked on the road where the driver insisted the house must be. A huge sign, faded through long exposure to the sun, proclaimed a development of luxury villas 'ready to move into.' A portakabin signed 'Sales and Marketing' had not been visited recently, judging from the pile of mail visible through the dust-encrusted glass door. Leading from it towards the sea was an asphalted road lined with lampposts, covered with sand, desert on both sides, piles of construction blocks, a rusting crane standing guard over it all. At the end of the road, just one solitary house.

It had clearly been occupied, and recently. Through the windows they could see furniture. A bedroom. A kitchen. A food processor on the countertop. But definitely deserted now.

"Shall we go inside?" asked Jason.

"We don't have keys. Let's ask the driver if he can call a locksmith."

"No need, I think. A pal of mine taught me how to open simple locks like this with a credit card. Let me try with the hotel room key." There was a moment of fiddling, then Jason turned his head triumphantly towards her. "Open sesame!"

It was obvious there wasn't anyone living in the house now. One kitchen cupboard full of packets of pasta, nothing except pots and pans in the rest. A tower of boxes of wine in one corner. Two bedrooms on the ground floor, sheets stripped and left in a pile. Jane was still exploring cupboards when she heard Jason shout from upstairs, "Jane, come up here! Now!"

At the top of the stairs, there was a small landing with a single, open door leading off it. Jason stood beyond it, shaking. Not his usual confident, urbane self. "Come." He beckoned at her. "And don't shut the door, whatever you do." Oh. No handle on the inside. Strange. She followed Jason into an almost empty room. No furniture except one long wide shelf like a kitchen working top and one chair against one of the walls. Then, through another door, a bedroom. A man lying down. An elderly man in a dirty grey tracksuit. Emaciated. Still. "Is he alive?" she asked.

"Yes, I am. Just about." An English voice. "Are you the Covert Ones, then?"

"Who?"

"The people who keep me here. Imprisoned. You stopped feeding me. I am extremely hungry."

"There's nobody else. How long have you been here?"

"Four hundred and thirty-three days. Thirty-two of them without food. Just water."

Jane scowled. Now Barry really had some serious questions to answer. No doubt he'd say it was all Arbuthnot's fault, of course.

Jason was for calling the police immediately, but Jane stopped him. "My husband must be involved in this."

"So what? You said you hated him."

"I do. Passionately. But calling the police here is going to give us a problem. They're bound to contact the British police immediately. I don't want to be sucked into Barry's shitstorm. And we don't want anyone to know about the two of us. Not yet, anyway."

Jason looked at her quizzically. "So, what do you propose?"

"I don't know. I'll think about it. Let's get him fed first." She went downstairs to boil up some pasta, leaving Jason with the man. He attempted conversation.

"I'm Jason. Who are you?"

"Jones. Ronald Jones."

# Virtually a Virtual Assistant

"So, progress report. Please." Laoban calling Latviana.

"The only emails coming into his office address are junk mail and bills. Well, almost all. Whatever he told you about everything going through official channels, all his business stuff is on his private email."

"Anything encrypted? It's just an ordinary Gmail address, after all. Definitely not secure."

"No. And there's not been one mention of that funny-named mineral stuff in any of his emails in the last week," said Latviana. "But I suppose they might use code words like we do. Or have other secure comms."

"I'm not sure Gideon Caesar is clever enough," replied Laoban, dryly.

"Well, there are lots of references to 'the product.' And he's talking about temporary interruptions to supply in some emails to what I suppose are his customers."

"Who are the customers?"

"If they are companies, there's no way of telling. All the emails are to what look like individuals, mostly Gmail and Yahoo addresses. But not standard dot com ones; country-specific ones."

"In Africa?"

"No. Malaysia, Australia, Mexico. Even some oddities like Georgia and Kazakhstan."

"Very international. Tells us nothing."

"Not a word in any of the emails that implies this is a mining company."

"I'm fairly sure it isn't. But he has paid the advance, so we have to deliver on this mission."

"There's one thing I think you might find interesting. The office email address is used to receive bills and send out remittance advices. Quite boring accounts stuff, but I found out a few things from them. The office you went to. He's only renting two rooms: 'reception' and 'consulting.' He only contracted them in March. Three months ago. He's also using a virtual assistant company in Sofia."

"Virtual assistant?"

"A remote PA. A VA. Secretary Plus. Paid by the hour. Working from home, usually in another country. And before you ask, because it's cheaper."

"And Sofia is the name of his virtual assistant?"

"Ha, funny. No. Sofia is in Bulgaria. It's Mariana, actually. He makes calls to her every day, too. So perhaps all the interesting stuff — if there is any — is going through her."

"Yes, that is indeed interesting. Get Toshio to hack Mariana's email, then. If it looks worthwhile, let's see if we can introduce an intermediary. A virtual virtual assistant."

"Who were you thinking of?"

"Why, you, of course."

# Humphry

Humphry knew his *nom de plume* invited ridicule, so used it only in the reading group and with his employers. He preferred the code name he had used in an earlier life, Hunter. In his opinion, it sounded modern and film star-ish and entirely appropriate to what was now his covert part-time job. Unfortunately, Laoban didn't agree.

A decade earlier, in his clean-shaven days, he'd been officially an RAF captain, but in reality what he called a spy-medic, being flown around the world and, quite literally, parachuted in at an instant's notice to remove the odd bullet, sew up a stab wound or two, things like that. Injuries incurred in the normal course of duty by real James-Bond-type operatives, but ones who lacked the capacity to avoid personal injury. All medical procedures were carried out with total discretion. At his happiest, he'd be a backseat passenger in a Typhoon and press his own ejector seat button at the appropriate moment. More often than not, though, he was forced to endure long and tediously slow journeys sitting on the floor of an ancient Hercules, being at some point unceremoniously pushed out of the back with little clue where he was likely to end up. Even so, all exciting stuff and good fun. Shame he couldn't tell anyone about it, being shackled for life by the binds of the Official Secrets Act.

Now officially retired — the reason given being that at the age of thirty-three, he was too old — he'd come down to earth with a bang, but this time without a parachute. He had landed a job as an A&E registrar at Whipps Cross Hospital. It claimed to be a major London teaching hospital, but the truth was that it was just a very big, very busy and rather dilapidated establishment in the further reaches of the East End. He still removed bullets and fixed stab wounds, but those inflicted by rival gang members of minimal intelligence, not by the skilled mercenaries employed by international criminal masterminds.

Whilst admitting to being a doctor, the others in the reading group knew nothing of his day job — well, often night and weekend job, too — just as he knew nothing of theirs. Rules were there for a reason. He just had to hope that none of the others ever came to the hospital needing his ministrations, but he figured that as long as he continued to specialise in gangland injuries, it was unlikely their paths would cross there.

Humphry, under his preferred name, Hunter, lived alone in a modern studio apartment overlooking the Thames in Heron Quays. It wasn't a council block, but could easily be mistaken for one, being part of the earliest and most basic of the Docklands redevelopments. Most of the other flats were owned by or rented out to Chinese students with rich daddies. From what he could tell, they were rarely there. No raucous student parties for them. Indeed, no noise at all. On rare occasions, he would pass one or two in the corridors and lift lobbies, but they paid scant attention to him, and he none to them. For weeks at a time, when the universities and colleges were on Christmas, Easter, or summer breaks, they scarpered off home (he supposed) and his block was more or less deserted. Just the way he liked it.

When he'd shared a lift with her one evening, about six months ago, he'd initially ignored the Chinese woman in the same way he'd ignored all the students, perhaps only noting that she seemed older and a lot better dressed than most. Not old enough to be the mother of one of them, though. When, a few moments after locking his front door, she rang the intercom, he assumed she was asking for directions. "Sorry, I don't know anyone else here," he shouted back.

"It's you I want to speak to," she said. "I have a business proposition for you, Humphry." Emphasising his name.

"My name is Hunter, and I'm busy. Sorry."

"Let me in so we can talk. You will like what I have to say. I brought a bottle of Cardhu with me. I believe it's your favourite?" She waved the bottle in front of the camera on the entry phone.

Either she was extraordinarily persuasive, or Hunter was off his guard and tempted by the whisky. Against his better judgement, he let her in.

"I brought cheese straws as well," were her first words after crossing the threshold. "Fortnum and Mason. They're very good."

The only women who had ever come into Humphry's flat had been the occasional hired escort, and the last one of those had been many months ago. None had brought whisky — or cheese straws — with them; rather, they had taken his money, and in the case of the last one, purloined other valuables, too. A sobering experience, sufficient to convince him that celibacy was preferable, though occasionally frustrating.

"What is it you really want?" he asked.

"May we sit down?" The Chinese woman moved past him, removed her coat, and answered her own question by taking a place at the end of the sofa.

"Glasses?" she inquired. "Ice?"

"One doesn't put ice in Cardhu. At least, I don't. Americans put ice in Chivas."

"And Asians. Very well. We still need glasses."

Humphry went to the kitchenette and extracted two tumblers from the dishwasher, congratulating himself for having remembered to turn it on before he left that morning. He placed them on the low table in front of the sofa.

"And plates? Or do you eat cheese straws from a paper bag?"

She sounded quite fierce, like a school mistress. Not someone to be argued with. Humphry certainly would, on his own, have eaten straight from the bag, but did as he was told, and found plates. He seated himself on the edge of the bed, facing her.

"You can sit next to me, you know. It's your apartment. I don't bite." Even though it sounded quite like she did. Humphry acceded. Didn't seem that he had a choice.

"You must miss being an agent," she told him. "I think you were a good one." Probably just as well he had sat on the sofa, then. The edge of the bed wasn't very stable, and he would definitely have fallen off. How did she know that?

"Hold on. I was simply a doctor."

"But a doctor for secret agents. And I'm told you were a better secret agent than many of your patients."

That was exactly what Humphry had always thought himself, though he had never expressed this opinion to anyone else. Not that he could remember doing, anyway. At least, not while sober.

"I'm in a position to offer you a part-time professional engagement."

"You mean being a private doctor?"

"No, a private spy. Real espionage. I can't guarantee you'll never have to use your medical skills, but no, serious research. Uncovering secrets."

"Who are you? MI6? CIA? Mossad?"

"The organisation I represent has nothing to do with government, Humphry. We uncover commercial secrets. A private enterprise."

"Industrial espionage?"

"We don't call it that. We prefer the term 'covert research.' The name of the organisation you'll be working for is CASCADA. Classified and Sensitive Commercial Data Acquisition."

Humphry tapped away on his mobile. "If I've got the right website, it says that you organise team-building trips for sales people."

"And so we do. Occasionally. Surely you wouldn't expect us to advertise exactly what we do, Humphry?"

"Then, exactly, what do you do?"

"That will become clear to you when we start working together."

"And what would be my role?"

"Obviously, that depends on the project. Each one is different in nature. Most will be part-time activity, a few hours a week, to fit in with your regular job. Sometimes, there may be some travel. We'll see. You'll enjoy."

"And…"

"Before you ask, yes, we'll pay you. Extremely well. Into a numbered account in Vanuatu."

"Where's that?"

"A long way away. I'll be in contact."

Leaving her glass untouched and the bottle on the table, she rose and left without another word. Humphry did not get up to see her out. When the door had closed behind her, he poured himself another large measure of whisky, munched a cheese straw straight from the packet, and wondered what this surprising turn of events would lead him to.

# Richard

Richard stood overlooking the foundations, observing the three men below him digging. Topless, in shorts. Watching the sweat drip off them on this hot July day, he was feeling bad for telling them to dig deeper, down to 1.8 metres, but they didn't seem to mind. "It's just work," the foreman had told him. Richard didn't really need to stay any longer. He could come back tomorrow or the next day when they'd finished, but his gaze was fixated on their rippling muscles. He forced himself to look away, conscious his body was beginning to get excited.

Once — was it fifteen years ago already? — he'd had a physique like theirs. Or better. Honed into shape by hours of daily exercise. The Lieutenant Commander never lost an opportunity to tell him that to be successful at his job, he had to be at the peak of physical fitness. He'd enjoyed the exercise — well, most of it — but it had never made any sense to him how his fitness helped him in his hours of painstaking evaluation of Chinese and Russian plans for massive infrastructure projects, poring over monitors, spotting where they may be sneaking in cables or electronic devices or even 'sleeping bombs' that might interest the grey suits in Whitehall. Roads, tunnels, undersea pipelines. Projects that cost billions and took years, sometimes decades, to complete.

And now? Reduced to supervising the foundations of a garage in the back garden of a semi-detached house in East Barnet that, once completed, would have zero architectural merit and possibly less necessity. Instructing workmen to break their backs and dig deeper just because it says so in Section

21 (a)(1.04)(x). Doing his job. They could have made the foundations just a couple of feet deep; the bloody garage would never fall over. Or sink. Or be destroyed by the roots of a tree designated as invasive, yet forty-two metres away and certainly not in Birnam Wood and capable of getting up and walking. It still had to be evaluated and reported on. Box ticked.

He had abs somewhere, though they had retreated to invisibility under a thickening layer of fat. The enduring evidence of a diet rich in burgers and fried chicken. Where a submarine-shaped roll counted as healthy eating as long as there was a solitary lettuce leaf in it on top of the other ingredients.

Richard's silent observation of the workmen was interrupted by the arrival of a young woman in the alley at the back of the house that formed the driveway to the garage. A model? Smartly dressed, for sure. Not a customary sight in a back alley in East Barnet. And certainly not at a building site. She was wearing a shimmering blue and green blouse and skin-tight, white, glossy trousers. Huge, black-framed sunglasses obscured most of her face. Strong yet alluring perfume. He could smell it even from where he was standing, seven or eight metres away.

"May I have a word?" she called.

"With me, or with the workmen?"

"With you. Can you come over here?"

Richard moved a plank, tested it for stability, and put one foot on it, bridging the gap. The foundations were only sixty centimetres wide. He should have been able to leap across easily, but something told him he shouldn't risk making a fool of himself in front of this mystery woman. He had to move the plank again to bridge the far trench, but he made it to the other side without incident.

"How can I help?" He put on his best customer service smile. He was used to dealing with fussy residents who didn't like the noise or mess of building works, or were paranoid about security, or dredged up unlikely complaints born of years of prejudice against certain neighbours. All part of the job. "I'm Richard," he added, "the Council building works inspector. I'm just here to make sure that the work is being done safely and legally."

"I'm not interested in building works," replied the woman. Her voice sounded a bit oriental, but with a posh western veneer. Public school educated? "I'm interested in you."

The woman was certainly attractive, and Richard imagined that, had he been inclined that way, he would have been flattered. But. On that score, she was wasting her time.

"I'm sorry? I don't..." He left the sentence hanging.

"I have something for you that I'm sure will make you happy."

Richard couldn't imagine what that might be. She had almost certainly reached the wrong conclusions about him, and it made no sense that a young fashion model would be interested in an overweight middle-aged building inspector. How to put it politely? "Well, you see, I'm quite happy already in my private life."

"Really? Are you? With all your skills and qualifications? You find this building inspector job satisfying? Given your talents?" Again, that clip in intonation.

"I really don't see the relevance of any of this. If I can help you with something to do with building control, that's different."

"No. This is a private matter. I have an interesting business proposal that I would like to discuss with you. You'll like it."

"I have a full-time job with the Council. I'm not in business, private or otherwise. And I can't moonlight. I have contractual restrictions."

"You have plenty of spare time. I can introduce you to part-time work where you can apply your true skills. Nothing that will compromise your contract. It'll make your life more satisfying and worthwhile."

Richard had decided he didn't like this woman, but what she was saying piqued his interest. "I can't discuss this now. This isn't the time or the place. I'm here in a professional capacity."

"Indeed. There is a sushi restaurant almost next to your offices. On the corner. Do you know it?"

"The one that used to be a pizza place?"

"That one. They have tables in booths. Discreet. I'll be waiting for you there at 5.15 tomorrow. Come immediately after work."

"It will be busy. There may be colleagues of mine there."

"Not there. We will almost certainly be the only customers."

# Beatrix

"You're a naughty boy. You know you're supposed to take the yellow pill when you first wake up in the morning. It's nearly lunch time now."

Mr Gills didn't react as if he had been chastised.

"I like to wait for you, Bea. That way, I know I get the dose right."

"There's no way you can get it wrong. Two tablets, all ready for you in the plastic box by the washbasin. One yellow. One white." Bea adjusted his pyjamas, plumped up his pillows, and pulled up the duvet. "You ought to put the heating on and get up. It's not good for you staying in bed all day."

"The electric's too expensive, dear. Can't afford to heat the place more than I already do. Not with what I pay you."

"Of course you can. You have a good pension. It's important to stay warm and eat well."

"I told you I can't afford it. I need to save my pennies for my daughters."

"Hmmm. Maybe. If they ever came to visit you. It's not as if it's far to travel from Watford." Bea didn't know why she bothered; it was the same conversation every time.

"For your lunch, I've got you the smoked salmon roulades that you like. All laid out for you. A bottle of sparkling water and a half of pinot grigio in the wine cooler. If you're good and eat it all, you might find a chocolate éclair in the fridge."

Mr Gills nodded.

"Do you need anything else?" she asked him. "Janice will come as usual in the afternoon to clean up the lunch things and get your tea ready. It's just that I need to get going now. I have a new customer to see."

"No, you're fine. See you tomorrow. Put the TV on to the racing and turn up the volume before you go."

Beatrix was no ordinary carer. At something of a loose end when her husband died a year earlier — apparently of Covid — she'd volunteered to help a friend who ran a home visit service and, through having lost most of her small coterie of staff through Brexit or the pandemic, was desperately short-handed. She'd expected to hate it, getting geriatrics out of bed, cleaning up behind them, on occasion literally making them cups of tea and making sure they took their pills, but the job turned out not to be that unpleasant. In fact, she quite liked 'being useful,' even if it didn't pay well. At least, she had for a while. It actually paid terribly. Not that her friend was raking it in. Her only customer was the local council, who paid a fixed fee per home visit, barely enough to cover paying her staff the minimum wage. Which is where Bea's psychological evaluation skills came into play.

She didn't need them to see how upset the 'customers' were at having visits limited to fifteen minutes a day. That was barely enough to say hello and make the tea. For Bea, who was nicely-off since the life insurance on her husband paid out and was just helping her friend, the time limitation didn't apply. If she wanted, she could stay as long as she liked. Most times, she didn't like, but for some customers, she was happy to stretch her visits out and have a friendly chat. Such conversations were a far cry from the psychological interrogations that she had subjected individuals to in her twenties, usually in basement rooms beneath embassies in dodgier countries, occasionally in the leafy surroundings of the English country houses that MI6 liked to use for 'residential debriefing.' Her customers now were nice older people incapable of plotting insurrection even if the thought had ever occurred to them. Whatever their minds might stray to in her presence, particularly the randy old men, they were up to nothing anymore, as they were physically incapable in every respect.

She quickly established that some of the customers she visited were quite well off and were only availing themselves of the free council services because 'that's what they'd been paying for all their lives,' and they simply weren't aware of any alternative. It was easy to trap them in conversation. Once she had established they were still thinking straight, even if they tended to lay the blame for the terrible service they received from the state on the last Labour government, never mind that was getting on for close to fifteen years ago, she could gently begin her sales pitch.

She set up her own company, 'Bea at Home' and invited select customers to contract her directly. She offered longer visits — several times a day if necessary — and a 24/7 call service. To guarantee the continuance of her rather extravagant fees, and as a demonstration of her powers of persuasion, she had the customers not only sign a lifetime contract but, fearing that a son or daughter might try to cancel it, also a Power of Attorney, giving her the control over health decisions if, or rather when, they became incapable of making their own choices. To cover the regulatory angle, she simply hired her friend and took over her business. "It's called a reverse takeover, Janice," she had told her. Janice didn't care what it was called, as long as it paid her better and eliminated most of her responsibilities.

It was unusual that Mrs Lin, the new customer she was going to see, did not have existing care arrangements. Janice simply told her she had rung the office, said that she had a recommendation from another customer, and that she wanted to see Beatrix — in person and on her own — as soon as possible. She'd refused to tell Janice how old she was, what was wrong with her or any other information at all. "I'll tell Beatrix when she visits me," was all she'd said.

Mrs Lin lived in a block of well-appointed expensive apartments in St John's Wood. Convenient for all the private hospitals, thought Bea as she waited for the security guard to raise the barrier to the residents' parking area. He hadn't known of a Mrs Lin and had made something of a fuss about her not having given Bea a magnetic card to lift the barrier, but a £20 note turned out to work just as effectively.

The woman who answered the door didn't look unwell. Or frail. Or old. In fact, she looked the picture of robust and excellent health. And fashion. Obviously not the customer.

"Good morning, I'm Beatrix. I've come to see Mrs Lin. Your mother?"

"My mother? She died many years ago. It's me you have come to see. I sent for you."

"Oh, I'm sorry. Perhaps there has been a mistake? We offer a personal care service for the elderly."

"The proposition I have for you is not directly related to personal care. Though that might prove useful."

# Pilot AKA Robert

Well, Robert was his *nom de plume*, as he liked to put it. One he really only used for the reading group. Nobody knew his real name. He'd almost forgotten it himself, it was so long since he had needed to use it. His business partners, Laoban and Latviana, called him Pilot. A name that Ronald Jones had given him. But apt, since that's what he was.

'Home' was a single storey wooden building in what purported to be a 'business park' in a field, in reality a collection of six big huts on a farm somewhere near Elstree. Still just about North London, but so isolated it could have been anywhere in the country. Lots of such 'business parks' had sprung up in relatively remote country locations across southeast England in the last twenty years. It was a way for farmers to make money from fields of no agricultural merit and entrepreneurs, generally speaking not very successful ones, to set up in an environment they could pretend was the future of business. Robert, having lived most of his life in South America, didn't much like England and liked its climate even less, but now that his job was here, the location suited him. City an hour or less away; airfield just five minutes.

According to the lease, no one was permitted to stay overnight in any of the office buildings, but nobody came to check. In fact, nobody ever came during the day either. Three of the huts weren't currently rented to anyone, their original occupants having gone bust long before the pandemic hit. The signs outside proclaimed the fourth to be a 'party supplies' company and the fifth a 'medical analysis consultancy.' The sixth, Robert's, was signed as 'Air

Taxi Services.' He never saw anyone come or go to the other huts, but then he was rarely there during business hours. Certainly, if the businesses were functional, they kept themselves to themselves.

It was approaching midnight when he got back from the Tuesday evening group. They'd had another beer or two to celebrate being given such an interesting project. (They were sure it was going to be interesting, though none of them knew yet just what it was.) Probably at least one beer too many, he reflected, bumping down the track from the farm gate to his hut. Especially since it was probably best to decode the rest of the instructions from Laoban before bed. And he had to fly the next day.

It never took him as long to remove his beard as it did to put on. This, at least, was something he could do still while slightly pissed. In fact, the alcohol helped numb the pain. It was easier to just rip off the faux hair and put up with the agony for a few seconds, but he had to be careful not to damage the postiche, as he would need it again in a few days. He looked in the mirror and slathered cream onto his chin. Amazing how removing a beard erased ten years from one's appearance. He had to look his handsome best for the girlfriend, though it was probably just as well they weren't meeting tonight. The key to decode the instructions may have been schoolboy stuff, but it was time consuming. Easier with a clear head. Something he did not have that evening. Still, better get on with it.

So, fly to Victoria Falls on December 16th. On a commercial flight. No idea of the routing; he supposed Latviana would take care of that. He probably wouldn't know until she gave him the ticket. There wasn't much additional information to decode. Laoban invariably kept what she shared to a minimum. Search for and neutralise an illegal diamond mine somewhere in Africa. Pack light, as if he was going on holiday. Estimated duration for the project: two weeks.

He was itching to get back to some serious espionage, and this sounded like it might be just the ticket. He missed the intrigue, the jetting about the world at no notice, the dressing-up, the fights with the nameless woman who was now monikered Laoban. Not that he complained. He was glad to be out of the clutches of Mr Smith and his never-seen namesake and whoever the associates were, who had abused him with threats to reveal his past whenever he asked — and asked over and over again — to get paid. He accepted it would take time to build up a new business from scratch. If anyone could do it, Laoban could.

But the work she had been bringing in up to now was trivial. Boring. The most interesting had been following a group of Chinese executives. They were suspected of trying to adulterate batches of a vaccine destined for certain countries so that they could continue to subjugate their governments by offering what they claimed to be a superior Chinese product. In fact, they hadn't been trying to do anything of the sort. They just wanted to steal the formula and some of the equipment used for making it.

That job, like all the others, had been on the ground in and around London. Hanging around street corners and lurking in cafés. Private detective agency stuff. Not proper espionage. Nothing international. Nowhere to fly to. And now that he had an overseas assignation, he would be travelling on a commercial flight, others at the controls.

Never mind. He had the whole of the next day free, and he could go flying. Not in the executive jets that he preferred, where he could enjoy dressing up as a captain and wear a peaked hat and a white shirt with four gold bars on the navy epaulettes clipped to its shoulders. He did, however, have the use of a Beechcraft, the property of a rather elderly Chinese man who Laoban said was one of her best friends. Mr Lin owned several restaurants in Gerrard Street, and he smelled of oyster sauce and money. Some months ago, soon after they started the company, Mr Lin had taken it into his head to learn to fly and, enthused by the first few lessons that he'd taken, had bought an aeroplane. Just like that. And not just any aeroplane, but a Beechcraft Baron, only a year old, the previous owner having been another short-term flying enthusiast with more money than sense.

It hadn't taken long for Mr Lin to become disillusioned with learning to fly. He said it took too much time to study for the theory and navigation skills tests that he would have to pass to show competence and get his private pilot's licence, time that he didn't have. He also resented the obligation to study; his chefs didn't need any qualifications and could deliver a stir-fried kung po chicken dish in forty-three seconds (he had supervisors who timed such things), so why did he need to sit exams to fly a plane? He did, however, enjoy the practical side of sitting at the controls and attempting to climb and turn and bank, just as long as he had someone of confidence by his side in the co-pilot's seat who could grab the controls if he did something stupid, and who would get him back on the ground safely. Robert, who had become that co-pilot of confidence, could confirm that Mr Lin was not safe to fly on his own.

When he didn't want an hour's flying practice, he was perfectly happy to allow Robert the free use of the plane. He even paid for unlimited usage of fuel. A bagatelle to him, but prohibitive to Robert had he needed to fund this himself. The plane was parked at Elstree aerodrome, just five minutes up the road from Robert's hut. It's a tiny airfield, with a short runway that can only be used by propellor planes. In fact, almost exclusively used for flying lessons. Robert liked it being so small, and he was well known to the part-timers who ran the control tower and the engineers in the maintenance hangar. They'd be discreet if it was ever called for. Tomorrow he'd fly out to Rotterdam to see his girlfriend and business partner, and, in between catching up on romance, try to discover whether Laoban had told her anything more about the new project.

# Latviana AKA Maria

It had been her idea to be based in Rotterdam. She had acquired Dutch residency when she was just eighteen, the result of strings pulled by the Ambassador in Minsk as a personal favour, in return for the many personal favours she had given him since her sixteenth birthday. That gave her the escape from Belarus she craved, away from the repression and the ever-prying eyes of the security police. On a personal level, they largely left her alone, being the daughter of a senior official of the KGB, or she would never have been able to spend so much time in the Dutch Ambassador's residence.

Despite having had a residency card for five years, she had never lived in the Netherlands until a year ago. Her former colleague, Laoban, now the boss of the company in which Latviana and her pilot boyfriend were junior partners, had insisted that they move apart and do their best to 'go to ground' after the successful conclusion of their last project. Successful from their point of view, but leaving them, as individuals, at serious risk of reprisals. Now that the Smith case was stuck in legal limbo, and since they had never been implicated, they felt they could relax a little. But until the legal matters were closed, they still needed to be careful.

So, better to be away from her previous life and contacts. Her residency in Holland brought her a new existence and legitimacy. She'd visited Amsterdam briefly when she first came to Europe, but she hadn't liked it. Too big, too busy, too many tourists, too expensive, too many 'professional' women who reminded her of her earlier life. Rotterdam was much better. Smaller, more discreet and, most importantly, with an airport that was big enough for scheduled commercial flights but also accessible for the private propellor plane currently flown by Pilot. He'd told her that when business picked up and they had international projects, the company would be able to afford an executive jet and he would register it there. He definitely didn't want to be seen around Biggin Hill, his previous air base.

She didn't need to learn Dutch for her job, but nonetheless studied assiduously until, after just two months, her teachers considered her accent-free. She moved into a nondescript apartment near the airport, where any others who gave her the time of day, on the landings or stairwell or at the supermarket, would all assume she was a Dutch native by birth. Not one of those East European immigrants they complained about.

Discovering a passion for a nearby store in a big blue shed that stocked affordable furniture and housewares, she furnished one room as an office, installed the best communications equipment that the nascent business could afford from the gargantuan red shed next to the blue one, and thus created their operations hub. A fly on the wall would have said she was just a secretary working from home, editing contracts, arranging meetings for Laoban, paying expenses. The fly might consider her an exceptionally slow typist, but then the fly would not know that the documents she worked on had to be encrypted. The fly might also conjecture that she was often bored, and the fly would be right. But Latviana didn't mind so much. She had faith. Faith that the good times were coming soon. The spying times. The profitable times. And now, it seemed her dreams were about to come true. It would be a good day tomorrow. A lucrative African adventure to plan and Pilot coming to visit. She would have company. Fun. And no need for an electric blanket to keep her warm in bed.

She reflected on how her life had changed over the last five years. Actually, less than five years.

Back in her home city of Minsk, she had been a star pupil at the private academy for the offspring of government officials, a natural at languages, and had graduated with perfect grades in English, German and Italian. Outside school, not for her the evenings spent with gaggles of girlfriends, hanging out in cafés discussing the matters of critical interest to teenagers and admiring each other's nails. Rather, she sought additional learning beyond the kind of education she could get at any school. When her father was home from his job at police headquarters, she hassled him to teach her extra-curricular matters of interest. She had no idea then if or when some of these things might become useful to her. "I really don't know why you are asking me about interrogation techniques," he would say. "You're really so much better at them than I am." And then he would laugh heartily and happily indulge her. She proved a useful daughter, far more competent and quick at computer skills than her father or any of his analysts at headquarters. Especially proficient at extracting secrets from the laptops of would-be revolutionaries.

Duly educated in how to threaten and intimidate successfully, she took advantage of a particularly delicate situation to request the favour she craved from Pieter Van de Graaf. She had met him at a swanky black-tie function in his residence, where he was entertaining a visit from Dutch politicians. Sent there in the guise of a waitress, helping her father out on a day when his regular female spy employee had called in sick, she had discovered precisely nothing from what she overheard in the function itself, largely because all the guests spoke in Dutch. An obvious oversight by her father, though she doubted his regular girl would have understood anything in this language either. Determined to bring back proof of her success, she attempted, for the first time in her life, to flirt with the Ambassador, and within an hour or so was in his bed. Needless to say, she did not reveal her new experiences to her parents, but her father was sufficiently happy with the few morsels of information gleaned from the Ambassador's diary that he did not delve into details of her techniques for acquiring them and gave his onward blessing to the weekly visits she paid to Pieter thereafter.

Naturally, she hid her passport with its new Schengen visa stamp and her brand-new residency card from her parents. With their willing support, however, she found a serious-looking two-week course in London that she could credibly claim would be useful for her university studies. She booked her flight on Belavia, made her father take her to the airport to see her off as her calculated insurance that, unlike some others ahead of her in the passport queue, she didn't get stopped, boarded the flight, breathed a sigh of relief, and three hours later landed at Gatwick, never to return.

In her trysts with Pieter, she'd successfully amassed a few thousand euros. Back in Minsk, they'd seemed a fortune, but it was obvious they wouldn't go far in London. Amsterdam must be cheaper? The budget flight cost her only £50, but it took mere hours there to realise that, whilst she might be a legal Dutch resident, life there was at least as expensive as London. She would need a job. Urgently. She'd also need to learn the language. It seemed to be true that everyone spoke English, but if she was going to live and work there, she wouldn't be able to rely on that for long. But she was a fast learner. And she knew from her previous experiences that the best way to get herself to her goal was to exploit the weaknesses of men.

A tattered sheet of white copier paper taped to a lamppost pointed to the location of an otherwise anonymous hostel. There was no sign outside, probably to avoid inspection or taxes, but it offered cheap accommodation that suited her just fine. She paid for two nights and then went shopping so she could ditch her unfashionable and poor-quality Russian clothing. Eschewing the upmarket shops, she found a chain store and, for less than a hundred euros, purchased a diaphanous dress suitable for daytime pickup plus a very short figure-hugging black one for the dinner dates she was counting on being invited to, two sets of sexy underwear, and enough costume jewellery to dazzle any man not in the diamond trade. It helped to be a petite size 41 and having more important concerns than the latest fashions, as she found everything she needed on the 50% off rails. Dutch girls must be big, she thought. The dresses were cheap tat, true, but they looked good on her body, and she'd only need to wear them once or twice.

A little flirting encouraged an extremely bored young man in a backstreet phone shop to find a shop-soiled but working phone in a drawer under his counter, and a few euros secured an untraceable pay-as-you-go SIM card.

Now all she needed was a man. A rich one. Preferably not too old or ugly. Single, and with his own apartment. Perhaps a banker? This idea had come to mind because, after wandering around the city centre, she was now standing outside a skyscraper covered in golden reflective glass, the logo of a major international bank on a big sign on the street in front of it. The time was just after five, and workers were streaming out of the building. She sat on a conveniently located bench and watched. At first, those who emerged were mostly young women, then young men in groups. By a quarter past, the exodus had petered out. Well, surely a successful, young, single male banker would not be rushing out of the door at five on the dot? Give him time. Patience. A few men leaving on their own rewarded her theory, but none looked the part. Patience. Just after six, she pounced. An exceptionally tall young man, she guessed in his early thirties, well-coiffured blond hair, smartly dressed, expensive-looking crocodile leather laptop bag slung over his shoulder. In her opinion, nervous. Possibly lonely. She could fix that last part. Worth a gamble.

She moved artfully in front of him as he passed by. "Excuse me, can you help me? I'm new in the city and have got myself lost." She bit at her lip.

The young man looked as if her coming up to him and asking for directions was the scariest thing that had ever happened to him. He visibly swallowed. She saw the motion of his Adam's apple. "Of course. I will. If I can. Where do you want to go?"

"I'm staying in Prinsengracht."

"Oh, that's not far. I am going in that direction, so we can walk that way together."

They set off in uncomfortable silence. About half a kilometre later, he stopped at a street corner with shops and a café. "This is Weteringstraat. If you keep going down this road, you'll come to the canal in about a hundred metres. That is Prinsengracht. You can't get lost any more." He smiled implying a goodbye and turned away down a side road.

"Thank you so much!" she called after him, taking steps to follow. "Please let me buy you a drink to thank you."

"I could not allow that, but if you have the time, I will buy you one. No?"

"I always have time for a nice man like you," she replied, and bit at her lip again to draw attention to her mouth.

They sat at a corner table, facing each other. She checked to confirm he was looking at her breasts, displayed in her recent investments, a half-cup black-lace bra clearly visible through her flimsy pale green voile dress. His eyes were certainly focused that way and looked appreciative. He was on the hook, but she still needed to land him, to be certain that he was attracted to her and wanted her. He had no wedding band. His jacket was expensive; she had viewed the designer label when he slipped it off to hang on the back of his chair. His wallet, in crocodile leather and opened in front of her when he paid for the beers, was fat with cards. In a stilted conversation — she having to do almost all the talking — she established his name was Hans, he had been divorced for five years, that yes, he lived on his own, and yes, he was an investment banker. He was terribly shy. He hadn't ever had the courage to use dating websites.

Hans didn't ask her much, but did want to know where she came from. Seeing on the TV screen on the wall behind him that the Latvian Prime Minister was visiting — at least she guessed that was what the subtitles meant (the volume being off and the channel obviously being in Dutch) — she told him she was Latvian. Worrying then that he might think she was an illegal, she made a point of showing him her residency card before he explained that she didn't have to prove it to him, as Latvia was in the EU too. Belarus most definitely was not.

They only had one beer before he said he had to go. "I work with clients in America, and they're just getting back from lunch," he told her. "But tomorrow is Friday, and I don't work late. Perhaps we could have dinner together?"

"I'd like that very much." She gave him her new number. He recoiled minutely when she pecked him on the cheek as her seal on their deal.

Assuming that, as in Minsk, it was a lady's prerogative to be 'fashionably late,' she wore her little black dress, sprayed herself with perfume from testers at a department store she passed on the way, and arrived at the Grand Amsterdam Hotel restaurant lobby at twenty past eight. She looked around and could not see her date partner. Only now did she realise that in her exultation at having captured a rich, single banker at her first attempt, she had failed to ask his surname. There had to be a lot of men called Hans in Amsterdam.

The girl at the reception desk didn't seem in the least surprised. From the description that Latviana gave, she said that a man matching it had indeed been there but had left at ten past the hour, complaining that he had been 'stood up.' Latviana had always been told that it was the Swiss who insisted on punctuality; obviously the Dutch did as well.

Disappointed and making to leave, the reception girl — who might have been Russian; Latviana didn't intend to find out — touched her on the shoulder and pointed to a table by the wall where a man was sitting with his back to them. "In case you're interested," said the receptionist, "his dinner date hasn't arrived, and I don't think she will, if she's the one he was with at the bar last night. Perhaps you want to try your luck?" Well, it didn't matter if the girl thought she was a prostitute, she was only a desk clerk in a restaurant herself, and a plain one at that.

Latviana walked a circuitous route around the restaurant so that when she came back towards the entrance she would be facing him. Older than she would have chosen, but smart-looking with wavy black hair and no wedding band. If he could afford to stay here, then he must have plenty of money. Deciding in an instant that she might as well get something out of the evening, she approached him. "Excuse me, I'm sorry. I'm looking for my dinner date. The girl at the front desk told me you were waiting, and I wondered for a moment if you might be him. But I see you are not. I think mine must have left before I arrived. I was so late. Just my luck. Sorry again."

"No need to apologise, ha ha!" Refined English. Obviously not a Dutchman. "My date should have been here nearly an hour ago. She's obviously not coming."

"Two disappointed diners tonight, then." Smiling, she moved away.

"That doesn't have to be the case — if you would like to dine with me?"

"You're very kind. But really? You don't mind?"

Eager was an understatement. He practically leapt from his chair. "I would be honoured. Please, please do join me. Call me Smith. What's your name?"

"Maria." Not her real name, of course, but a nice one, a common one. "Don't you have a first name, Mr Smith?"

"Everyone calls me Smith. Just Smith."

"Do you live here, Smith, or are you just visiting?"

"Just here on business for a few days. From London. Ha ha." They'd said nothing in her English lessons at the Academy about the use of 'ha ha.' She wondered what it meant, or if it was just a nervous habit of his. What was the word? Yes, an affectation. Quite irritating for the listener. But still. "And you?"

"I'm from Latvia. I'm planning on staying here. Looking for a job."

Smith seemed to know a lot about Latvia and have friends in Riga, whereas, despite it having a long border with Belarus, she knew nothing about the country at all, so she frequently had to steer the conversation in other directions. But they had an enjoyable discussion. And a more enjoyable meal. Latviana AKA Maria was starving, having eaten nothing except a tray of chips in the morning, and Smith was thrilled to have a dining companion who was not only young and sexy but also hungry and a lover of fine food — and perhaps other things as well. She was intelligent and desperate. He had decided she could be useful to him.

To Latviana's surprise, Smith made no attempt to seduce her, or get her back to his room after dinner. Perhaps he wasn't staying there? Perhaps he wasn't into girls. Much better, though, he invited her back for lunch the next day "to discuss a potential job in London." Within days, she had flown back to London, been installed in what Smith called a 'safe house,' and given a Latvian passport that Smith told her she must have lost and that he'd found in a drawer in his office. It took very little longer for Smith to discover all her various talents, including in the bedroom, send her on an intensive Spanish course, and appoint her as his Latin America Project Coordinator.

But now that chapter in her life had closed. Smith was in prison. She was in Rotterdam. There was an African espionage — whoops, sorry, covert research — mission to be arranged, and the boyfriend was flying in tomorrow. Happy times.

# Logistics

"Are you sure you are talking through the new scrambler?"

"Of course I am," replied Laoban. "Why would you doubt it?"

"It's just that your voice sounds just like you," replied Latviana. "I'll need to do something about that."

"What are we supposed to sound like? Robots? You sound like you, too. So, fix it if it's wrong. But let's get down to business."

"Turn on the video so we can see each other. Little red button in the bottom left of the screen, looks like a camera."

"You are stupid sometimes. I know what to do. Remember who's in charge round here."

"Yes, Laoban. Ah, I can see you now."

"What on earth have you done with your hair?"

"Do you like it?"

"No, I certainly do not. Most unprofessional."

"All the blondes are dying their hair in snazzy shades these days. Don't be jealous just because your hair is dark."

"But pink? Seriously?"

"With a streak of green!" Latviana grinned and swished her head from side to side.

"Horrible. You're acting like a child. Go and dye it a natural hair colour today. I won't have one of my operatives looking like a punk rocker. Or a child's cuddly toy."

"But Laoban, the whole point of my job is that none of our clients or targets see me. I thought the idea was that nobody suspects me of being involved in covert research."

"True, but we don't want anyone suspecting you of anything. And I'll need you in action on this project. With those colours, you *will* get noticed. And for all the wrong reasons. Solve the problem!"

"I'll think about it. Now, tell me about the project. In detail. Everything I need to know. So I don't need to spend hours coding and decoding stuff."

"Our client is concerned that a Chinese competitor has discovered — and may be preparing to exploit — a mine for praseodymium."

"What on earth?"

"I knew you'd ask that. It's some sort of rare metal. Used for a few everyday things, but our client thinks that the Chinese have found a new use for it. Something to do with semiconductors."

"But the instructions you gave the team said it was a diamond mine."

"You think that the word 'praeseodymium' is in the code book?"

"True. The client is a competitor of these Chinese miners, then?"

"Something like that."

"And where is this mine?"

"They think it's somewhere on the Caprivi Strip."

"And where's that?"

"In between Botswana and Namibia. It's technically part of Namibia, but used to be Botswana. I think they've given up treating it as disputed territory. Nobody much cares because it's almost impossible to get there. Could be anywhere in that region. Or maybe not there at all. We might be chasing a wild goose." She liked her English idioms.

"How come the client doesn't know exactly where it is? Mines are big, aren't they? Can't they find it with aerial photos? Satellite imagery? Google Earth?"

"Apparently not. If it was a fully functioning mine, yes, it would be huge. But the client says they're probably just sinking test holes, finding out what's under the surface. Small scale. They believe the mine is hidden in the jungle and invisible from the air. If these competitors find what they're looking for, they'll pay off the government and become their preferred mining partner."

"Why does the client care?"

"Because they're digging for the same commodity, but somewhere different. That's common knowledge, but the Chinese test mine is being kept secret. If it exists."

"What is this praseodymium like?"

"What it's like doesn't concern us."

"But maybe it does," retorted Latviana. "What if it's dangerous? Radioactive?"

"No, it's not dangerous. Just valuable."

"Wouldn't the locals know all about it? Aren't those jungles full of native tribes?"

"There aren't any locals. Nobody for hundreds of kilometres. Plenty of elephants, so I'm told. They might never forget, but they don't tell." She smiled at her clever turn of phrase.

"How are our people going to find the mine? If it's there? There's nothing in their CVs about being jungle trained or any experience like that. In fact, I'm not sure any of them have even been to Africa. They might be eaten by lions."

"They've all gone through survival training. They're good. They'll manage. Though I admit they will need some on-the-ground help. That's something you and I need to discuss, but I have some ideas."

"Why do we need to send four of them? We've had enough work getting just one disaster-prone individual out of trouble in the past. But four?"

"Call it intuition. I'm convinced we need them all."

"If you say so, Laoban. Now, you're telling me that the focus is on this strip of land in Namibia or Botswana. Why did you tell the team they were going to Victoria Falls? That's in Zimbabwe."

"It's the nearest airport. Well, the nearest one that it's easy to get to from London. More discreet, too. Lots of tourists fly into there."

"And after there? How does the team get to the mine? If it's there."

"Land, water, I don't know. That's your job to work out, Latviana."

"And what's their cover? What do they say that they're going for?"

"A holiday, of course. Remember that we're supposed to be a travel agency. Lots of people go to Africa on holiday. Looking for lions and elephants, of course, not for a praseodymium mine."

"Ah. Spies on safari."

"Exactly."

"And what do you want me to do while they're searching for the lost ark?"

"Sorry? What do you mean?"

"Never mind." She concluded Laoban didn't go to the cinema or read popular fiction.

"Just do what you always do. Stay nearby. Somewhere from where you can reach them if needed. Keep an eye out. Just in case anything goes wrong. Oh, and very important. Monitor those email accounts."

"Can't you ask Toshio to do that? I'll be busy and travelling."

"No, the fewer who are involved, the better. Whenever you'll be out of contact for more than twelve hours, say, message me and I'll monitor them myself."

The call over, Latviana adopted her travel agent mindset and started googling routes from London to Victoria Falls. No point in leaving the team to plan their own flights. In her opinion, with the exception of Pilot, they'd struggle to locate a bus to Piccadilly Circus from Oxford Street. She quickly discovered it was difficult enough to find four different routings for the four agents; it was near impossible to get them all to arrive on the same day. She remembered the old days, when she could simply have arranged for them all to fly in to some better-connected airport, and then have Pilot jet them to an airstrip closer to where they needed to be. But the old days weren't good. Soon, she was sure, the new days would be better. At least what she did got recognition from Laoban. Not like working for Smith. After their relationship had changed to a purely professional one, he'd treated her like the rest. Like shit on his expensive shoes. Not that he'd be wearing those anymore. Not where he was now.

Anyway, back to the job in hand. Getting the team to Victoria Falls was one thing, but they then needed to get to where they actually needed to be. Wherever that place was. She searched for Caprivi Strip on Google Maps. A long green band of land. However far she zoomed in, it was just green. No roads, no villages, no nothing. A river dividing it from Botswana. All green land there, too. No proper roads, but a few tracks on the Botswana side, indeed one that ran parallel to the river. But nothing to indicate what it would be like. The first time that online maps had failed her.

So, Plan B. Time to WhatsApp Pilot. Thank goodness they weren't using PDAs like in Smith days and were embracing the twenty-first century. Latviana had set the incoming message tone to a 'ping,' though. Unlike everyone else from those times, she'd missed the pings. She tapped out a message.

'Do I have time to get some maps couriered to Elstree before you fly out?'

Two grey ticks. No answer. Hopefully, he hadn't left yet. But no, five minutes later, a reply.

'You've got two hours. Where are they coming from?'

'Stanfords in Covent Garden. Assuming they've got them.'

'OK. Have a biker pick them up and take them to the Village Hotel. Tell him to message me when he's near. I'll meet him there.'

Latviana had no idea what maps she needed, but luckily found a remarkably helpful cartography specialist at the end of the phone. She explained that they urgently needed maps to plan self-drive safaris in Botswana and Namibia, biggest scale possible, and he not only seemed to understand exactly what she wanted and have the right ones in stock, but was happy to take a card number over the phone and put them by the till for the courier to pick up. Total time from sending initial WhatsApp message to maps in Pilot's hands: one hour and twenty minutes. Result! A tribute to her remarkable logistical efficiency.

Less than an hour later, another ping. 'About to taxi. ETA 16:50 if ATC is nice to me.'

So, an hour and a half to shower, change, fix makeup, and get to the airport to meet him. Perfect timing.

And bringing the maps provided the ideal excuse for Pilot to come to Rotterdam. Latviana was still nervous that Laoban would discover their relationship. Back on their last mission together for the Smiths, pushing back on her lascivious tendencies, he'd managed to convince Laoban he was gay, while demonstrating to Latviana that he most definitely wasn't.

# Recovering from Starvation

Ronald wasn't enjoying his spaghetti. "Where's the sauce? And it's overcooked, pasta should be *al dente*."

"For a man who's had nothing to eat for a month, you're a damned awkward customer," said Jason, who had taken over from Jane as 'mother,' feeding the bed-ridden invalid one strand of pasta at a time. "I know that it's probably not the right thing to give you, and we may have cooked it wrong, but that's all there is. Like it or lump it."

Jane adopted a more conciliatory tone. "We'll get you something else, but you'll have to wait."

"I can survive a little longer. It's difficult eating this. I can't chew. Can you bring me soup?"

"Of course. Oh, and I could purée something. There's a food processor downstairs. We'll go to the shops. Wait here."

"As if I could go anywhere. I can hardly make it to the lavatory anymore."

Jane and Jason went downstairs and walked back to the waiting limousine. "He needs a doctor. Probably hospital, too. Let's get back to the hotel and make enquiries."

Mateo, the concierge, was already eating out of Jane's hand, a state she had expected to achieve considering the tips she had given him before, but the sight of a hundred-euro note was certainly enough to ensure his total dedication. And discretion. Asked if they could talk somewhere away from the hotel lobby, he instantly placed a 'back soon' card on his desk, murmured "follow me," and led them to a remarkably luxuriously appointed office.

"The manager's," he told them, locking the door behind them. "He won't be in until the evening."

Mateo might have been able to fix most things, but obtaining totally discreet medical attention on the island proved beyond his superpowers. He was more than sorry, but since the start of the pandemic, the police authorised and monitored all hospital admissions. In any case, the island's hospital could only really cope with minor emergencies. Anything serious meant travelling to the capital, Praia, on another island in the archipelago. However, there might be a solution! The talk of having to travel to the hospital had obviously reminded the concierge of something, as he apologised and broke off the conversation to make a call. While he talked, his smile grew, and though she didn't understand what he was saying to whoever was at the other end of the line, Jane could tell he had come up with something by way of a solution.

"That call was to my friend who works at the airport. They often handle medical emergencies, tourists who have heart attacks, things like that. He said there is an air ambulance flying out tonight at 22:00 with only one passenger. If you are generous with my friend and the pilot, they will put your man on the same flight. And then, on arrival, he will be taken straight to hospital."

Agreed that this would be an excellent solution, Jane and Jason returned to the limousine hovering at the kerbside. Mateo stopped them before they could get in. "You can go now but come back at 18:00. I will find you another vehicle more appropriate for when you go to the airport."

"That makes sense. But now we also need some food to take to the patient. Where do you suggest we go?"

"The buffet is closed at this time, but go round to the kitchen and ask for Eloisa. Tell her I sent you. She will give you a takeaway box. Choose what food you want and bring it back here."

Back in the limo for now, they first cruised slowly down the main street of Santa Maria, stopping at every cashpoint, each time extracting the maximum of fifty thousand escudos. About five hundred euros. For the first time, Jane appreciated her husband having so many credit cards and using the same PIN for every one of them, and was pleasantly surprised that the banks hadn't stopped them when Barry was taken into custody. What she and Jason didn't like so much was everyone staring at them, perhaps because of the limousine. They probably thought they were film stars. Some tourists even took pictures of them. Well, it couldn't be helped. As soon as they had exhausted the island's totality of ATMs, they were almost relieved to be heading back to the house.

It didn't look like Ronald had moved an inch, but he was awake.

"What did you bring me?"

"Vegetable soup. And fish and potatoes. I'm going to go downstairs and liquidise those now," said Jane.

"All out of a packet, I suppose."

"All out of a five-star hotel, actually. And later you're going to fly to a hospital where they can look after you properly."

"Do I have to travel in a coffin?"

Jane laughed, not understanding why he looked so serious. "I certainly hope not! You look alive enough to me. Anyway, we'll be back to collect you later."

Back at the hotel, the friendly concierge was waiting for them. "I have the perfect transport for you outside. The driver will help you. He knows what to do, but he doesn't speak English. I am sure you will manage. But now you have just enough time for an early dinner before you have to go."

The 'perfect transport' turned out to be a white SUV with 'AMBULANCE' painted down each side in red and a prominent red cross on the bonnet. The driver was wearing a white coat with a red cross embroidered on the breast pocket. Was it a disguise, or was he really a medic? Jane didn't care.

He may not have spoken English, but he knew exactly where to go. Unsurprisingly, and fortunately, the street was still deserted. The driver drew up in front of the house, opened the back hatch, and pulled out a stretcher, pointing to Jason to pick up the other end. Inside, the driver took Jason by the arm and pointed alternately to the patient and the bathroom.

"We're leaving," Jason told Ronald. "You need to go to the bathroom first."

"Help me, please," came the reply. Jason was unamused at having to support the man to the toilet, but did it all the same. "I'm glad I decided on a career as a fitness instructor and not as a geriatric nurse," he told Jane when it was done.

"I may be older than you, and weak at the moment, but I am *not* geriatric!" Then, to Jane, "Thank you for dinner. It was delicious. Best thing I've eaten in a month!" followed by a coughing fit that was probably an attempt at laughter.

Ronald collapsed onto the stretcher, and the driver-medic and Jason got him down the stairs and into the waiting car. Before closing the hatch, the driver took out two white coats for Jane and Jason, then pointed to a rear-facing seat in the back, next to the recumbent patient, and indicated that was where Jason should sit. Jane, who was quite happy dressing up as a nurse and had already made herself comfortable in the front next to the driver, found the situation rather entertaining. "You can give him some fitness instruction as we go, darling. He looks like he needs some!" Jason grimaced.

At least they didn't have to go far. In less than fifteen minutes, they were driving up the ramp to the airport terminal, though they went straight past it, continuing to the end of the building, then turning right and halting at a door marked 'Executive Aviation.'

The driver barked some instructions, presumably in Portuguese, but it was obvious he meant for Jane to go with him and for Jason to stay with Ronald. The personal trainer attempted some conversation, but even though the spoon-fed meal seemed to have put some colour into the invalid's face, he was clearly only semi-conscious. He did manage to mouth "where are they taking me?" to which the only answer Jason could give was "hospital, somewhere."

The Executive Aviation terminal was devoid of executives. In fact, it appeared devoid of life altogether. Just a few sofas and low tables and a water cooler in the corner. The driver led Jane through a door and down a corridor, then into an office where another white-coated man was standing. Definitely a doctor, this one, since he had a stethoscope around his neck. The essential qualification. He held out his hand to Jane and introduced himself as Marco. He spoke English!

"I understand you have a patient for me to take to hospital?"

"Yes, please. He's in the ambulance outside."

"How old is he, and what is wrong with him?"

"I don't know his age, but he looks at least seventy to me. Until we found him this afternoon, he'd been trapped in a room and had eaten nothing in the last month."

"Dehydrated too?"

"He had water, but very possibly."

"Mateo told me you need this to be very discreet? Are the police after you?"

"No, I'm not in trouble with the police, but the situation is delicate. I found him living in my house. So yes, I need total discretion. Please."

"I have another patient going to hospital tonight. I can take your man in the other bunk as long as he does not need continuous medical attention or drips or transfusions?"

"No, he's conscious. Just very weak."

He spoke a few words in Portuguese to the driver, who evidently understood them as instruction to leave them alone, and went out, closing the door behind him.

"You understand this is risky for me? And expensive for you?"

"I do. How much are we talking about?"

"Five thousand euros. Plus the hospital fees, of course."

"All I have is three thousand five hundred. Well, the equivalent in escudos. The cash machines wouldn't give me more."

The doctor was unhappy. "The fee is five thousand. I'm sorry, it's not negotiable. Can you get more tomorrow?"

"I think so. But I can't leave Ronald here until then, surely?"

"No, that will not be necessary. Three thousand five hundred now, then you give the other one thousand five hundred in an envelope to Mateo tomorrow. Agreed?"

"Agreed. What about the hospital?"

"When I deliver him there, I will tell them that I think he is covered by the same insurance as the woman I already have on the plane. She is quite old. I think we can say they are man and wife. That will get him admitted, but the hospital will discover the truth very quickly. Maybe in two or three days. My friend there will send you an email, and you will need to send him the funds immediately to pay for the hospital."

"Can I pay by credit card?"

"No," the medic laughed. "You have to pay my friend there in crypto. He will tell you how much. One week at a time. He will settle up with the doctors and the hospital."

"Crypto?" Jane looked blank. "What's that?"

"You have not heard of bitcoin?"

"Oh, yes, but I don't have any. I know nothing about it."

The man opened a drawer of the desk, pulled out a wad of papers, riffled through them and drew out one page. "Here are the instructions. It tells you all you need to know."

"You've done this before."

"A few times." The medic grinned.

Jane scanned the page, folded it, and put it away in her handbag, remembering as she did so to pull out the money and give it to the man, who counted it slowly. Satisfied, he put it in an envelope and locked it away in the drawer. "I will come now to help my colleague carry the body onto the plane. The pilot wants to leave in twenty minutes, so we have little time." He led Jane through a different door, this time directly onto the apron. "Look, that is our plane," pointing at a small, white, unmarked jet parked close to the terminal. The driver had already brought the car up close beside it. He and the medic pulled the stretcher out of the ambulance and went to climb the steps into the plane. Jane and Jason stood watching. "Good luck, Ronald," she called. "Get well soon!"

Within moments, the men came back down the steps. "A pleasure doing business," said the medic. "Don't forget tomorrow."

Jane nodded. "I forgot to ask. Where are you taking him?"

"Luanda."

# Victoria Falls

"Welcome to Zimbabwe, Mr Grimes." A short in stature, rotund in shape, bald on head, broadly smiling in face, black man holding a placard with his name on it was standing right in front of Humphry, blocking his path as he exited customs in Victoria Falls.

"Oh, er, yes… that's me," he replied, recovering his composure, having momentarily forgotten his temporarily adopted surname.

"My name is Aaron, and I am your local guide here. Did you have a good flight?"

"Better than I'd expected. Some people told me Ethiopian was a rubbish airline, but I thought they were quite good. Didn't like having to wait in Addis Ababa airport, though. I suppose everywhere in Africa is so uncivilised?" Looking around at the gleaming glass and metal building and at the man greeting him, he instantly regretted his words.

"No, sir. I am sure you will discover that most of us here in Africa are very civilised." He smiled. "At least as civilised as your natives are in England, anyway."

Humphry recognised the need for a change of subject. "Are you my driver? Are we going straight to the hotel?"

"I am indeed your driver. But first we need to wait for half an hour or so for the flight from Joburg to arrive. There is a lady joining the same safari as you who is arriving on that flight. I trust you are not too inconvenienced by a short wait?"

"No, no… the travel agent told me that there were four of us on this safari. Have the other two already arrived, then?"

"One gentleman arrived a few hours ago from Nairobi. My colleague has already taken him to the hotel. The other gentleman will join you there. He is flying in to another airport." That's going to be Robert, reasoned Humphry. Bet he got given a better routing. Probably first class, too.

He passed the wait in silent contemplation until Bea came trotting through the doors, ignoring him and heading straight for Aaron, who was now holding a different placard with the name 'Babbage.' Must remember that we aren't supposed to know each other, thought Humphry.

Aaron's greetings having been repeated to Bea, she turned to Humphry. "Beatrix Babbage," she introduced herself. "You must be Humphry Grimes. I understand we're going on the same safari! Such fun! I'm sure we'll be the best of friends in no time." She rattled off her fake introductions at great speed. Humphry smiled and acquiesced, apparently happily, to the suggestion of friendship to come. Aaron told them to follow and strode off towards the car park. "Cutting your beard short makes you much more handsome, and twenty years younger," she whispered, checking first that Aaron wasn't looking and couldn't overhear.

***

Comfortably installed and luggage safely stowed in Aaron's minibus, they drove away. In silence. Humphry felt he needed to say something appropriate and positive. "I'm really looking forward to the safari. I've never seen lions. Up close in the jungle, that is. I've seen them in the zoo, of course. Have you been on safari before, Miss Babbage?"

She winked. "No, this is my first experience of anything quite so… exciting."

Bea and Humphry passed the next hour in inconsequential safari and holiday-related chatter, very little of it invented, and none of it previously known to the other. Take the reading group away, and they were strangers, seemingly with nothing in common. When the conversation died, they looked out of the windows to see they were trundling down an empty road through deserted countryside, lots of trees on both sides of the road. "Should we be looking out for wildlife?" Beatrix queried their driver.

"You might see some birds or a mongoose crossing the road," Aaron replied. "But this is not real safari country yet."

"Where exactly are we going?" asked Humphry, belatedly realising the only information Laoban had imparted to them was that they would be flying to Victoria Falls and then going on a safari, and that they were only allowed a 10kg hand-luggage-size wheely case each. Aaron must think it odd that he had two passengers who had no knowledge of the itinerary and had arrived with significantly more baggage. But, then again, no doubt he was used to idiot tourists.

Before answering, Aaron pulled over to the side of the road and turned to face them. This looked serious. "We are driving now to Kasane. You will stay there tonight."

"Where's Kasane?" Bea now. "Well, where in Zimbabwe? Are we going south or north?"

"East, actually," replied Aaron. "And Kasane is in Botswana, of course, where your safari takes place. We will cross the border in about ten minutes." The passengers did their best to contain their surprise. They hadn't yet got used to management providing them with incomplete, confusing, or deliberately wrong information. Aaron fished inside the glove box and pulled out two padded envelopes. "I'm sorry. I should have given you these before we left. Your itinerary and travel vouchers are inside."

Just as well Laoban reminded us to bring our pads with e-book versions of Le Carré, Humphry thought, scanning the itinerary and seeing that, despite looking suitably innocuous, there were plenty of things that would need decoding. At least the first line was in plain English and made sense. 'Leave Zimbabwe on your original passport. Enter Botswana on the new one.' He fished deeper into the envelope, located a booklet, and, after first checking that Aaron wasn't watching, pulled it out. An Irish passport. His picture. His birthday — well, right day and month, but a year later. In the name of Humphry Appleby. "Ye gods," he muttered to himself.

He looked over at Bea and pointed at the passport. She showed him hers. Beatrix Potter. "What joker dreamed these names up?" They would never find out, but it was Pilot and Latviana, who thought they were hilarious.

But there was no time for further discussion, as they had reached the border.

Leaving Zimbabwe was easy enough. Hand over passport to the officer, watch him stamp over the visa bought an hour earlier for fifty dollars, take passport back. Now for the sleight of hand.

Aaron drove the minibus forward about a hundred metres. "Botswana," he announced. Really? In the middle of the road, a dirty muddy puddle. To the side, what might once have been a shipping container, painted white and with a window cut into one wall. "First walk through the steriliser, then go to the window with your passports," Aaron instructed. Steriliser? "The water there. It is to stop foot and mouth disease." The water in the trough was brown with bits of vegetation floating on the surface and didn't look like it would sterilise anything, but they did as they were told. Bea was thankful that she was wearing trainers. Aaron drove the bus through a wider, deeper, and even dirtier puddle.

It transpired that the woman behind the window in the container wasn't there to check passports. She was the health examiner. "Yellow Fever certificates!" she shouted at them. Unnecessarily loud. Humphry knew that the real Humphry didn't have one of those, but he trusted Laoban would have planned accordingly and delved back into the padded envelope. There it was, a buff-coloured card confirming that Humphry Appleby had been vaccinated in Dublin five years previously.

Health requirements satisfied, next stop immigration. A rather basic wooden hut, but architecturally a step up from the container. Push passport over counter, officer stamps and returns it. Four seconds? Three? Are they competing for the world's fastest passport control? No checks? What if they were criminals? Or spies?

"Twenty minutes to the lodge," announced Aaron, slamming the doors and driving off. Within a kilometre they reached civilisation, or at least a road with houses and petrol stations and shops strung out along it. Not a cohesive village, rather a few single-storey buildings peppered into the wilderness along the verge. Nineteen minutes later — Humphry was timing it, thinking he should take a first step towards getting back into efficient spying mode — they pulled up. "Kasane Safari Lodge," announced Aaron. "You will stay here tonight. Be ready here in reception with your cases packed tomorrow at twelve exactly. A hotel driver will take you to the airport."

"The airport?" asked an incredulous Bea. "But we've only just flown in. We're not leaving! We're going on safari."

"To get to your safari lodge, you have to fly. From here, from Kasane airport. Your lodge is up country, about one hour from here. There are no roads. You can only get there by plane." A porter came to unload the bags, Aaron bid his passengers goodbye and drove off.

As they followed the porter towards the reception desk, a petite white woman with bleached blonde hair, dressed in a brilliant blue uniform, a yellow sun embroidered on the jacket pocket, rushed towards them. "You must be Beatrix and Humphry," she beamed. "I am Maria, from Caprivi Tours. Welcome to Kasane. I hope you had a delightful journey and are looking forward to your safari?"

Niceties duly exchanged and keys collected from reception, Maria informed them they would all meet for dinner and a briefing at seven. "Two others will be joining us. Mr Rodgers is already here," she said. Hmmm, thought Bea. That's obviously Richard. Another joke surname. "And Mr Hammerstein?" she hazarded. Maria looked lost. Obviously, she hadn't seen *The Sound of Music*. "No, there is no Mr Hammerstein. Our other guest is Mr Ludlum, and he is arriving from Gaborone this afternoon." Robert Ludlum, eh? And nobody is supposed to guess that we are secret agents, mused Bea.

# Kasane

Duly checked in, key in hand, Bea followed her escort to her room, or 'rondavel' as the snooty receptionist called it, in something of a daze. The considerably overweight African walking in front of her was dressed like a middle-aged boy scout, with khaki shorts, a khaki shirt, and a khaki cap. She'd managed to stay alert until now, but twenty hours of travel and the heat of the midday African sun were finally taking their toll. The effort of raising her eyebrows when she saw how the staff at the lodge were dressed was the final straw on her sleepy camel's back. She therefore paid no attention to this new guide's non-stop patter, no doubt honed through many years of conducting guests to their rondavels and explaining the facilities and rules of the establishment. As soon as the door was opened, she shooed him away and collapsed on the bed, instantly unconscious.

Several hours later, she was roused from the deepness of her slumbers by someone hammering on the door, followed by them telling her in an extremely loud male voice that dinner would be served in one hour. Opening her eyes, she transitioned from coma to shock in an instant. Where on earth was she? Above her head was a roof made of tree trunks and twigs. A pukka fan rotated slowly beneath it.

Realisation crept in, and she remembered she was in a safari lodge en route to a secret mission. But where, precisely? Some place in Africa, for sure. Botswana, was it? It must be near Zimbabwe, she decided, as they had only driven an hour or so from the airport.

Turning her head to one side and then to the other, she examined her room. Not only was the ceiling made of wood, the walls were made of tree trunks, too. The window was gauze, not glass. Splayed across the middle of it was a green lizard. Disturbed as she moved to sit up, it raced away to hide behind a curtain.

She supposed that was normal. Lizards live here in the jungle. That one was small and green. It couldn't be dangerous. Anyway, lizards aren't creatures that spies should be scared of.

The rondavel was large. Like an apartment. A bungalow. Lots of furniture — in Bea's opinion, most of it unnecessary — also all in wood. A brown study. Opening doors, she discovered the shower was in the open air. No roof, a twilight sky overhead. A fence around it to protect her modesty. The weather being warm and the water being hotter, she understood how tourists would consider this luxury.

It was just as well that her phone had a torch function, as night had fallen and the path from her room was in total darkness. No artificial lights to guide her way. But no need. Overhead, there was a wonderful starscape, such as she had not seen since her early childhood staying with her aunt out in the country. Clear summer nights were more frequent in England then. Now there was so much light pollution. She vaguely recognised a few constellations, but couldn't remember their names. She meandered along the path, passing a few other rondavels, avoiding a large tree root that hadn't yet been commandeered for building materials, until she met a dead end. The wrong way, then. Rustling sounds from the trees. Mustn't be scared. I'm a secret agent, she reminded herself.

Returning, she now saw the lodge building ahead suddenly lit up from within. Head down, concentrating on the patch illuminated by her phone so as not to trip over anything on the gravel, she walked headfirst into the man scout who had been her guide earlier.

"What are you doing out here alone, Miss Potter?" It sounded like a reprimand.

"I'm going to dinner." Surely that much was obvious.

"You must never walk to or from your room alone in the dark. I told you before. It's too dangerous."

"Dangerous? You mean I could trip?" Harry. She suddenly remembered his name. Couldn't have been totally out of it earlier.

"No. You might get attacked! Lions. Leopards. Many animals." Bea hadn't thought about that. Perhaps she should have listened more attentively to the guide when he led her to the room. Stayed conscious for a few minutes longer.

"Next time, you call out to me when you wish to leave, and I will come to take you."

"Won't the animals attack you, though?" It didn't seem likely to Bea that a hungry lion would distinguish between a black man in khaki and a white woman in a Laura Ashley dress. If anything, the lion would probably prefer the man, at least this one. More flesh. Much meatier.

Harry patted the rifle at his side and nodded knowingly. Bea hadn't noticed that before.

They arrived back at the reception desk. "After dinner, you wait here. I will come." He turned and left her alone. The lobby area was enormous. A vast wooden deck with lots of rugs and sofas, coffee tables loaded with well-thumbed books of pictures of animals and birds. A bar in one corner, but no barman in residence. Framed photographs of zebras and leopards and elephants and giraffes on the wall. A blackboard headed "Today's Sightings" on which someone had chalked 'Lions x 12, Wild Dogs x 8, Hyena x 1,' proving she really was in Africa, in the jungle, in safari country.

A loud honking made her start and turn her head toward the noise. Not a siren sound she recognised. Not mechanical. It was coming from the fence at the edge of the deck, opposite the wall. She approached and peered over. In the light from the lodge, she could see a pool below with, yes, an elephant siphoning water over himself. Amazing! So close! For sights such as this had she come to Africa!

The restaurant looked empty. Either there weren't any other people staying, or if there were, they hadn't come to dinner yet or were keeping themselves to themselves.

"Your table is outside, on the balcony," murmured the waiter. "Your friends are already assembled."

Bea didn't think of them as friends, not yet at least, but could understand why this oddly dressed young man was thinking they might be.

"Thank you," she replied. "Your outfit is very unusual. Is that how waiters dress here in Botswana?" If nothing else, Bea thought, it was impractical for serving food. A flowing bright yellow smock covered with various patterns in red and black, accompanied by a matching pillbox hat, and a drum that looked like it had been made from an outsized coconut shell strung around his neck.

"No, madam, I am not the waiter. He has gone to the bathroom. I am one of the dance troupe. He just asked me to look after the guests while he is away." He smiled patiently at this white woman. Her confusion was explained. Though she hadn't been expecting a dance troupe any more than she had expected an elephant to wander up and drink from the swimming pool.

The reason for the restaurant being empty became apparent as Beatrix passed through it and discovered another wide deck on the other side. With warm African nights, alfresco dining was clearly preferable to being closeted in an air-conditioned glass tank. Or, at least, that's what all the other guests had decided on. Not many people, but more than enough to quell the idea of the place being deserted. Another waiter lurked there, this one dressed for the part. "Caprivi Tours?" he enquired. "Your table is over there."

She could see the team already gathered together around the furthest table and made a little wave before remembering that she wasn't supposed to have met any of them before. Except for Humphry, of course, since they had shared the minibus. And the young woman who had met them in reception – Maria? She walked towards them, holding out a hand ready to be shaken.

"Hello everyone, I'm Beatrix Potter."

Robert rolled his eyes. "Playing the joker, I see. There's no need for that. We're far enough away from other tables for them not to hear us."

Bea returned her hand to her side. "I was expecting you to tell us about *The Bourne Initiative*. Or at least this safari initiative."

Robert looked mystified.

"Your last book," Bea reminded him. "We must read it after we finish Le Carré."

"It's just as well nobody who might overhear us would understand what you're talking about, Bea," said Maria. Latviana only to her close friends. "You're a covert researcher, remember?"

"And you're our tour guide, Maria?"

"Until you leave Kasane, yes. From tomorrow, though, you're on your own."

She was interrupted by the waiter, asking for drinks orders and displaying a wine list. Richard, always the first to react when alcohol was on offer, reached out and grabbed it. "I think we should celebrate the start of our safari with a bottle of fizz!" he pronounced.

Maria fixed him with a stare and waved the waiter away. "Frankly, it's better you all keep your heads clear. If you insist, you'll have to settle for a glass of house wine. Champagne isn't included in the budget."

"Why? James Bond drank like a fish. I don't mind paying," said Richard.

"With what? You have no *pula*. And before you ask, neither have I."

"I have a credit card."

"Not in the name of Richard Rodgers, though."

Richard nodded glumly and called the waiter back. "I'll have a glass of house red wine. The one that's included with the meal."

The others, suitably admonished by Maria, settled for water and were joined by Richard after he had taken one sip of the wine and spat it back into the glass.

Dinner was served from a buffet, wherein lay various indeterminate stewed meats, all equally tough and flavourless, a selection of exotic vegetables — if one can describe plantain and yam as exotic — and a monstrous dish of spaghetti. Despite it being cold and congealed, the team discovered that was the best option once it was livened up with liberal dollops of tomato ketchup. Humphry, to his surprise, found a pot of Marmite on the counter and recommended adding a scrape of that as well.

Although quizzed throughout dinner, Latviana avoided explaining the plan for the next few days or answering any of their questions, insisting that everything would be addressed in their planning meeting the following morning. Unable to extract further information, finding the desserts even less tempting than the savoury dishes, and in the absence of alcohol, there was no reason to go on being sociable. By eight o'clock they were on their way back to their rondavels in a crocodile — a term Humphry pointed out as unsuitable given where they were — led by Harry, the rear guarded by his similarly clad colleague, Paul.

# The Planning Meeting

Each of the team found a note pushed under their door when they woke in the morning. 'Your Caprivi Tours Guides will be expecting you for a safari orientation meeting in the Green Conference Room at 8.30.'

Said room could easily have held a hundred people. The four covert researchers occupied front row seats. Latviana, immaculate and coiffured as Maria in her travel guide uniform, dressed more appropriately for welcoming millionaires onto a luxury yacht than guiding a bunch of middle-aged English tourists on a safari, stood waiting for them. Beside her was a big plasma screen, displaying a rotating series of pictures of wildlife. "That's only there in case anyone walks in," she explained. "You'll be looking for an illegal mine, not a giraffe," she said, pointing at the current image on the screen, "though you'll no doubt see one or two of those along the way.

"So, as you know already, my name is Maria." Worth reminding them, especially Rob, that she didn't want them using any other name. "First, health. It's still the dry season, so there shouldn't be any mosquitos, but let's not take the risk. Malaria tablets." She handed out blister packs of tablets to each of them. "Take one now, as soon as we finish here, then one every morning."

Humphry the doctor interceded. "There are fourteen tablets here. We need to go on taking the tablets for seven days after we leave the malaria zone. So, do I surmise that you only expect us to be here for a week?"

"If you are there longer, we will give you more. Now, the itinerary."

She explained they would leave the lodge immediately after the meeting and fly in a small plane to another lodge, much smaller than this one, in northern Botswana. That would be their base, and they would be the only guests. The staff there had been security screened, background checked, and apprised of their objective. Two of their skilled rangers would join the mission. After an initial day or two of orientation, they would set out in search of the mystery mine. Which direction they went in and how they managed their mission would be entirely down to them and the rangers from that point forwards.

Richard asked the first question. "The original instructions said we were looking for a diamond mine. Now you say praesidium?"

"Not praesidium, praseodymium. Diamonds were just to give you the concept." Richard looked sceptical. Maria was already irritated with him from the previous evening. She shook her head. "And because it's not a word in the code book, of course."

"What is this stuff, then? And what does a praseodymium mine look like? Something like a coal mine?"

"No, the client says open cast. More like a quarry," replied Laoban, materialising from behind the screen, dressed identically to Latviana AKA Maria. "He thinks it will be an exploratory mine, so manual digging, no machinery."

Disregarding the answer, the faces of every member of the team registered something between surprise and shock. "Where did you come from? Have you been here all the time?" asked Beatrix.

"No, I have just arrived."

"Are you coming with us?"

"No, and before you ask, I will be leaving as soon as this meeting ends. No more questions about me!" she said, her shrill voice rising an octave. Then calmer, "Now, questions about your mission."

"Why do you need all four of us to go? If the lodge is sending two people, surely you only need one of us?" asked Robert.

"The two people from the lodge are rangers, not researchers. Their role is simply to guide you. Each of you has unique skills, and we might need any or all of them. Equally importantly, we need other people who see you or that you might meet unexpectedly to assume you're tourists. Your cover story. As a group with guides, you won't raise any suspicions. Just one or two on your own would be very unusual in safari country."

"Is it likely there will be a lot of other tourists?" asked Beatrix. "I have a friend who went on safari in Kenya, and she said that there were jeeps everywhere, hundreds more people than animals."

"Not where you're going. Botswana is expensive, so there aren't so many tourists. The lodges are small and a long way apart from each other. Nobody else will be staying in your concession. The other lodge nearby is closed for renovations. So, if you come across another jeep with people who look like tourists, be suspicious. And suspect that they suspect you."

"What if they don't look like tourists? They might be workers, or filming animals, or something," enquired Robert.

"Assume danger. Always. It is possible that another lodge will send out a team of workers or replace their staff, but we don't expect that anywhere you are going. And it's the wrong season for making documentaries." Laoban maintained a withering stare towards Robert. "Remember that your mission is to discover information. Covertly. You are not there to disrupt whatever they're doing, illegal or otherwise. Try not to be seen."

"And if we are seen?" asked Beatrix.

"Then you're tourists who have strayed off the beaten path."

Humphry took over the questioning. "How often should we report back?"

"Once you have located the mine, mapped its coordinates, taken many photographs, and gathered as much detail as you can safely get, you are to return to the lodge where you're being based, and they will call us to send a plane to bring you back."

"You don't want us to send daily updates?"

"There's no mobile phone coverage in the whole of that area. Sometimes there's a patchy signal from Namibia, but latching on to that would be very risky. We must assume that because the mine is secret, there will be a lot of security and any electronic communications in a wide area will be monitored. Leave your phones in airplane mode at all times."

"But when we are in the lodge, we can call you from there?"

"No, the lodge has no mobile signal, and there's no wi-fi. They have just one fixed line back to their base."

The entire team looked perturbed. They hadn't expected to be totally out of contact with the world. The thought of being unable to call anyone, no internet, no WhatsApp… How did real tourists survive for days away from social media? And, more to the point, how would covert researchers manage without electronic communications?

The meeting paused while everyone took it in. Latviana and Laoban appeared to be enjoying the consternation on the team's faces. After what felt like an age, Latviana held up her hand. "Don't worry. You won't be able to make calls, but we're giving each of you one of these devices." She triumphantly held up a rectangular orange and black block of plastic, a little smaller than a mobile phone. "This is a satellite tracker. I'll be monitoring where you are. I can send you short text messages. In an emergency—"

Laoban interrupted to stress, "And ONLY in an emergency!"

Latviana continued, "Here on the back, there is an SOS button. Press and hold it for ten seconds and help will come."

"Where from?" asked Beatrix.

"The nearest emergency services."

"They might be a hundred miles away, though."

"Probably. Don't expect anything to happen quickly. Especially in Africa."

"Can't we message you?" asked Robert. "These look like kids' toys. Proper satellite phones work both ways."

"Not with these devices." Robert frowned. Surely Laoban was charging the client enough to kit them out with the best equipment?

Latviana ignored him and went on. "But you can send me a simple standard message. Here, there are four buttons." She turned the gadget over and pointed at buttons that were indeed labelled 1, 2, 3, 4. "We assign standard messages to each. But first you have to press the 1 button four times in a row. That's just in case you press a key accidentally. For example, when you are successful in your mission, press 11111. If you are returning to base without finding anything, press 11112."

"And if one of us gets attacked by a wild animal?"

"Any big problems that you can't fix yourselves but can wait for us to provide help without involving emergency services, like being eaten by a lion, press 11114. If you still have hands and fingers." She half laughed, her contempt for the team showing through.

"What's button 3 for, then?" asked Richard.

"If something unexpected happens that will delay you completing your mission and you need more time, press 11113. That way, we won't be concerned if we know you will be stationary in one place for an extended time."

"But you can message us?"

"I will only send a message if it's critical. If I do, the SOS button will glow red. Press 4444 to retrieve the message. Press anything else and I'll know you are in trouble. Or that you've forgotten the code."

Humphry decided he had better change the subject before Richard said something sarcastic. "What if we don't find the mine? How long do we carry on looking?"

Laoban looked down her nose at him. "The client is confident it's there, so I'm confident you'll find it." To Humphry's ears, it sounded more like a threat to not fail than a vote of confidence in their abilities.

"Are you sure that it's somewhere near the lodge you're basing us at?"

"As sure as we can be. The client says it's definitely somewhere in that area. You're going to the furthest, the most remote lodge that's in use. All the land between here and there is regularly traversed by safaris, so we can be certain it's not there."

"Surely local people would know about it?" said Richard. "You can't dig a mine without people knowing."

"The client says they cannot have started to dig on a commercial scale yet. He believes they're checking out the territory and staking their claim. They'll have had to do some digging, of course. We assume they'll have built some sort of hut to live in and assay any samples. We know no more. Our client needs to know where they're looking and what they're doing before the Chinese tell the government what they've found and claim the concession."

Humphry was going to make a comment about how the Chinese always seem to be stealing other people's businesses but thought better of it. Was Laoban herself Chinese? He had never been able to work it out.

Richard had another question. "But, even so, local people would know?"

"There are no local people. No villages for a hundred kilometres in any direction. Only the lodge. The staff at the lodge have offered to sound out their colleagues in other lodges and friends in the villages where their families live. You English call it the jungle drums, I think. If they find anything, they'll tell you. They will point you in what they think is the most promising direction."

"Isn't it dangerous having the lodge staff know about our mission?"

"We have not told them all the details, of course. They believe the people you are searching for are looking for rare plants in the jungle that they can farm to make pharmaceuticals. And carrot and stick techniques tend to work well in Africa."

You mean bribes and threats, thought Humphry. Not things he was happy about, but as long as it was just a matter of calling a spade a shovel and not having to use it himself, he could turn a blind eye to this small corruption. Again.

The meeting over, the team went to their rooms to pack. Latviana turned to Laoban. "What you just told them about the lodge staff being told that those people are farming plants for drugs. Did you know that?"

"No, of course not. I had to tell them something, though."

"Well, I got word from our man in Belgrade this morning. I had to ask him to keep an eye on Mariana's emails while I was travelling here."

"And?"

"There's been a flurry of emails in the last few days. Mariana's definitely handling all the interesting stuff. She must be getting her instructions from Caesar and feeding back to him in those daily phone calls. Most of the correspondence is with somebody in Colombia. A lot of it's about Africa. Nothing at all about mining or that weird mineral. They use code words, but our asset in Belgrade is convinced that Caesar's principal business is importing drugs."

"Now that really is interesting. I wonder what we're going to find, and why he wants us to look for it."

# Into the Delta

The hotel minibus disgorged the team outside the Kasane airport terminal. We could be anywhere, thought Robert, who had more experience of airports than the rest of them. Just another large modern glass and steel construction. Incongruous in its style compared to its surroundings and in its size given the few people around, none of whom looked like passengers. Inside, there was a row of check-in desks and an illuminated departure board, but other than the word 'Departures' and a flashing time display, it was blank. Nowhere to go. No planes going anywhere.

"Where's our flight, then, Maria?" demanded Bea, pointing at the board.

"Don't worry. Private charters to the lodges don't show up there," Latviana said, doing her best to sound reassuring. That wasn't something that came naturally when she was at her most relaxed, let alone at times like now when she was stressed out. She surmised it would be less aggravation shepherding a group of hyperactive schoolchildren than this coterie of nervous wrecks.

The team, who had acted happy and enthusiastic at dinner last night, had been subdued, or perhaps terrified, in the morning meeting. The reality had finally begun to seep into them.

As for Latviana herself, the team's questions and reactions had caused her to lose most of the little confidence she had in their ability to undertake the mission. Even her beloved Robert. She'd expected him to become their natural leader, but they seemed to be coalescing around Humphry. He reminded her of Ronald Jones. Well, true, Jones hadn't had a beard, and he was at least twenty years older. But Humphry was proving to be just as much of an idiot and an irritant. Admittedly, not as much as Richard, in her opinion the dumbest of them all.

She led them through an unlabelled door to a room devoid of anything other than a long bench table, on which lay four rucksacks. "Repack!" she ordered.

Seeing their incomprehension, she continued. "You're now officially on safari. You can only travel with one item. You may be trekking, so you'll need rucksacks. You can't carry suitcases through the jungle. Pack everything you need into a rucksack and weigh it. No more than ten kilos. Leave everything else here."

It was certainly true that, except for Robert, the team had arrived with inappropriate and excessive luggage. Unsuitable under any circumstances, in Latviana's opinion, but definitely not appropriate for the African bush. Richard, who, when she'd first met him the day before, had considered one of the more practically minded members of the team, was travelling with a gargantuan cabin trunk. Beatrix was at least relatively light, but her roll-aboard case was bright mauve moulded plastic, and she had a backpack something like a young child might choose, a full-scale illustration of a penguin complete with wing flaps as the pocket covers. Robert, of course, was the consummate professional. He had the right sort of luggage. Naturally, she was biased, though, having worked with him for a few years and more recently forged a romantic attachment that in the present situation both were forced to hide. But where on earth had Laoban got these other people from? They reminded her of characters in some ancient black and white comedy films she had seen in the cinema in Minsk as a little girl.

Richard was the first to complain. Of course. "I can't fit in everything I want to take."

"I have told you, take only what you need. Leave the rest behind. Laoban made it clear to you that ten kilos was the limit before you left London."

"Maria, what will happen to my case and bag?" Beatrix wailed, clearly perplexed over the fate of her penguin out of its geographic habit and without her conservation. "I'm really rather attached to them — especially Pingu."

"Beatrix, you may be sure that I'll take care of them," assured Latviana, insincerely. She didn't add that she intended their cases and whatever remained in them to end up in landfill or an incinerator before the day was out.

The team carried their new rucksacks back out of the room. There was a little more activity now in the terminal, and one of the check-in desks was open, with two young men standing behind it. They didn't look like airline staff. Seeing the team file out, one of them lifted a card on the counter in front of him and called out. "Mr Appleby!" Nobody moved. Latviana prodded Humphry. "Sorry," he mouthed back to her as he approached the desk. His bag was grabbed and tagged, and he was presented with a boarding pass. Just like any other flight, except that the piece of card in his hand simply had the words 'Boarding Pass,' his name, and nothing else.

"Mr Rodgers!" Not so straightforward. "Your bag is too heavy. Eleven kilos!"

"It says ten point eight on the scale."

"Still too heavy. Take something out."

Richard, embarrassed, unzipped the bag, rooted around, and pulled out a pair of cowboy boots. "Probably no good for trekking in the jungle, anyway," he muttered.

To the surprise of each of them, not only was there a spacious departure lounge but conventional airport security too. Duly scanned and deemed unlikely to be terrorists, they stood at the vast window and surveyed the tarmac outside. Six or seven planes were lined up, all of the single-engine propeller type, all but one quite large. Robert alone knew that those were Grand Caravans and was itching to talk about them, but he had to restrain himself, aware that his new colleagues didn't know that he was a pilot. Unsurprisingly, their own transport was the one small plane. They manoeuvred their way in through a door at the back, Richard banging his head and swearing in the process, and levered themselves into the four passenger seats. A young man in orange overalls brought up the rear, pushing a trolley laden with their four rucksacks, which he then unceremoniously tossed onto the floor behind the passengers and shut the door.

At the front, a very tall, very slim, and very freckle-faced young man climbed into the pilot's seat. He had the greenhorn appearance of an eighteen-year-old, which gave none of them any comfort. Smart white shirt plus a tie, the latter seeming somewhat incongruous in a tropical climate and the midday sun. The baseball cap that topped it off had a Pan Am logo. Robert hoped this plane wouldn't go the same way as that long defunct airline. "Welcome aboard!" he called out. "I'm Gaz, I'll be flying you up to the lodge today."

"I didn't expect anyone here to be white skinned," whispered Bea to Richard.

"Judging from his accent, he's South African."

Bea nodded slowly, realising her lack of knowledge about Africa. She would need to retrain her preconceptions and, if she had any prejudices (she didn't think she had) eliminate them pretty smartly. The pilot was waving for their attention, and she was distracted from further introspections.

Gaz rattled through a safety briefing. Not quite like the ones on big commercial planes. With no life jackets, no oxygen masks that might fall from above, and no long-shot hope of being able to get out of one's seat to go to the non-existent lavatory at any stage in the journey, arguably there was no point. "There are two doors, one at the back that you came through, one at the front next to me. In the event of an emergency… scream." He laughed. None of the others joined in.

Robert couldn't resist an observation. "What about the third door? The one on the right side by the co-pilot?"

"Ah," replied Gaz, brightly, "but there is no co-pilot today, and that door is broken, anyway." Seeing Beatrix in panic mode, he added, "Don't worry, though, the plane has been fully checked over by the mechanics only this morning. I'm assured it's in perfect flying order." With which, he turned in his seat, pulled a few levers towards him, put an old-fashioned key into a lock on the dashboard, pulled out a knob, turned the key and the machine spluttered and vibrated into life.

Humphry, sitting in the row behind and watching Gaz with some fascination, was transported back to his early childhood and car journeys in his father's Humber Sceptre, already ancient when he was an infant. It sounded and felt the same, just that his dad's car didn't have a big propellor rotating rapidly in front of the windscreen. The Humber had felt safer, though. And that was before they had left the ground.

However, after the noise and vibration increased, the speed picked up and, with a bit of swaying to left and right, the plane was airborne and flying. The passengers visibly relaxed and looked out of the porthole windows, enjoying the panorama. Above, a clear blue sky. Beneath them, a wide river; to either side, as far as their eyes could see, a patchwork quilt of grass, shrubs, and clumps of trees, sometimes interspersed with streams. No towns or villages, not even a house.

"Where's the jungle, then? Does Africa even have jungles?" asked Richard of no-one in particular.

"That's it, below us," replied Bea. "Don't you watch the natural history programmes on television? Jungle doesn't only mean impenetrable forests of trees, you know."

As if on cue, Gaz turned his head towards his passengers. "Look. Down to your right. Elephants."

Indeed, there were. Not just one or two; twenty or thirty, maybe more, all different sizes. Marching in single file across open grassland, heading for a destination only they knew.

Humphry, Richard, and Bea spent the rest of the flight scrutinising the landscape, searching for more wildlife. Gaz pointed down towards what he claimed was a field of buffalo, but it just looked like another patch of grassland to the spies. Possibly a few spiders speckling the grass. Too high up to tell.

Robert, by contrast, kept his eyes ahead and on Gaz, itching to get his own hands on the controls but knowing that he couldn't appear to know anything about flying. His collaborators believed him to be a plumber by trade, a subterfuge insisted on by Laoban. He'd never quite fathomed why his aeronautical skills had to be kept secret from the others, but Laoban was the boss, she who must be obeyed, and so he went along with it. Not hard to do in the reading group, or even as a passenger in a big commercial plane, but here, putting his life in the hands of a juvenile aviator seated just within touching distance in front of him, he seethed with frustration. Admittedly, Gaz was holding the joystick and adjusting the throttle from time to time, but judging by the way his head was rocking from side to side, he was listening to music on his headphones rather than paying any attention to the sound of the engine or attending to air traffic control. Feeling the little plane yawing gently left and right, Rob itched to jump into the co-pilot's seat and teach the 'Captain' a thing or two about trim control.

Richard suddenly recoiled from his seat, falling against Robert, seated to his right. "Now's not a good time to get intimate, Richard."

"Don't be silly, Rob. I just got surprised by the fellow passenger nobody told us about." He pointed at a small green frog, now contentedly spreadeagled on the window to his left.

"Those little fellas get everywhere," laughed Gaz, who had turned his head to see what was going on. "They're more interested in the view than most of the guys I fly."

After over an hour of flying over landscapes as near identical as made no difference, Gaz appeared to jump to life, banked, put the little plane into a steep dive, and landed it on a gravel strip that nobody else, not even Robert, had seen coming. The engine phutted and died, the propellor made its final revolution, and an uncanny peace reigned.

"Welcome to Dreamtime Lodge!" exclaimed Gaz. No lodge was visible. Just a clearing in the bush where the plane had landed.

Gaz opened his door, jumped out with youthful vigour, and walked round to open the back door. As he did so, a big, dark green, open-top Land Cruiser materialised from behind the vegetation and approached. Not so much leaping as falling out of the front seats were two jolly-looking, corpulent men dressed in khaki shirts and shorts, one wearing a matching peaked cap, the other a pith helmet. The picture reminded Humphry of a comic strip he'd enjoyed as a child.

"Greetings! I am Jimbo, your guide, and this is Pascal, our tracker, and your Man Friday." Richard was taken aback by the 'Man Friday' description. He wasn't even sure that anyone who, like him, had taken the Council's obligatory Diversity Training (or 'Woke Brainwashing', as some of his colleagues had described it) would ever choose to admit to being called a Man Friday. "The lodge is a twenty-minute drive."

As they clambered on board, Bea seriously regretted having worn a skirt — after all, where did she think they were going? Pascal busied himself, first loading their bags into the back of the truck, then extracting bottles of water from a cold box and handing them around. Humphry, swimming in sweat, decided it was more useful poured over his head than down his throat. Although they didn't copy his example, none of the others objected to being splashed. Pascal, unsurprised, simply gave him another bottle to drink from.

Then they set off, Jimbo at the wheel, first pushing a way through the bushes, then onto a heavily rutted dirt track. No relaxing ride this. Rather, the impression of travelling on a mobile trampoline. They'd only driven a minute or two before Pascal pointed at something in the distance, and they screeched to a halt. "Impala! Lots of them!" The team peered in the direction he was pointing. All they could see was grassland and clumps of trees.

"You mean near the trees over there?" enquired Robert, with no especial enthusiasm.

"Impala. A breed of deer," tutted Bea. "Can't you see them? Don't you know anything about wildlife?"

"No, actually," admitted Robert.

Jimbo smiled. "You will learn a lot very quickly here, Mr Robert."

"Well, I can't see any deer at all. No animals. Only trees. Oh…" Grasping the concept that wildlife spotting meant looking for very tiny shapes a long way off, he now focused on a small herd of animals that were heading their way.

"We will wait a little and see how near they will come to us," advised Jimbo. "Meanwhile, we need to know your favourite tipples." Pascal had a notebook out and was looking expectantly at Humphry, in the first row behind him.

"Tipples? Drinks? Here? Now?"

"Not now. We want to make sure we have the drinks you like on board for sundowners," explained Jimbo. "On our afternoon safari treks. We always celebrate in the evenings."

"Excellent idea," said Richard. "Never turn down a tipple."

"Anyone would think we were here on holiday," muttered Humphry.

"Officially, we are," Robert reminded him. "And having a 'tipple' or two to relax sounds good to me. I like red wine!" he said louder, now addressing Pascal.

"Merlot or Pinotage?"

A choice of grape varieties compounded the implausibility of their situation. Here they were, all alone on a dirt track surrounded by green and brown vegetation, a herd of antelopes meandering towards them, on a mission to hunt for a mystery Chinese mine, and this was the time and place to place their orders from a bar preference menu?

Drinks orders taken and impalas retreated, the bouncy castle resumed its route. It was a long drive. Much longer than the twenty minutes Jimbo had told them. "Are we nearly there yet?" pleaded Bea, who was suffering more than the others, her backside perched painfully over a spring in the seat.

"You sound just like a five-year-old," snorted Humphry.

"What would you know about children?" retorted Bea. Humphry looked away and kept silent, stung by her retort.

"We'll be in Paradise in another ten minutes," said Jimbo. "Enjoy our safari on the way."

"Paradise, seriously?" asked Humphry.

"The name of the lodge you are staying at."

"I thought the pilot said it was Dreamtime."

"That's the other lodge, near that air strip. The pilot thinks you are going there. But you're not," said Jimbo. "But look, elephants!" Indeed there were. An extensive family. Large and small, most intent on destroying a thicket of small trees to the side of the track. One massive individual was standing in the middle of the track ahead, facing them down. They screeched to a halt.

"He is the boss," said Pascal, not that any explanation was necessary.

"Not quite like our boss," whispered Robert. "Although I suppose her skin is probably just as thick." Those around him suppressed giggles.

They remained still for a few minutes. Eventually, the gigantic beast decided that habitat destruction was more to his liking and lumbered off to join his delinquent family.

"Why are they breaking down the trees?" asked Bea. "I'm surprised there are any left."

"It's the dry season, and it's the only food they like at this time of year," replied Pascal. "The trees will grow back fast when the rains come. Lots of trees, lots of elephants."

Resuming their journey, they rounded another thicket of trees to find a clearing, another runway. "This is the airstrip for our lodge," said Jimbo.

"So why didn't we land here?" asked Richard.

"Your agent insisted. She said we should use the other one so the pilot would think you were staying at the other lodge in this concession. We're almost there now."

The lodge only became came into view at the last moment, being hidden from sight until then by a dense treeline. Outside it waited a welcoming committee: one man, also dressed in what they now realised was the regulation boy scout uniform, and two women in pink housecoats. Presumably the cooks. Women who didn't aspire to being girl guides, introduced as Hilda and Glenda.

Jimbo and Pascal helped the team out of the Land Cruiser, and the other man stepped forward, enthusiastically shaking hands and introducing himself as Joshua, the lodge manager.

"I was expecting you to be Chinese," he said. "The lady who came to make all the arrangements for you was Chinese, I think?"

"I think I know who you mean," replied Robert. "Not sure that she's Chinese, though."

"She is your travel agent, correct?" Well, that pre-empted the risk of any of them blurting out that she was their boss. They all nodded.

Joshua led the party down a path and into the lodge proper, which was basically an enormous wooden deck on which were ranged a long table on the right-hand side and sofas and chairs to the left. In front of them, open to the world, was a view over a river. Beyond that was grass that stretched to infinity, apparently the property of a herd of buffalo.

"The other side of the river is Namibia," explained Joshua. "The Caprivi Strip. It used to belong to Botswana until the British gave it away a hundred years ago. Bastards." He said the last part without thought, though it brought no rebuke, just sympathetic nodding.

So this was where they were heading, reasoned Humphry to himself. Surely nowhere here to hide a mine? "Is it all flat grass, like that?" he asked.

"No, downriver it is forest. You will see. Tomorrow. But first the important things! One, the bar is there," pointing to the side with the sofas, "and two, meals are served there," pointing to the table. "The bar is always open. Just help yourself. Anytime." Richard grinned. Just the invitation he needed.

"Pascal will show you to your huts. You will find essentials for your mission on your beds."

The 'essentials' turned out to be camouflage clothing, hats, and binoculars. All things that Latviana assumed would never have occurred to the spies to bring with them. In that, she was, of course, correct.

# Our First Game Drive – Humphry

I'm really not a morning person, and being 'knocked up' (if you'll forgive the expression) at 5am was very much a rude awakening. I hated early calls when I was in the RAF. I had never liked them before, and certainly haven't ever since. I wouldn't have been enthusiastic even if my head had been clear and I'd slept well. Yesterday evening it took us no time at all to realise that one reason there was a free, open-all-hours bar was to ensure lodgers were always so inebriated that they wouldn't notice how bad the food was. We'd all been rather restrained until dinner was served. We all agreed we were starving, but one quick pass of the food counter changed our priorities, heading for the bar instead to grab a bottle of vino each to dull our tastebuds and sensibilities.

Dinner was described as a buffet. I suppose this was technically correct. Six or seven dishes of food set out on a counter for us to help ourselves to. Lasagne. Moussaka. Parmigiana. Bolognese. All essentially the same — layers of mince and pasta. You get the picture, I'm sure. But what you can't get from reading this is the smell. Or the taste. Indescribable on both counts. Heaven only knows what animal they had minced up for the meat element of the dishes. And the rancid cheese on top defies description. It was unbelievably disgusting but nourishing enough, I admit, when washed down with a bottle or two of Pinotage. And — Richard's idea, I blame him — a couple of whiskies as nightcaps after that. After which I vaguely remember the boy scouts conducting us to our huts in the dark. Very vaguely.

The only one of us who stayed sober was Bea. I think. I think Richard poured her a vodka and orange before dinner, the drink he always brings her, but I'm sure she was abstemious after that. Perhaps there wasn't so much need for fermented grape lubrication with the vegetarian options, which to my untutored eye comprised three varieties of overcooked yams and beets. Yuck. Plantain too, their name for green bananas. I suppose it's a way of justifying not leaving the fruit long enough to ripen. I'm sure chimpanzees enjoy them. Are there chimpanzees in the African bush? We haven't seen any. Not even a monkey so far.

All three guides — Joshua, Jimbo, and Pascal — joined us for dinner. They even went back for second and third helpings. Just drinking water! They either really enjoyed the meal or had been starved for weeks beforehand. I suspect the latter. And, of course, nothing beats 'free' as an employment perk.

It turned out we weren't on our own. There was one other man, English judging from his accent. Well, as far as I could judge from him only saying 'Good evening' and 'Good night.' Freckled face, short dark hair. He kept to himself, arriving some time after we had started eating, sitting at the top of the table, drinking just one beer, and leaving as soon as he had finished. His presence came as something of a surprise, as Maria and Laoban had told us we would be the only guests. Laoban told us she had arranged it so that we would have the lodge to ourselves and be able to perform our mission surreptitiously.

Robert asked Joshua about the stranger. The story went that he had been supposed to fly out two days ago, but his agent had forgotten to book a flight for him. Now he would leave in the morning. Robert was insistent he'd seen him before somewhere. That was probably his imagination, though. He looked like a nondescript character to me. Mister Average. He scarpered before any of us could talk to him, anyway.

Back to the early morning reveille. The day before had been baking hot, so leaving the hut before dawn was a shock to the senses. It was freezing. How can temperatures change so much? A trusty guide — I think it was Pascal — led me up the garden path from my hut to the lodge. The others were already there, none looking any better than I felt. Our first breakfast awaited us, this time not at the table but seated on camp chairs around an open pit fire. Just the four of us and Joshua; Jimbo and Pascal stayed hovering in the shadows. There was coffee — well, mysteriously flavoured dark brown water, but at least it was hot — and muffins, which Hilda, who told us she was the chef, had baked herself. Not bad at all. Made me hope she would serve muffins for dinner rather than the disgusting filth we had suffered the night before.

Joshua leaned in towards us, waving that we should do the same towards him. Time to be conspiratorial, then. He spoke almost in a whisper, furtively. "Your agent explained your special safari needs to me. Today is an orientation day. Now, this morning, Jimbo and Pascal will take you on a game drive. A reconnaissance. I think none of you have ever been on safari before. Am I correct?" Nods all around. "Then you need to do this, and you will enjoy it. You will see many animals, lots of different antelopes. Elephants for sure. And buffalo. If you are lucky, you may see lions, or even a cheetah or a leopard. It can be dangerous in the wild. You do not understand that yet, but I think you will after the drive. And it will show you the lie of the land for your mission."

He took a big gulp of coffee, slurping noisily, but had not yet finished with his disclosures.

"After our morning drive, you will come back here for lunch and a rest. In the afternoon, when it gets cooler, we will take you out on the river." What river? I wondered. Joshua must have noticed my expression. "It is just there, a hundred metres away," he said, waving his hand to the right, "and on the other side is the Caprivi Strip. Namibia. When you return tonight, you can discuss your plans for your mission. I think it might be better that you do that before you visit the bar?" He grinned. I had to admit he had a point.

Noting the enclave was over, Jimbo approached the table carrying a large wooden board with battered edges and a map pasted onto it, so yellowed it appeared antique. He stood it up against a chair and extracted a torch from a pocket to use as a pointer. "We are here," he pronounced, illuminating a scratched-out patch. "River runs here" — he waved his torch right and left — "and our concession is marked by the black line."

A concession, we learnt, meant the area of land leased from the government by the lodge, and this one was huge: 40km from west to east and over 20km from north to south, delineated to the north by the river. In outline, it was roughly rectangular with jagged edges, and we could see it was criss-crossed by tracks, none of them going anywhere in particular. Just for safaris, it seemed, driving around hunting for wildebeest or whatever. Only one was a road. Of sorts. "This one," he said while pointing a fat finger at one track running parallel to the river, "is the supply route. Truck comes once a week with oil for the generator and other supplies. And food." That might explain why dinner smelt so appalling. Minced meat delivered a week ago and left in the tropical heat? Well, I haven't got the runs. Yet.

We readied ourselves for the ride. Robert was already dressed in khaki. Matching the guides' uniform, except that his hat was wide brimmed rather than a cap. An Indiana Jones wannabe, then.

Jimbo took the wheel while Pascal hauled himself up into a single metal-framed seat right at the front, perched over the front bumper. "Is that so you're the first to get eaten?" I asked him. At least he smiled.

"No, I do the tracking. It is easier to look for wildlife this way. If I spot any that might be dangerous, I will wave. Jimbo will stop the vehicle and I will get inside. Up till now, I have always come back alive that way." He grinned.

I chose to sit at the back of the mobile trampoline, otherwise known as a Land Cruiser, thinking I'd get a better view, but quickly changed my mind and moved forward with the others. I was squashed in, but there was much less bouncing. I've grown out of that part of my life. Many years ago.

We headed west, first along the so-called highway, then deviating onto tracks that ran roughly parallel. Jimbo said it was to avoid meeting any trucks that might be coming in the opposite direction, not that any were expected. A bigger advantage from my perspective was that the track, being less traversed, was less rutted, and although the ride could hardly be classified as smooth, it was at least less of a bone breaker.

Discomfort aside, I have to admit it was a wonderful, sensual experience. The sun came up, the air was warm, the sky was blue, and the grass was green. No, there weren't any red roses. And most of the grass was brownish. But there were herds of impala, so many that we didn't even bother to stop, the occasional kudu, and the unpronounceable tssessebe. Several other varieties of antelope, too. Don't ask me to remember which is which. I do remember the wildebeest, simply because they really do look like wild beasts. A big herd of them was following an even bigger herd of zebra. They graze together. Something to do with the comparative length of their teeth, but I forget what. No other vehicles, no other humans. Just us and the animals, in what felt like a vast expanse of bush. Or prairie. Or savannah. Or veldt. All the same thing, apparently.

Robert had brought a camera with a lens longer than my arm — the total opposite of one of those tiny discreet Leicas that us secret agents are supposed to carry. How he got it into the ten-kilogram allowance I cannot fathom – probably some sort of special dispensation. He kept asking Jimbo and Pascal to stop so he could take photos. He must have snapped hundreds. I wondered if he would be able to remember the difference between an impala and a springbok when he came to look at the pictures later. I knew for certain that I wouldn't, even if my life depended on it!

After we'd been going for around an hour, Pascal pointed to something in the distance, and Jimbo twisted the steering and sped away across open country. Off the track now — but a smoother ride! Pascal kept pointing. "Do you see it?" he asked repeatedly. We all peered into the distance. All I could see were several trees and shrubs and lots of grass.

"What are we looking for?" I replied.

"A leopard. Under that bush, just to the right of it." He got down from his jump seat and got into the vehicle next to Jimbo. As he said he would.

Even looking through the binoculars that were on my bed when I arrived, I struggled to see anything. Bea and Richard couldn't see it either. But Robert, with his long lens, located it. "Spotted!" he remarked. Indeed, when we saw the picture in the screen on the back of his camera, it was certainly spotted. But then, all leopards are. Jimbo kept driving towards it, slowly now, until we were less than five metres away from our quarry, which seemed to be quite contentedly sleeping off breakfast. It paid no attention to us. A remarkable, thrilling sight.

But, also, quite a worrying one. I knew that we would have to undertake most of our mission on foot, and that meant we might get close to wild animals. Or, rather, that they might get close to us without us knowing. There were not just leopards but lions out here too, and who knew if they might be partial to a morsel or two of English spy? They must crave some variation in their diet from impalas. And none of us could run as fast as an antelope, for sure. This leopard was nourished, resting and didn't care, but what if he or she had been hungry? If we couldn't spot one until we were practically touching distance away, what hope would we have for saving our skins? We weren't carrying guns, and anyway, we wouldn't want to shoot; the noise of a gunshot would eliminate any surprise, especially here in this environment, total tranquillity save for the twittering of birds and the occasional distant snorting of an elephant.

The survival training I'd been put through in the Air Force was rigorous enough, but the only ferocious beasts we encountered were our own sergeants. Had we met an enemy, that problem was always to be solved (or not) by guns. On this trip, all we would have would be our wits. And however hard we tried, we would always be at a disadvantage. Cats, big and small, are the masters of stealth.

Pascal went back up front and we drove off, leaving the leopard dozing. In the ten minutes that we were parked a few metres away, he'd taken absolutely no notice of us, or, if he had, knew that we weren't a threat. Pascal pointed out that from the animal's point of view, the creature that was watching it was the Land Cruiser, which was the size of an elephant. Too big to kill. Not aggressive, anyway. Would be a nasty taste of metal if bitten.

# Where to Hide a Mine? – Richard

The track went on and on. And on. The landscape hardly changed: open grassland, bushes here and there, occasionally a clump of trees. No significant cover for anything.

"The green season hasn't started yet," Pascal told us. "Usually it begins in November, but it's been starting later and later. You've heard of global warming?" Indeed, we all had. Pascal assured us that when the 'green,' meaning rainy season started, trees and bushes would sprout as if awoken from a dream and then there'd be plenty of cover. Meanwhile, most of the trees we passed had been savaged by elephants. "Elephants are terrible," said Jimbo. "They destroy everything in their path. There are just too many of them."

I couldn't stop wondering how an illegal mine — if, indeed, there was one — might remain hidden from satellite imaging in an open landscape like this. Pascal's next comment provided a plausible answer. "The Caprivi Strip is different. You will see this afternoon when we go out on the boat." His explanation was that the land was so well irrigated by the river and its tributaries that the trees didn't need to wait for the rains.

The only evidence of mining that we saw that morning was that performed by termites. Countless huge termite mounds punctuated the landscape. They were remarkable architectural triumphs of insect engineering and collaborative effort, some even resembling the façade of a church, several at least as big as small chapels. No sign of the miner termites themselves, though; they were presumably busily engaged doing whatever termites do underground. That, I supposed, would be one way of disguising a mine; build a big enough termite mound, or a construction that looked like one, and work under that. Would a particularly massive termite mound stand out in a photograph taken from space? Would anyone even think of looking? I thought back to my army intelligence days and tried to remember whether we'd ever looked at termite mounds. Highly unlikely. With scarcely populated, wide-open landscape like this, representing no military risk, we'd probably never studied any aerial photographs of here. If we had, I don't suppose we would have taken any notice of them. Just blips on the landscape. Anyway, until today I wouldn't have recognised a termite mound, let alone been able to speculate as to how big they could be.

I'd figured that my principal role in the team would be to identify places offering cover to a mining operation so that it wouldn't be visible from space. Now that I was down on the ground, it seemed a daunting task. It was obvious no mine was on this concession, as Jimbo and Pascal and their colleagues would know about it. There wasn't any human activity here other than the lodge, with its ten guest rooms and five staff (ten if the rooms were full). So, assuming it was operating at maximum capacity, that meant no more than thirty people including guests within nearly a thousand square kilometres.

We'd been driving for close on three hours when Jimbo pulled off the track and parked under one of the few large trees that were dotted around. "Elevenses!" he exclaimed. OK, it was actually nearer nine o'clock, but we'd been going since six and a break from the juddernaut was welcome. Not that they allowed us out straight away; first, the guides went to check that there were no snoozing leopards or lions or hungry hyenas anywhere in the neighbourhood. Satisfied that we had the place to ourselves, they returned to the vehicle.

"It is safe to get out now," we were told. "The ladies' toilet is behind that bush," Pascal told Bea, handing her a black plastic bag. "Paper inside. Bring it back after you finish. No littering is allowed." We men were led behind another bush opposite. All very discreet.

By the time we wandered back, stretching our legs, Pascal had already set up our 'elevenses.' Remarkably sophisticated. He had folded down a grille hinged over the front radiator to make a table — in reality, a large shelf —

and covered it with a white tablecloth. Set out on it, bone china cups and saucers and a milk jug. Tea and instant coffee then came out of thermos flasks, but what can one expect in the middle of nowhere? Pascal had even brought tubs of biscuits, which were near-impregnable lumps resembling moon rock. "Homemade," he announced, proudly. We looked at each other, remembering the quality, or lack of it, of last night's dinner. But remarkably, they were quite edible, and excellent exercise for the jaw.

Bea arrived with her left arm outstretched, dangling her plastic bag between two fingers as if it might be radioactive. Leaping up in anticipation of her dropping it onto the mobile breakfast table, Jimbo snatched it from her and hid it somewhere in the vehicle.

I remarked on not having passed another vehicle. "You're the only ones here," replied Jimbo. "The other lodge is empty this week." It wasn't silent, though. I could hear an engine. Very faint, but definitely an engine, and, although close to being inaudible, it was getting slightly louder all the time. I cupped my ear to hear better. Jimbo nodded. "The plane coming to pick up the other man." Perhaps anticipating my next question, he said, "It won't be coming over here. He's going to Maun. It's in the other direction." So now we were definitely on our own.

Our guides packed up the breakfast things in a large metal trunk and loaded it into a space under the floor at the back of the Land Cruiser. "Let's go for a walk," announced Jimbo.

"For any particular reason?" asked Bea.

"Your mission will be on foot," replied Jimbo, "so you need to start learning basic bush trekking tactics and observation skills. You don't have long to pick them up, so we should start now."

Pascal handed Jimbo a couple of pieces of khaki, which turned out to be leggings, or rather the bottom half of their trouser legs, which they zipped onto their shorts. Pascal pointed to Richard. "Shorts are only for the vehicle and the pool. To walk, you need long pants. Today will be OK, but remember for next time."

"To stops snakes and insects?" asked Bea.

"No, nothing stops them," replied Pascal. "To stop you from getting scratched by plants. They help with leeches, too."

"Leeches?" Bea shuddered and for the first time that I had noted, looked a bit scared. "Like in old medicine?"

"Exactly. In some places, there are a lot of leeches. They will suck your blood! Women extra tasty!" Jimbo grinned broadly, almost lasciviously, but I couldn't quite see him as an African vampire. Not that I had any idea what one looked like; when we'd read Dracula in the group, they'd all been Transylvanian and had pointy teeth, not brown decayed ones. "We will give you special leech socks at the lodge to carry with you on your mission." Leech socks were apparently more like half leg trousers with elastic tops. "Uncomfortable, but sometimes necessary," he advised.

Pascal appeared at Jimbo's side, clutching a pair of rifles, and handed one to Jimbo. I raised an eyebrow; the firearms looked ancient. Catching my look, Pascal said, "I know what you're thinking. But they are in working order. Only to use in case a predator attacks us."

Jimbo was now standing to attention, rifle butt on the ground, in full drill sergeant mode. "Now, line up! Tallest at the front, shortest at the back! I will lead, Pascal will take up the rear. You will be safe with us." Probably true if it was only a matter of a wild animal attack. I was far less confident that they could fend off a murderous gang of illegal miners. Were we ever to come across them, they would almost certainly be much better armed and more inclined to violence than us.

"When you can, walk away from the wind so your scent goes ahead of you. Animals find prey on scent carried by wind. It gives us more chance to spot any risks. If you walk into the wind, they can come up behind without us seeing them." That seemed like good advice. Things I should probably have known already, but in the army, we weren't worried about big cats, and human enemies didn't rely on sniffing out sweaty soldiers. Jimbo proudly rolled out the fact that human nostrils are about 250,000 times less sensitive to chemical scents than those of animal predators. I'm sure he's right, I thought.

"Now, let's walk. Keep quiet. If you sense danger or need help or have to say something, raise your arm and Pascal will stop us when it is safe. When I raise my rifle, stop."

The reasoning behind the single file in order of height was that this was supposed to confuse any watching predators, though how this logic had been arrived at remained unexplained But we did as we were told — Robert behind Jimbo, followed by me, Humphry, Beatrix and Pascal — and strode off in single file across the plain and towards a small coppice of acacia trees about half a kilometre ahead of us. It was straightforward going at first; the terrain was flat, vegetation was sparse, and wildlife was nowhere to be seen. If the wind was towards us, it wasn't impeding our progress because the air was completely still. And getting hotter by the minute.

As we approached the trees, there was more vegetation; not grass — we were later told that anything bright green would have been munched within moments of venturing above the ground by some antelope or other — but a deepening tangle of dry and dead-looking twigs. I suspected that Jimbo had brought us there deliberately so that Robert would scratch his legs and learn his lesson about sporting long pants in the future. Judging from the swearing, he did just so. "Silence!" instructed our leader, in a very loud whisper.

Silence was impossible, as the crackling of the carpet of twigs as we walked over them sounded like jungle drums to my ears compared to the total pin-drop quiet while we were traversing the savannah. "Not a problem," whispered Pascal. "They'll think we are elephants." So much for my studious attempts to keep my weight down. 'They' proved to be a pair of tsessebe — or possibly oryx, they were dark brown anyway — who made a swift exit as we approached. Presumably we had disturbed their elevenses, a feast on young branches. As further experience proved, all breeds of antelope are incurable nervous wrecks. Poor things. They must waste a lot of energy running every time they hear a twig snap.

In the conversations the team had earlier when planning our mission, we had assumed that since no mining activity could be spotted in aerial photographs, that meant that there must be tree cover. There, standing in the acacia wood, it became clear that it wasn't possible. The trees were light and deciduous. In the dry season, like now, they offered no significant shade. And they were prone to destruction at any time by elephants, giraffes, antelopes and heaven knows what else. We would have to think again. How were they hiding the mine? Was it even there?

We resumed our march, once again in single file, completing a circuitous journey back to the Land Cruiser, en route encountering nothing scarier than a rather large monitor lizard who was much more interested in sunbathing than in us. Oh, and a family of warthogs, snouts to the ground, like the other residents only interested in searching out a tuft or two of edible vegetation. Or in our case, something more substantial and hopefully tastier than last night's dinner. Lunch beckoned.

# A Meeting of Minds – Beatrix

Our morning game drive had been so exciting, I'd quite forgotten we weren't on a holiday but there on an important mission. That was until Jimbo got us all marching round a big field. The thought that we might need guns, which we didn't have, and in my case didn't know how to use, was disturbing. If this mystery mine was really there, it would certainly be guarded. Now we knew that even if they weren't expecting humans, they'd be armed with guns to repel itinerant beasts of the forest. Why hadn't Maria prepared us for that? She had seemed knowledgeable. So cool and efficient. I'd have tried to poach her for 'Bea at Home' if she had been working for anyone other than Laoban.

The best bit was when we stopped under a clump of trees. Since we were standing still, Robert's legs were no longer being scratched by bushes. However, a colony of ants had now decided they might be tree trunks and were busy clambering up them to investigate. I suspect the others were as amused as I was watching the spectacle. It didn't last long; Jimbo pulled an aerosol from one of the many pockets sewn into his scouting outfit and zapped the invaders right up inside his shorts. Whatever was in the can gave Rob another version of pain. All very funny!

It was a long, hot drive back to the lodge. It is a very big concession, and we had been taken all the way to the western boundary. Jimbo told us it was twenty kilometres back, but with the tracks being so badly rutted, it felt much further. When we had left at daybreak the air was decidedly chilly, and I'd gone back to my room to get an extra sweatshirt. By eleven, though, it was sweltering. Pascal said it was thirty-five degrees. It felt like a hundred to me. Bounced up and down in the back row, dusted with sand and drenched in sweat, the drive seemed interminable.

The men weren't so affected. All they were interested in was food. Gannets, they really are. All I wanted was a shower. Nice and simple. I wasn't expecting any surprises. When I had bathed the night before, it had been dark and I'd been tired from travelling, so I suppose that explains why I hadn't taken a lot of notice of the rondavel's construction. Now it was broad daylight, of course, so the first thing I saw when stepping into the shower was that there was no wall on one side. It was totally open with an expansive view of the river and savannah beyond. Nobody could see me from the lodge, fortunately. I just had to trust that the hippo poking its head above the surface of the river had seen a naked, white, middle-aged woman before. One doesn't want to get hippos overexcited. He looked quite relaxed, but with the rest of his body under water, who would know?

Although my ablutions meant I was the last to arrive in the dining room for lunch, there was plenty of food left. Probably because it was all salads. Indeterminate root vegetables chopped into small pieces and swimming in salad cream. Grated carrot in salad cream. Beetroot slices in salad cream. You get the drift. On the table was cold floppy toast and pots of Marmite, in my opinion a colonial legacy the British should be ashamed of. The men grumbled that there was no meat, but ate the vegetables anyway and washed it down with beer. I went to the bar in search of something non-alcoholic and discovered a fridge full of cartons of cranberry juice. "Every week they send us this juice, and nobody ever drinks it," Hilda, one of the cooks, told me. I thought it tasted nice. Attractive colour too.

While we were eating, Jimbo gave us an interesting lesson on antelope differentiation. In a lot of cases, one can only tell which is which by the colouration or pattern on their hind quarters. Useful, since they almost always run off when spotted. Unfortunately, although it was only an hour or two before we saw more, I'd by then already forgotten how to recognise the different species. Not that the knowledge was necessary or in any way relevant to our mission.

Lunch over, the guides sloped off to their quarters, giving us what they said was an hour's R&R. Nobody felt like dozing; we were all becoming quite psyched up for our mission. We spent the time gathering our thoughts and discussing what we had learnt in the morning. Our fundamental difficulty was, of course, where these mendacious miners might be set up. We assumed they would want to stay hidden, or at least be as unobtrusive as possible. There would be quite a lot of them — somehow or other we arrived at an estimate of at least fifteen to twenty. They'd need a building to sleep in, digging machinery, and transport. We hadn't seen any sort of place where all that could be hidden from view, aerial or otherwise. The land was just too open.

We couldn't approach them by vehicle, as they would be sure to hear us coming. Anyway, with the racket that the Land Cruiser made, we wouldn't hear them, and we figured they couldn't do any mining, however small scale, without making noise. So, we would need to move on foot. What we had seen so far of the landscape was flat terrain; not difficult for walking, but we would probably only make slow progress since we would have to keep a watchful eye out for dangerous animals. With the heat of the sun, we'd need to travel in the early morning and late afternoon, though Robert had a theory that since the predators liked a midday nap, it might be safer for us to walk then. Mad Dogs and all that. Robert said he would consult Jimbo. I was pretty sure he'd be unenthusiastic.

We decided it would be safe to assume that we wouldn't just suddenly stumble on their camp or the mine. Most likely, we would hear sounds long before we got close or come across tracks and signs of human activity. Hopefully far enough away from them to be able to approach with stealth and relative safety.

We would have to camp at night; that would mean carrying tents and provisions. We'd seen tents rolled up as if ready to go by the desk at the entrance to the lodge. What would we take as provisions? Presumably Maria had arranged all that. Humphry and Richard, who had both been in the military, were unperturbed. "The freeze-dried survival sachets that they make for the army and for space travellers are way more delicious than last night's dinner," Richard declared. He didn't make them sound very appetising, but I suppose all we cared about was calorific nutrition. Nobody dared say that we might have to rely on whatever food was sent to us by the lodge kitchen.

How many days would we walk for in the same direction before we retraced our steps or chose another route? After much discussion, we concluded three days should be the limit. Then we would decide whether to return or continue or go left or right.

At that point in our discussion, Joshua came back to the dining area and joined us. We told him what we were thinking.

"Yes, you are right. You will have to go on foot and travel during the day. You will go with Jimbo and Pascal. They are strong men and will carry the tents and emergency provisions. In the evening, when you reach a safe place to camp and can hear nothing and are sure that you have not been seen, they will radio me and I will bring the vehicle to you with fresh supplies."

"I thought there was no signal and no phones here?" I said.

"We have CB radio. Like a walkie-talkie. It is just short range, very noisy, but good enough."

"But surely anyone nearby can pick up a CB radio signal?"

"Your tour operator lady, the Chinese one, gave us some new handsets. Modern, not like our old ones. She said they were special. Safe to use, but not all the time. Just like this, once a day. When we know it is safe. And for emergencies, of course." Grinning like it was the most unlikely thing that could happen. "If Jimbo does not call me, I do not come. If he says it is urgent, I come any time, day or night."

Humphry whispered to me. "This is all terribly amateur, don't you think? It wouldn't be like this if MI6 were organising it."

"Have you ever worked for MI6?" I asked him.

"No, no. I was in the RAF."

"You watch too many James Bond films," I told him. "This is as good as it gets. Believe me." I trust he understood from my expression that I knew. I couldn't say more since I had signed the Official Secrets Act. But he had a point. Spy missions really ought to be organised better, even if they just involved a bit of light industrial espionage in the jungle, as we were doing. But from the way Joshua had described it, Laoban had at least thought through some important practicalities.

Just as Jimbo and Pascal arrived to take us on our afternoon adventure, we heard the deep-throated hum and splutter of a plane overhead. "Wait here!" said Joshua, looking worried, like the guides. We sat back at the table while Joshua ventured out from under the canopy. We could see him scanning the horizon.

"Very unusual," he told us when he came back. "A two-seater, a Piper Cherokee. Not one of ours. Flying over the Namibian side of the river, but definitely coming to look at us. Must be Namibian if it is flying west. We have never seen it before. We are lucky you did not go out to the boat already or they would have seen you."

"Would that matter?" I asked. "This is a tourist lodge. They'll think we're tourists."

"Officially, the lodge is closed for renovation from yesterday. We have to register that with the government. No more tourists until February."

"Could it be the government checking up on you?"

"Not our government. When inspectors come, they come by road. The office tells us two days before they are coming."

We waited twenty minutes in case the plane returned, and then walked down to the jetty to board the boat.

# A Cruise Down River

It wasn't the sort of boat that any of them had ever seen before, but it floated. An aluminium raft? A giant punt? Bea described it best — as an enormous ten-metre-long aluminium roasting tin with posts stuck on to each corner supporting another flat sheet of aluminium, doubling as a roof and an upper deck.

"The waterways around here are very shallow," Pascal explained in his new role as captain. He'd even acquired a peaked cap, though he hadn't changed out of his scout uniform.

"I thought it was a big river?" observed Richard. "We're a long way from the sea."

"This is not the main river. We are going there now," replied Pascal, firing up the outboard motor.

The slow cruise around the waterways would have been relaxing, had it not been for the evident concern that the guides had shown when the plane had flown over, and the fact that ever since they kept nervously looking upwards. The waterways were still, mirroring the sky, and for most of the time they ploughed a straight course down the middle. Herons perched on the bank, watching for fish. The occasional kingfisher was spotted. Sometimes they had to divert around a dark grey island in the middle of the river. "A resting hippopotamus," Jimbo told them. "We must not upset his afternoon siesta. He would never let us forget it. Hippos are the most aggressive and dangerous animals around here."

Richard expressed his surprise. "They don't look dangerous. Just big lumbering giants."

"Don't you believe it. They can run like crazy. Next time you see one with its mouth open, check out those teeth."

"At least we won't meet any when we are trekking overland, I suppose."

"That's true."

The team scanned the vista. Open grass plains on all sides, lots of birds, the occasional solitary elephant — Jimbo explained they were randy bachelors who had been kicked out of the herd by a jealous leader — and not a tree in sight. Not a soul here, and definitely no mining activity. When they turned into the main river, however, the opposite bank was densely forested.

"Namibia," announced Jimbo. "The Caprivi Strip."

"What is there beyond the trees? More tourist lodges?" enquired Humphry.

"No," replied Jimbo. "That is what you westerners call jungle. There are a few villages along the trucking route, but those are more than one hundred kilometres away. But we think this may be a good place for you to start looking. Joshua spoke to one of our pilots a few days ago, and he said that he had heard of some Chinese tourists bribing a pilot to fly across the border in recent weeks."

"Why would they bribe the pilot?"

"They're not licenced to cross the border and there's no passport control. Flying under the radar. Literally! Have to fly very low!"

"Maybe that was what the plane we saw before was doing."

"Maybe." Jimbo didn't look convinced.

They cruised slowly along the riverbank, passing the occasional lazing crocodile and spotting fish eagles perched like sentinels on the top of trees, spaced out at consistent hundred metre intervals as if they had agreed between themselves that each would be responsible for standing guard over a specific stretch of the river. And catching its fish. At one point, a cacophony of high-pitched screeching and rustling in the trees alerted them to the antics of a troupe of vervet monkeys. Negotiating a bend in the river, Pascal steered the boat across to the opposite bank to avoid running into a large family of hippos. There were dozens of them, all practically invisible, with just the front of their heads and two eyes sticking up out of the water.

Around the bend, a sandbank had been commandeered as a resting place for a similarly large contingent of crocodiles. Immobile, soaking up the afternoon sun to refuel their cold-blooded bodies and jaws held wide to show off their canines. An idyllic place. Lots of wildlife, no humans, a peaceful early evening, the sun now lowering in the sky.

"We need to get back," said Jimbo, which Pascal took as a prompt to steer the boat into an adjacent inlet leading away from the main river. Not that they got far that way. In no time at all, the boat ran aground on a sandbank. This was an inconvenience that the guides must have been used to, as Jimbo and Pascal simply picked up long metal poles that were lying on the floor of the boat along the sides of the hull and moved to stand at the front of the boat, manipulating their poles in an effort to push it off. The team gathered round to watch but were promptly told to move away. "We need your weight at the other end to get the boat moving," instructed Jimbo.

"Wouldn't it be better if we just got off?" suggested Richard, pointing to the grassy bank they were next to.

"Only if you want to be some croc's supper," retorted Pascal, laughing and pointing to Richard's right where one was emerging from the grass, curious to find out what was going on and if human flesh might be an easy addition to his daily diet. Fortunately, at that moment the guides got the boat dislodged and restarted the outboard, so they could return to the main river and turn down the next cut.

It was only a few minutes before they saw the lodge ahead of them, much to the team's surprise. Such a long voyage, yet so little distance covered.

A Land Cruiser was parked on a grassy bank by the side of the river, a picnic table set out beside it, topped with an array of bottles and glasses. Joshua standing proudly to its side. The boat pulled ashore. "Ahoy sailors! Sundowner time!" Joshua announced, grabbing the rope that Jimbo threw him and tying it to a wooden post on the bank.

"This is the life!" said Richard, mixing himself a generously large gin and tonic.

"I don't think we deserve this special treatment," said Humphry. "We're here to work, after all."

"Work is tomorrow. You need to relax now. This is something that we do for all our safari guests," advised Jimbo. "Every afternoon around this time, at the end of the afternoon game drive. Or in this case, the afternoon cruise. As the sun goes down, which is why we call it sundowners."

All of a sudden, the peace was shattered by an explosion somewhere off in the far distance. A gunshot?

"Too loud for that. Dynamite." Joshua seemed very certain. Everyone turned to him.

"Is that usual?" asked Humphry. "What is dynamite used for around here?"

"I've never heard it before. Not here, anyway. Perhaps it's your miners."

In further discussion, the guides' unanimous opinion was that the sound came from the Namibian side of the river, the direction they had just come from. Confirmed by a second and even louder blast two minutes later. Jimbo pulled a pair of binoculars from the Land Cruiser and scanned the horizon. "Look over there," he said, handing them to Robert, "you can see the vultures circling."

"Does that mean there's a dead animal down there?"

"Not when so many of them are circling like that. They've been scared by the explosions."

Joshua refreshed their drinks, restoring their good mood. "At least you now have a good idea where to look. You can start your expedition tomorrow. Let's have a toast to a successful enterprise!" Lifting a cheese biscuit taken from a tin Pascal was offering with one hand and clutching his refilled glass in the other, Humphry adopted the role of toastmaster. "To the mission! To success! To us!" After practically choking on his biscuit, he pronounced it the hardest, stalest, and most foul-tasting snack he had ever put in his mouth. "I can't imagine even a hungry vulture liking these."

"And you haven't seen what's for dinner yet," giggled Beatrix, going to the table to refill her glass of cranberry juice. Joshua stopped her.

"We had better hurry back, I think. I can hear a plane. Sounds like it's coming this way. Jump in." The others strained their ears but could hear nothing; nonetheless, they followed the instruction, and were driven the short distance back to the lodge, leaving Jimbo and Pascal to clear up the sundowner drinks table. Although the plane was now audible, the sound like that of a large trapped wasp, it quickly died away again. Nothing to worry about right now.

After a quick wash-and-brush-up in their rooms, the team returned to the deck and assembled around the table. Time for dinner. The kitchen ladies stood to attention, ready in their pink coats to serve whatever delicacies they had hidden under the lacy doilies covering the dishes on the counter in front of them.

"The sun now being well and truly downed, it's time for an apéritif, or at least a stiff drink to dull the palate," suggested Richard. Always the first to the bar.

"Not yet," asserted Robert. "We've already had a sundowner. Or two. Or three in your case. We need to plan tomorrow while we have relatively clear heads. Let's sit and talk before we eat."

They huddled over the table. Covert operations. Don't want that moth on the wall to overhear anything. Joshua was the first to talk.

"There's a sandy bank about two kilometres downriver where we can bring the boat ashore. You can start your mission from there. We need to leave early, maybe four thirty, so it's still dark when we arrive."

"Why so early?" asked Robert.

"I'm sure you don't want to take the risk of being spotted from the air."

"Surely that's just as likely at any hour, day or night?"

"No, the single-engine planes we use here don't fly at night. If one comes at all, it will be at least an hour after dawn by the time it reaches here from the nearest airfield. So, you see, you have time to reach tree cover." Joshua looked around. Then had an afterthought. "Also, any crocodiles on the sandbank will be sleeping. They're only active in daylight."

"We'll have to take your word for it," muttered Robert, not reassured. "And I suppose your earlier plan for following us in the vehicle to bring fresh supplies can't work if we're on the other side of the river."

"Correct. You will have to carry more camping equipment with you. Jimbo and Pascal will carry heavy things and supplies like food."

"Tell him not to bring any of those rock biscuits. My jaw still aches, and I think I loosened a tooth," grumbled Humphry.

"You should all carry water, of course. Hopefully there will be many streams so you will find fresh water easily. Pascal will carry sterilising tablets."

"So, all we need to carry is our own clothes, tent, and sleeping bags? Jimbo and Pascal will bring the food?"

"And their guns. Just in case. If you walk for two days and decide not to proceed any further in the same direction, you can go back to the sandbank. Jimbo will send a code on the CB, and I will come with the boat at night with fresh supplies."

"And what is the range of the CB?"

"Depends. Something between ten and fifteen kilometres. But, as you have seen, the other bank of the river is only two kilometres from here. So not too far."

"Any suggestions for what we should do if we can't get back to the river for any reason?"

Joshua seemed quite amused by the idea. "I was told you were pros. Lie low. Go native! Catch a fish, kill an animal, eat plants!" He was the only one who was finding it funny. "But careful with the plants. Some of them are poisonous. And watch out for snakes. Although they are very good meat. Very tasty." Such reassuring words. "And scorpions!" Joshua collapsed now in gales of laughter.

Richard, who had been itching to go to the bar, pushed his chair away from the table. "I hope you're going to manage without that when we are on the mission," said Humphry. "I knew you like a drink, but now I'm seeing you every day, I'm thinking you are borderline alcoholic." Richard glared, and a heated discussion looked bound to ensue, but Joshua raised his hands and then put one finger to his mouth. "Listen," he whispered.

The faint sound of an engine. Not the generator or a plane or a car. Something else. Getting louder.

"Go to your rooms and keep the lights off," said Joshua. "We'll call you when we know it's safe." Led by Jimbo, trailed by Pascal, the team left down the gravel path to their rondavels.

# Unexpected Visitors

Joshua went to retrieve his rifle from his office before going out of the lodge and looking around. Nothing visible yet, but he could definitely hear a vehicle; still some distance away, but closing fast. No deliveries expected until next week, and the tanker only drove in daylight. The sound of the engine was getting louder, and now he had glimpses of headlights flickering through the trees. It seemed to take ages before it came into clear view, though perhaps it was only five minutes. A Land Cruiser. A night safari? Impossible, surely, as there were no guests in the other lodge on the concession, and it surely couldn't have come from anywhere else.

Finally, the vehicle drew to a halt right in front of Joshua, the headlights both illuminating him and preventing him from seeing who was inside. Two men jumped out, now recognisable as the guide-caretakers left in charge of the other lodge while it was closed to visitors.

"Tobego! Kabelo! What are you doing here, and at this time of night?"

"HQ sent us. You're not answering the landline."

"It hasn't run. Of course I would have answered it if it had." Joshua led them into his office and picked up the receiver. Dead. No dialling tone. "That's strange. It was working first thing this morning. They called to ask if I needed a diesel delivery. Anyway, what's the emergency that makes you drive all the way out here at night?"

"Hilda's mother has fallen ill. They say she's going to die any day now, and she wants her daughter at her bedside." Hilda being one of the cooks.

"They're sending a plane in the morning to pick her up and drop off someone else to take over from her."

"I don't need a replacement. We don't have any guests. Probably not until February."

"Well, that's what they said."

"I have an idea," said Joshua, trying to think quickly. "Take Hilda back to your lodge, call HQ and tell them to send the plane to your airstrip. And not to send anyone new."

"Man, why? You can't expect us to drive back tonight," said Tobego. "We're staying. We'll go back in the morning. I can smell food, and we're hungry!"

This was the last thing Joshua needed. The Chinese woman had been crystal clear. If the mission went off according to plan, she'd pay him a bonus. A lot, enough to go back to his family, build a big house, strike out on his own. His dream of his own travel agency could come true in less than a month. But fail, and he wouldn't just be stuck in this out-of-the-way hole for ever; he'd be stuck in his own hole inside it. Not so much carrot and stick as passion fruit and revolver. And now, this problem had materialised out of the indigo night. The team was confined to their rooms with no idea what was going on. Tobego and Kabelo were good friends, but had arrived unwanted and at the worst possible time. HQ would be sending a plane tomorrow, and, potentially far more problematic, bringing a new worker on board. Probably someone unknown. Certainly untrustworthy. In the current situation, anyway. And Hilda, his best cook, was leaving. Even Joshua, his palate dulled to the point of ageusia through nine months of Hilda's catering, believed dinners could be improved. Putting Glenda in charge of all the cooking would only be worse. Well, it might force him to diet. Shed a few pounds? Has to be a silver lining somewhere.

He was roused from his contemplations by Kabelo. "Wow, man, you made the girls cook all this food just for you three guys?" Laughing loudly as he piled a plate high. "It's good stuff, this fried chicken," munching on a drumstick.

And Tobego. "You said you didn't have any guests?"

"We don't," stuttered Joshua. "Closed for a month. Like you."

"So why is the table laid for seven?" Good point, something Joshua hadn't thought of.

"Oh, they just get into the habit, I suppose."

Fortunately, Joshua was saved from having to invent any new excuses, since the men were now far too busy eating to ask any more questions. Joshua interrupted their demolition of the buffet. "You came to tell Hilda about her mother, and all you've done so far is eat. You let her serve you chicken without saying a word."

"Not our job, man. We were expecting you to tell her."

Well, someone had to do it. Joshua left them to clear the desserts, wondering to himself how anyone could eat two pink jellies, let alone four or five, and went back to the kitchen. "Hilda, come with me to the office," he said in as gentle a tone as he was able. Once there, they sat down, and he told her of the news that the men had brought. Unsurprisingly, Hilda was distraught, breaking down in tears. "They're sending a plane for you tomorrow," Joshua told her. "You'll be with her by nightfall." Those words didn't console her. There were more hysterics than before. He tried again. "Go and be with Glenda. She'll look after you tonight."

"No! I hate her!" Well, he wasn't expecting that.

"But you have worked together here for months. You share a room."

"No, we most certainly don't!" Joshua looked surprised. "We can't stand each other. She goes and sleeps in room 12." The rondavel that was perpetually under construction. Isolated, away from the other rooms. At the end of the path. Joshua realised he hadn't ventured down there for months. "The only friend I have is Masha, at Dreamtime."

"But you never go to the other lodge," said Joshua.

"We used to work together until I got moved here. We still talk every afternoon on the landline. While you men are snoring." She choked back tears. "Except we couldn't talk today. The line is cut."

"Well, it's not working. But it's not been cut."

"God, you men are hopeless. Don't tell me you didn't see the cable hanging down from the post outside?"

Joshua was embarrassed. "I haven't been out the front since morning. We went on the boat this afternoon."

"Jimbo is supposed to patrol, check that everything is OK. How can we feel safe here if someone can come and cut the only outside line we have, and you don't even know about it?"

"I'm sure nobody came and cut the line."

"What do you think did it, a giraffe? Decided a phone cable might taste better than a eucalyptus branch?" A flame of anger ignited in her, her grief temporarily forgotten. "I don't want to be here anymore. Get your friends out there to take me to Dreamtime." A rather inappropriate name for the other lodge, considering that it was so dilapidated and run down. "I can be with Masha there until the plane comes. If it comes." That was certainly a point that Joshua hadn't considered. When HQ was paying, air transport was totally unreliable. It had taken three days to get their last guest out. There was no guarantee that the plane for Hilda would come tomorrow. But what she said was helpful; Hilda had provided the credible excuse he needed to get rid of the unwanted visitors. "Wait here then," he told Hilda.

Joshua returned to the dining area. "Stop drinking our beers," he shouted.

"Why? Nobody will know."

"I'll know, and HQ made me send in an inventory yesterday. But that's not the issue. You're driving."

"Ha ha! No drink drive rules in the jungle," joked Kabelo. "Anyway, we said we're not driving anywhere tonight."

"Oh yes you are," retorted Joshua. "Hilda wants to go. She won't stay here. Her friend, Masha, is at your camp. Get going!"

"Don't believe you, man," drawled Tobego. "We've always been mates. Good to have a night here. Grab a beer yourself."

Hilda appeared then, out of her pink housecoat now, clutching an enormous bag. "Let's go, guys," she said, scowling at Tobego and Kabelo, who were opening new cans.

"OK, OK, we'll go. Let us finish our beers first."

"No way. We go now. Did you come because of me and my mother or to have a party?"

The men reluctantly rose from the table and sloped back through the entrance to their Land Cruiser. Neither offered to carry Hilda's bag. Joshua thought he had better be the gallant one. "Not safe driving at night," Kabelo said as he got back in the driver's seat.

"You know all the tracks as well as I do," replied Joshua. "You could drive back in your sleep."

"He'll probably do exactly that," said Hilda from the back row. "After all he has had to drink."

Kabelo started the engine. Joshua leaned over the door towards him. "Don't forget to call HQ tonight and tell them the plane needs to come to your lodge. And not to send a substitute!"

The men, moody about being kicked out and forced to drive back, looked as if they were ignoring him, but Hilda replied. "I'll remind them. No, that would be a waste of breath. I'll do it myself." She was no longer tearful, now her usual fierce, proud African mama self.

# The Mystery Deepens

With the unwelcome visitors — and Hilda — gone, Joshua could finally get the team back to the deck. He realised he hadn't seen Jimbo or Pascal since the visitors arrived and started by going to the men's quarters.

"We thought we had better lie low too," said Jimbo.

"Good, probably for the best. Did you know the phone cable was cut?" Jimbo and Pascal looked blank and shook their heads.

"Where? How?" said Pascal.

"I don't know where, but Hilda said she saw the cable hanging down from a post, so it must be nearby. She assumed you'd have seen it on your patrol." He looked at Jimbo, who hung his head. "Sorry, boss, no time today. Too busy with the visitors. We'll fix it in the morning."

"You won't. You can't. You both have to leave with the guests at 4.30. I hope I can do it myself when I come back after dropping you off on the other side." They looked at each silently for a long moment. "On second thoughts," added Joshua, "we could go out now with our spotlights. At least see what the damage is. You can tell me how to fix it, too, Jimbo. Let's go."

Jimbo and Pascal got up, anything but enthusiastic, and followed Joshua to the store cupboard where they kept the two spotlights that they used for night safaris. Joshua picked up the first one to hand and turned it on. Hardly a spotlight. A candle would have been brighter. "They haven't been charged," said Joshua, angry now. "And look, this other one was left switched on."

"Sorry boss. Must have forgotten," replied Pascal, looking sheepish.

"Well, plug them in now to charge. We'll need them for the boat in the morning. Jimbo, bring our guests. They must be famished."

Jimbo went to collect the team, returning with just Richard and Robert. "Humphry is not answering," he told Joshua. "He's not in his room."

"He must have gone out on his own. Idiot. We told everyone not to walk the path in the dark. We'd better all go. I'll bring the rifle to be on the safe side. What about Beatrix, though? She's not here."

"I didn't go to her room yet," said Jimbo. "When I couldn't raise Humphry, I came back here."

"Well, let's call for her first."

Beatrix was staying in the rondavel furthest from the lodge building. Joshua, Jimbo and now Pascal, too, stood in front of her door. They hammered loudly and heard her voice. "I'm coming, just a minute."

The door opened. It wasn't Beatrix who stood on the threshold, but Humphry. In shorts. Shirtless. "I came to keep Bea company," he told them. "I thought she would be afraid." Followed out by Bea, looking a little dishevelled.

Joshua, unsurprised, chuckled. "Don't you want to get your shirt?" he asked Humphry.

"Oh, of course." He went back into the bungalow, glad that blushes didn't show in torchlight.

"I must remind you again, do not walk outside at night without a guide. It's dangerous."

"I know, but my hut is just next door, only ten metres or so."

"Enough time for a crouching leopard to pounce," replied Joshua, not waiting for a reply but turning and walking back to the lodge, followed by Bea and Humphry, tailed by Jimbo and Pascal.

In the dining room, Robert and Richard had already assessed the damage done to the catering by the earlier visitors. "Who were those greedy beggars? How many of them were there?" asked Robert. "There's hardly anything left here."

Joshua scanned the buffet counter. "There's plenty of stewed vegetables," he said, pointing at one dish, "and plenty of salad." He indicated a platter of what looked like raw cabbage.

"And one chicken wing," said Robert, purloining it. "Not sure the Colonel would be very proud of it, but it's quite tasty."

"Yes, it was fried chicken tonight," replied Joshua. "Let me ask Glenda to bring out some more and see what else she can find."

"They finished all the chicken," were Glenda's words as she emerged from the kitchen. "I'll bring the lasagne left over from yesterday."

"Remind me never to suggest to anyone that they should come to this lodge for fine dining," said Humphry, this time the first to the bar, selecting a fresh bottle of Pinotage. "This one's just for me, by the way. Get your own," he told the others.

"Remember you won't get much sleep. We need to leave at 4.30," said Joshua.

Hunger silenced criticisms, and the team set to work on plates of cold vegetables and colder lasagne. Both spiced up with liberal additions of Marmite. "It actually tastes less bad when it's cold, don't you think?" suggested Robert. There were only grunts from the others.

Bea pointed towards Pascal, who had moved away from the group and was sitting at a table far away from them. "Is he using a mobile phone?" she asked.

"Looks like it," said Humphry, getting up and walking over to investigate. Pascal, seeing him approaching, looked furtive, hurriedly tapping at the screen.

"I was told phones didn't work here, Pascal."

"I'm just looking at photos of my family, Mr Humphry." He turned the screen, showing a jolly-looking woman with two little girls sitting on her lap.

"Your wife and daughters?"

"No, I am not married. My sister and her children."

Humphry returned to the table. "He's just using it to look at pictures, would you believe?"

"Dirty pictures, I suppose," replied Bea.

"No, family. Sister and nieces."

"Hmmm. Then I'm not sure why he went over there and was hiding his phone under the table." They looked over again, but Pascal had already left.

# An Early Start

Assembled around the fire pit in front of the lodge, nursing coffees, the team appeared to the guides to have undergone an overnight transformation. Dressed identically in camouflage khakis, matching brimmed bush hats, and carrying their backpacks, they exuded professionalism.

"Are you all ex-military?" asked Jimbo.

"Not me," replied Beatrix. "I think all the guys used to be?" Humphry and Richard duly nodded. Robert looked away.

"Are you sure you are up for this, then?" Jimbo continued. "It can be tough going for a woman." Typical sexist male attitude, thought Bea.

"Don't worry. I learnt outdoor survival in the girl guides." No point in telling him the truth. Anyway, Official Secrets Act and all that.

"Your call, Miss Beatrix. You have to stay with us. I'm not carrying you back."

"Maybe I'll be the one who has to carry you."

Robert coughed loudly. "Listen up, team. Packing check before we leave. Sunglasses."

"Check!" The team shouted in unison.

"Binoculars! Walking poles! Sunscreen! Head torches! Charging pack!" The list continued.

Down at the landing stage, the boat looked different. The roof and the poles in the corners had gone. It still looked like a big roasting tin, but now with no trivet. "Makes it lighter. Easier for me to get it off the sandbank on my own," explained Joshua. "And you don't need a roof to keep the sun off when it's night." True. Not only was there no sun, but the air felt distinctly chilly. It would be colder still on the water.

Jimbo and Pascal stood in the front corners, training spotlights — now fully charged — on the banks, while Joshua sat at the back, nursing the outboard motor and steering. Once they reached the river proper, he killed the engine, stood up, and grabbed a pole from the hull, Jimbo and Pascal doing likewise.

"Now we punt," explained Joshua. "So we are quiet. Just in case. The current helps us." Which it clearly did, as the boat drifted along at a reasonable pace, the three guides just dipping and pushing with their poles every twenty or thirty seconds, more to keep the boat from drifting towards the bank than to propel them forward. Under the crystal-clear African sky, with no mist and no clouds, the heavens presented a truly amazing panoply of stars. A gibbous moon provided more than sufficient light to see their way. No spotlights required now.

"Won't you need the outboard to get back again, Joshua?" asked Humphry.

"Yes, of course. But I will be on my own. And I will be fishing." Joshua pointed to rods and a net lying beside him. "If the plane comes or anyone sees me, they will think nothing of it."

"You'll have fresh fish for your dinner, too." Humphry felt a pang of jealousy.

Mercifully, the sandbank where they alighted was devoid of crocodiles. Or at least none that were visible in the pre-dawn half-light. Jimbo and Pascal jumped off first, followed by the team. Joshua passed over huge rucksacks to the guides. Without any doubt much heavier than the ones the team were carrying. Richard tried and failed to lift one. Jimbo and Pascal had no such problems, each effortlessly hoisting a pack onto the other's back. "What on earth do you have in those?"

"Supplies. Useful stuff."

"How much do they weigh?"

"Fifty kilos," replied Jimbo. "Didn't you do endurance training in the army? Our sergeant major told us every soldier had to do it. He came from England too. I remember it well. He said you guys do sixty-four kilometres across the Brecon Beacons, wherever they may be. He made us do sixty-four kilometres across bush terrain."

"I was in the Air Force. They only made us do twenty K, and much less weight," replied Humphry.

Richard felt humbled. "Ah. I was in the Army, but all I had to endure was a desk job. Most of the time, anyway. Lots of bodybuilding, though." Seeing no reaction from the other two, he asked, "Robert, Beatrix, did you have to do that sort of training?"

"Our professional training was rather different," replied Robert cryptically. "Listen, we can't stand around chatting. We need to get started. That direction looks promising — at least there's a sort of path into the trees. Looks like it was made by some helpful elephants. What do you think?"

The team started to move but were stopped by Jimbo. "Remember what I told you about walking in line? Me in front, Pascal at the rear. We all need to be safe. We might or might not find what you are looking for, but wild animals will certainly find us. Every two hundred metres or so, we stop for a moment. Look around and listen. Understood?"

Whilst none of the team really felt comfortable taking orders from Jimbo, what he said made perfect sense, and they duly stepped into line. "There, you see. Now you are the crocodile." Pascal enjoyed his joke. Again.

Two hours and perhaps five or six kilometres passed, with nothing happening more exciting than scaring a few antelopes who had been lurking in the trees. The elephant tracks hadn't stretched very far; it seemed that the troupe had turned left after a few hundred metres, and Jimbo told them that direction would simply take them back to the river. He extracted a machete from his voluminous backpack and hacked to clear a path forward when necessary. Even when it wasn't, they were making plenty of noise just walking through the dry undergrowth. The going got slower. Creepers and horizontal tree roots too thick to be cut impeded their path, the occasional fallen dead tree forcing them to deviate from their route. "I can see why the elephants didn't come this way," said Humphry.

"How far does the forest go on?" asked Richard.

"We don't know. As Jimbo told you yesterday, we know there is a road in one hundred kilometres, so it must stop there," replied Pascal. Amused by the dejected look on Richard's face, he added, "But I'm sure we'll find clearings soon."

"It's nothing like the Botswana side. Flat and easy there. No forests."

"There are many forests in Botswana. Just none in the Okavango Delta, where our lodge is."

Beatrix was surprised that there was so much noise in the jungle. At none of their frequent stops did they experience silence. There was no wind, but the trees still swayed and creaked. They didn't see many birds, and those there were didn't sing so much as croak or make chattering noises. At one point, the antics and shouting of a large family of baboons drowned out everything else and made them wonder why they were bothering to try to move silently.

Another hour, and a wide expanse of savannah opened up in front of them. They had reached the end of the forest. For now, anyway. "We stop and rest here," said Jimbo. "While we still have cover." He stamped down the branches and bracken under a tree to make space to sit, and the others followed suit, but were stopped from sitting down. "Wait. We check it is safe, nothing alive underneath. Nobody wants to sit on a snake." He and Pascal walked round the area, poking the brushwood with sticks, conversing with each other in low tones. "OK, you can sit now. But stay alert!"

"We already agreed that the four of us would take turns in being on watch guard in every rest period. One hour each. I'm first," said Robert, lifting his binoculars to his eyes and scanning the horizon.

"Good, but one of the two of us will also stay watchful at all times, day and night," replied Pascal. "For some things we may be better observers than you."

"Really?" said Robert, sceptically. "Seriously?"

"Really, Mr Robert. The cheetah over there, for example. Do you think it might attack us?"

"Where?" Robert scanned all around again and couldn't see anything resembling even a tabby cat. Cheetahs were big, weren't they? Pascal wasn't even using binoculars. Robert thought he was just making it up.

"Two o'clock. To the right of the bush."

Robert trained his binoculars in the right direction and fiddled with the focus. "There are four bushes over there."

"The nearest one."

"There's nothing there." A moment later. "There's something on the ground, looks like a log."

"Not a log. A cheetah. Very dangerous, if she was awake. She's lying down, probably sleeping. Keep watching. If she moves, alert everyone."

"She's a very long way away, though. Can't be much of a danger, surely?"

"A hungry cheetah runs at a hundred kilometres an hour. It could be here in thirty seconds."

Bea shuddered. "What else should we be most afraid of?"

"Lion, leopard, cheetah, buffalo, elephant, wild dog. Most of the others will simply run away. Like that tsessebe." He pointed to a startled antelope that had emerged from the forest, which had now found a tasty patch of long grass.

"The cheetah has noticed," said Robert. "She's sitting up now."

"She's going to come after the tsessebe. She's just checking that there are no other predators around that she might have to compete with."

Jimbo had taken out a flask and some plastic cups from his rucksack. "Coffee," he announced, pouring and then handing out the cups.

Bea took a sip and screwed up her face. "It's got sugar in it!" she exclaimed.

"Sorry," replied Jimbo. "Drink it anyway. It will give you energy."

Five minutes passed. Then ten. Nothing new spotted. Tranquillity. No sound of mining or anything other than the murmuring of the bush, which they were getting used to: birds, rustling in trees, faint and distant snorting and braying. Then, as if launched from a slingshot, the cheetah raced, feet hardly touching the ground, towards the fated antelope, who noticed it just too late to escape into the forest. "Lucky cheetah," observed Jimbo. "Over ninety percent of the time their prey escapes. Now she will have meals for a couple of days. If the wild dogs and hyenas don't get here first."

"Lucky us too," said Humphry.

"We need to move before the scavengers arrive. It's going to get busy around here," said Pascal.

"It'll be hot too," added Jimbo. "We should stay as close as we can to the perimeter of the clearing. More shade. Less risk of being seen."

"Even by cheetahs," said Richard.

Humphry grimaced.

# Making Tracks – Robert

Laoban and Latviana call me Pilot, and that's appropriate. Flying's my game, and I get frustrated and irritable when I have to spend time on the ground. I know it's supposed to be good for one's health to walk ten thousand steps a day — or is it six? Or four? The advice keeps changing — I just find it boring. Tedious.

But not in the African bush. At first, I was jealous of the eagles and vultures that flew over us. Why weren't we born with wings? However, by the end of the day, I'd had to admit to my fellow trekkers that walking in the bush was fascinating. True, we hadn't found the mine we were looking for. Yet. But we were in no special hurry, and our mission, which forced us to walk, meant we saw and learnt things we would never have discovered riding across country in a 4WD. Nor, of course, flying over it.

Unlike my fellow travellers, the military had never got its paws on me. Not that their training was proving to be much help for them here in Africa. Humphry knew how to land with a parachute, and had been taught some basic survival skills, useful only if he conveniently landed next to a hospital, hotel or supermarket. Richard had trekked across the Cairngorms in Scotland, but that turned out to have been on an Outward Bound course when he was still a teenager. Bea had been given the longest and most practical training. She wouldn't say where, but from the clues she dropped (she's into penguins like other women like cats) I'm guessing Antarctica. And you don't need to know anything about Africa to realise that's not a lot of help.

We saw animals, of course. Lots and lots of them. Mostly one or another kind of antelope. But also a herd of buffalo, a family of giraffes, a few elephants in the distance. Near enough to enjoy the view, but none close enough to give any cause for concern. No more big cats after the morning's cheetah. All very exciting, of course, and a world away from taking my sister's children to the zoo, but what I found really fascinating were the things one needed to know in order to survive in the bush.

The days are hot, and even with a hat and walking in the shade most of the time, it's thirsty work. One needs to drink a lot of water, which is heavy to carry. It wasn't even midday when Pascal told me we had already drunk ten litres of water between us. More than a litre and a half each? Not so surprising, I suppose, but it still seemed a lot. The subject came up when our trek took us near a pond, and Pascal went to refill the empty bottles. "Nobody here now," he said, "but there'll be a crowd around just before nightfall." Not humans; the crowd he was referring to comprised all the animal species we had been observing, and those who were lurking somewhere, unseen by us, the night prowlers. Did he expect us to drink the same water from the same muddy hole as buffalos and elephants? Indeed he did, though he had an ingenious filtering bottle to separate out the worst of the brown bits, and tablets that fizzed when he dropped them in the water to sterilise it. The result was still brown and tasted of bleach, but was perfectly drinkable.

Occasionally, we would come to a halt while Pascal studied the surrounding ground. Sometimes he would confer with Jimbo, then both of them would wander around, looking this way and that. I didn't understand what they were doing until Pascal pointed down to what he said were recent animal tracks or fresh droppings and explained he was working out which way the beast or beasts had gone, and how long ago. This was jungle forensics; he would suddenly bend down, pick up a piece of dung and brandish it proudly in front of my eyes. "How long ago?" he would demand. It was like a game I always got wrong. "Yes, if this was the morning, I would agree this would be six hours old, but now it is mid-afternoon, it might only be two or three. Morning cold, afternoon hot!" Then, another time, he would point down with his finger and move his arm quickly out in an arc, pointing in another direction. "See those tracks? Wild dogs! Went that way!" Well, better they went away than came to attack us.

Most times when he found evidence that animals had been there before us, he'd pull out a phial of talcum powder he carried and sprinkle a little between his thumb and forefinger. "Always check which way the wind is blowing," he reminded me. The air felt still to me, but it was true that one could always see the direction the powder drifted.

Pascal, latching on to me as someone interested in learning about jungle things, impressed on me that one must never pass by any water source without refilling all the empty bottles. "Man can't live without water," he kept repeating, like a mantra. This water pan, just a shallow pool perhaps ten metres across, was the first we'd come across, and I asked what we would have had to do if we hadn't found any. After that, he stopped at bushes that had pods which were juicy when sucked — so a source of water — and a huge baobab tree that he clambered up to retrieve a cupful of water, saved from morning dew or past rainfall, that lay stored between two branches. I was just glad that he was there to look after us. On my own, I'd have run out of water with no idea how to find more.

After water, fire. When we reached a point where our guides decided we would camp for the night, I watched Pascal start a fire by rubbing two twigs together. Something everyone has probably heard about, but few actually know how to do. Well, I didn't, anyway. You can't just take any old twigs, rub them together and hope for the best. The correct technique, passed on from generation to generation of bushmen, is to take a long, straight stick of one type of wood and, holding it between the palms of your hands, twizzle it back and forth, all the while pushing down the end of the stick against a flat piece of another specific type of wood with an indentation carved into it to stop the first stick from slipping. Use the wrong kinds of wood or get the technique wrong and nothing happens. Oh, and chant the magic spell while you're doing it. I'm not convinced that's essential, but that's what he did. Pascal lit a flame on the end of the straight stick in less than a minute and used it to light a fire of dry wood and leaves that Jimbo had collected while he had been twizzling and chanting.

We drew more water from a nearby stream — such a narrow and overgrown one that I would have walked straight over it had Jimbo and

Pascal not shown me. We refilled our bottles, but this time, with a fire going, the guys boiled the water. They still added the bleach tablet. Just to be on the safe side. The team watched in silent appreciation of the sterilisation ceremony. Except for Richard, who was getting on our nerves. I swear that if I'd heard him make one more joke like "tastes just like Chardonnay," "looks like a pisco sour," or some other reference to drinks, I would have slapped him.

After everything Pascal had been telling me all afternoon about jungle plants and the wildlife we'd seen, I was quite hoping that the guys would be planning something like roasted springbok for dinner, with a vegetable dish made from bush plants for Bea. Sadly, that was not to be. "Another day, if we run out," said Jimbo. But at least our meal wasn't reheated leftover lasagne carried from the lodge. Instead, it was sachets of dried vegetable soup, which tasted rather weird when reconstituted with bush stream water laced with bleach, and chocolate and nut breakfast bars. Two each! Laced with the promise of the same dinner tomorrow and the next day and the one after that. I drifted off to sleep, dreaming that I'd convince the guys to catch and roast that deer tomorrow.

I hadn't been asleep long when Richard shook me awake. "Hyenas!" he said in a loud stage whisper. "Three of them!" While he went on to wake Humphry and Bea, Jimbo handed me a long stick. "To keep them away if they attack," he told me. I knew nothing about hyenas, of course, but would have thought that Pascal shining a bright light in their eyes would be enough to scare them off. It seemed to have the opposite effect, as they continued to walk towards us. "They must be really hungry. Hyenas don't often attack humans."

All six of us lined up, side by side, holding our sticks in front of us like spears. The hyenas stopped and eyed us, no doubt assessing who would be the tastiest or have the most meat on them. The answer to that question, Jimbo, had a solution. From the embers of the campfire, he lit some twigs and tossed them at the dried-up undergrowth on the ground in front of us. That took no time to catch light, and, at the sight of the flames, the hyenas raced away at speed.

The little blaze quickly grew into a minor inferno. All the vegetation was so dry that it took all of us half an hour of stamping on the ground, pouring flasks of water and piling sand to put the flames out. An object lesson in how forest fires can start, though I imagine that repelling a hyena attack is one of the least likely causes.

Rather than go straight back to sleep, it was time for my turn at guard duty. With the return of peace, I spent a contented hour scanning the surroundings, illuminated only by starlight, undisturbed by predators.

# Dawn Chorus

"Did you hear that?" Richard suddenly woke, poking his head out of the tent and looking around. The buzzing noise was much louder now. "What is it? A hornet? Some other massive insect?"

"Shhh," whispered Robert. "It's a drone."

"We must be very near them, then."

"No, it's our drone. My drone. Bought it online last week. I thought it would be useful. I'm looking to see if there's any evidence of life up ahead before we make a move."

"But if any people are around, surely it will make it obvious that we're nearby."

"I hope not. I'm keeping it close to the tree line."

"Laoban didn't tell us you had a drone."

"She doesn't know. It's very basic, very light, folds up into this little case. It's short range, so I mustn't let it get very far away."

"Can I see the pictures?"

"Not until it comes back and lands."

"Doesn't it come with an app so we can watch in real time?"

"Better ones do, but not this one. And… no signal. Wait." Robert manipulated switches and joggled the joystick on the device he was holding, looking up all the time. Richard followed suit. The buzzing intensified. The drone appeared from over the trees, and came in to land. Robert picked it up. "You see? Very small, very light." He ejected a memory card from a slot in the base and pushed it into his camera. "Now let's see what's around us."

Trees, mostly. The pictures were black and white and not of very good quality, but clear enough to see that the route up ahead looked more or less the same as that which they had traversed the previous day. "How do you know which direction we're looking at?" asked Richard.

"The number in the corner of the screen. So, this one is 275, roughly looking west." Robert scrolled through the pictures.

"No point to keep heading northeast, then," said Richard. "Looks like that way we'll run out of forest cover very soon. Since what we're looking for is hidden, it isn't going to be on open ground, is it? I suggest we change direction and head northwest." Robert, immersed in studying the pictures, ignored him.

"Look again at this northeast picture. What's that blob — just there? It's too black to be a bush." By now, Humphry and Pascal had raised themselves, and together with Jimbo, who had been on guard duty, they all peered at the miniscule image. A sea of out-of-focus light grey grassland with a dot in the middle. "Shame your camera hasn't got a bigger screen," remarked Humphry.

"That's an elephant. Solitary male," pronounced Pascal. "But this, over on the left edge of the picture, looks like a vehicle. A Land Cruiser, but smaller than ours." Nobody else had noticed it before, but now that Pascal had pointed it out, it was quite clear. Robert paged through all the photographs, but that was the only one it appeared in. "It's driving across open country," said Jimbo. "No tracks."

"I'll send the drone back up to get better pictures," said Robert.

Jimbo held up his hand. "No, too dangerous. It makes too much noise."

"You've got to be near it to hear it, though."

"It's past dawn now. It will scare the baboons nearby. The enemy may not hear the drone, but they'll certainly hear a family of blabbering baboons."

"Well, we'd better head that way to investigate," said Humphry. "Which direction?"

"The picture was thirty degrees, so that edge must be roughly due north of here, I think."

"We don't know if the truck was coming or going, though," said Beatrix, materialising from behind the bush that the guides had designated the ladies' lavatory.

"Since there is no legal place for it to come or go to around here, that doesn't matter," said Robert. "Either we find them, or we find the place they abandoned."

"But first, breakfast," announced Pascal, proffering cups and unscrewing his thermos flask. "How did you make hot coffee?" asked Beatrix.

"I heated the water in the fire pit last night, after you had gone to bed. No sugar!" he said, smiling at Beatrix. "And there are biscuits."

"Those same lumps of rock you gave us yesterday morning?" asked Humphry.

"Drop them in your coffee. After you drink, you will be able to eat the biscuit. Tastes better too." Humphry did as he was told and drained his coffee quickly. Having expected to find a soggy mess at the bottom of the cup, he was pleasantly surprised to find that the rock had stayed in one piece and was, indeed, edible. Quite pleasant, in fact.

# Praise the Lord

Jimbo, in the lead as usual, held up his left hand and cupped his right to his ear. The team stopped and listened, most looking nonplussed. Pascal, however, pointed to his right. "Voices," he whispered. "Not far." He moved from his place at the rear of the line to the front and conversed quietly with Jimbo. "Wait here a little. Stay quiet. We are going to look for the best route." Beatrix wondered how such big men could move so silently in the forest with so much dry vegetation under foot. Every footstep she made crackled, but she heard nothing as they walked away.

The guides weren't gone for long. The team got back in line, and Jimbo led them slowly, meandering their way between the trees. The wood there was clearer, with less undergrowth. Almost as if someone had cleared it. Humphry tapped Jimbo on the shoulder and pointed down to their left. A cigarette butt. He bent to pick it up. "Delicados," he read. "Is that a local brand?"

"Never heard of it," said Jimbo. "But now we are in Namibia, so I suppose it must be from here."

Pascal interrupted, pointing ahead of them. Now they could all hear talking. Male voices. Too far away to hear what they were saying, but it sounded like two men having an argument. Then banging. Then what could only be a chainsaw.

Doing their best to tiptoe and stay silent, they followed Jimbo in the direction of the noises. As they got nearer, they could hear branches falling, but they must have been small ones, as there were no crashes loud enough to suggest they were felling trees. Jimbo stopped suddenly and signalled for the others to lie down. They looked ahead. What they saw was not what they had been expecting. They were on the edge of a small open plain with neatly trimmed grass, giving the impression of the lawn in front of a stately home. Except it was a large wooden construction. A lodge, like the one they had been staying in but somehow, even from a distance, looking more upmarket. There was a large, raised deck with tables and chairs on it and steps leading up to it from the grass. Thatched huts, rondavels, ranged in an arc on either side.

"You told us there weren't any lodges on this side of the river," Richard whispered to Jimbo.

"Well, none that we knew of. None that are open, for sure. Some rangers told me that local people said there were one or two that had been built over here long ago but that they'd never been finished. The lodge company ran out of money. If any existed, they would be derelict by now."

"Well, this one exists, and it doesn't look derelict, does it?"

Three men stood in the clearing. One big, burly African wielding the chainsaw. The other two watching, brandishing not chainsaws but what looked very much like machine guns. Those two were definitely not of any African ethnic group. Swarthy skin, but not black. Short. Latin features. Definitely not Chinese. As soon as the sawing stopped, they resumed their argument.

"Sounds like Italian or Spanish to me," whispered Beatrix.

"Spanish," confirmed Robert. "Latin American Spanish. I think they're arguing about how big an area they've been told to clear."

"Shall we go back?" asked Richard. "Whatever this is, it's not a mine, Chinese or otherwise, and I don't like the look of those guns."

"I think we ought to investigate," replied Robert. "Remember that officially, there's not supposed to be anything or anybody here. At the very least, we need to report it in."

Bea weighed in with an opinion. "So, it's a lodge that nobody knew existed, or one local people believed to be derelict. It's not on the map, and nobody goes there. Yet it's not derelict, and there are people here. It's very suspicious."

"Too late to go back now anyway," said Humphry. "They're heading this way. They must have heard us."

"May as well stand up and be counted, then. We're going to look even more suspicious lying down here."

"Who are you?" said the slightly taller and much fatter one of the two. They were speaking English now. The other man stood back, brandishing his gun. "AK47," whispered Richard to Robert, who just nodded.

"We're tourists," replied Humphry. "On safari."

"You can't stay here. We're fully booked."

"That's all right. We didn't even know the lodge was here. We are trekking." Seeing the incomprehension on the Latino's face, he added, "Exploring the jungle. Camping. That's why we have our guides here." He pointed to Jimbo and Pascal.

"You cannot camp here. You must not be anywhere near here. How did you get here?"

"Walking, of course. Why is that man pointing a gun at me?"

"We are security. We keep our people safe. You could be terrorists. Where do you come from?"

"We're English. On vacation. We're staying at a lodge near the river."

"You come to hunt animals? What have you killed?"

"No, no, we only take photographs. We're not hunters. We don't have guns."

"What about them?" He indicated Jimbo and Pascal. Humphry had forgotten that they had rifles slung round their necks. He was saved from answering by Jimbo.

"We only carry rifles in case we are attacked by predators." It didn't seem to be a word the Latinos understood. "Lions. Leopards."

The bigger Hispanic grunted. "Put them down on the ground. Follow me. You need to talk with our leader."

Abandoning their single file formation, they followed him alongside one another, the other Latino marching behind, keeping his gun trained on their backs. They climbed the steps to the deck. "Take off your backpacks and put them down there," the lead Latino instructed them. "Wait here." His partner moved around to be in front of them, keeping his gun poised and waving it left and right.

The team stood, looking at each other nervously, waiting for 'the leader' to appear. They weren't expecting a Chinese praseodymium miner, whatever one of those looked like. They certainly weren't expecting the tall, corpulent African who appeared, dressed in a dark carmine cassock and wearing a dog collar.

"My children, welcome to the Benevolent Heart of Christ Mission." He had a deep, booming yet melodious voice. "I am the Reverend Pastor Wellington, but you may call me Father. I am sorry that you have walked so far to come to Jesus, to find that there is no room at the inn." He smiled at his own joke.

"Honestly, we didn't know you were here." Humphry took on the role of spokesperson for the group. "Father." That stuck in his throat. "We'll leave you in peace and resume our trek."

"But no, of course you will not. Sancho and Benny here will drive you to town."

"That's very kind of you, but there's no need." The prospect of two gun-toting Latinos driving them anywhere filled Humphry with the dread of a one-way destination ride — the kind of scenario where old-time gangsters got 'whacked.' "We came to walk, and walk we shall."

"I am sorry, but that will not be possible. It is not safe in this area."

That prompted Jimbo to speak up. "I and my partner here, Pascal, are skilled trekkers. Our guests will come to no harm, Reverend Father."

"I do not doubt your skills in avoiding wild animals, but there are other dangers here, and I cannot have it on my conscience to allow you to leave on foot. We will transport you to town, and you will be able to arrange safe passage back to your lodge from there."

"I am sure that God will watch over us and keep us safe," piped up Beatrix, mistakenly calculating that this intervention might help them.

"I am His representative on Earth, and He commands me to keep you safe by having you taken under our safekeeping as far as the town. It is decided. God has spoken."

While the lead Latino, presumably Sancho, engaged in a whispered conversation with the self-styled Father, the team pondered their fate, glancing sideways to one another. In their heads, they each doubted they had many options, if any at all.

Robert, who had one of the satellite devices that Latviana had given them in a jacket pocket, wondered whether he could reach it discreetly and find the right button to press without being noticed. Probably not; he knew that whatever he pressed, the gadget would beep. He hoped she wouldn't send any message to them while they were standing there, as that would make the thing beep too. Things definitely wouldn't end well then.

Humphry had no notion of what a Christian mission in the middle of the jungle should be like, but if any still existed in post-colonial times, he couldn't imagine this one being typical. Why the guns? Why the anxiety to get them removed a long distance away?

Their thoughts were interrupted by the priest.

"My men here have another urgent job to do before they can drive you, so you will wait in our visitor hut until they are ready. I will see you again to bless you and wish you all a safe journey." With that, the Reverend turned on his heel and went back through the door he had come from.

Sancho raised his gun. "This way."

They were led out of the lodge, opposite from where they had entered, and down a gravel path. At its end stood a solitary shipping container. Dark blue peeling paint, with 'Global Logistics' spelled out in huge lettering on the side. Incongruous, to say the least. How had that arrived in the middle of the bush?

Sancho lifted a hasp and pulled one of the end doors open. "You wait in here," he instructed, his colleague Benny almost pushing them forward with the butt of his gun. "Water over there." He pointed to boxes in the far corner. "Not long," he added as he slammed the door shut on them.

# The Visitor Hut

It was not what any normal person would describe as a visitor hut. It was almost in total darkness but for a sliver of light seeping in from beneath the doors. Just about enough light to stop them from colliding into each other once their eyes had adjusted. And hopefully enough to find the water. That was definitely a priority. The temperature in the container was stifling, the air stale and dry. They knew it was over thirty degrees outside; what might it have been in there?

In the weak light and with a lot of shuffling and fumbling, Richard — only recognisable by his voice as he shouted 'eureka' — found a box in the corner, full of bottles. He opened and sniffed one. "This one's some sort of cleaner. Smells of chlorine." He felt around the box; there were more boxes both underneath and next to it. "Better!" he announced. "This one is gin. I think."

"Stop it, Richard," said Humphry. "We know you like a drink, but what we want now is water. And to get out of here, of course. Keep looking."

A loud crash followed by louder swearing. "There's a lot of stuff here. Just tripped over what feels like a spade. There are more boxes. Hang on." There were scuffling noises. Then, "Found it, I think. You'll have to come over here, but be careful."

"I can just about see where he is now," said Beatrix to Humphry and Robert. "If you're not sure, hold on to me and we'll move together."

"I can see, too, now," replied Robert, after downing a bottle of near-scalding water in one. "This container is full of tools. Pickaxes. Whoops,

I think that's a pneumatic drill. Perhaps they really are thinking of mining here."

"Can't imagine anyone trying to mine with a pickaxe," said Humphry. "Especially not Our Father. Or whatever his name is. Looks like the only tools he ever uses are a knife and fork."

"Shhh. Can you hear machinery?" asked Beatrix.

"Probably their generator," replied Pascal.

"No. More like a pump," offered Jimbo.

"It's neither of those," said Richard. "It starts and stops and makes a grinding noise. I hear those noises in my day job. I'm pretty sure it's an augur."

"What's an augur?" asked Jimbo.

"A big mechanical drill for boring holes in the ground. Small ones are used to make holes for posts, bigger ones for digging foundations. They're probably digging holes for fenceposts around the area they were clearing when we arrived."

"Or maybe digging a mine?" ventured Beatrix.

"Good point. It would certainly work as the sort of tool that's needed to drill test bores to get samples of the soil underneath, to test for the minerals they're looking for. But it depends how deep they need to go. They would need a big pneumatic version if they wanted to dig deeper than six foot or so. It'd be huge and noisy. Probably hear it from the other side of the jungle."

That was about as much excitement and conjecture as they could take. Airless. Sweltering. The team collapsed on the floor, crawling close towards the door with the crack under it, and lying flat to take in gulps of fresher air. At least it gave the impression of ventilation. "I keep thinking of all those poor immigrants who died, starved to death, locked in a container like this one. It was in the news the other week. I suppose that at least it wasn't hot like this. It's cooler in Essex."

"Don't be so morbid, Bea," remonstrated Humphry. "Let's save our strength. They're going to let us out."

"Isn't drinking hot water bad for you?" asked Richard, of nobody in particular.

"I don't think it can be," replied Beatrix. "I have a friend who only ever drinks hot water. Swears by it. Boils the kettle but refuses to drop even a slice of lemon in the cup. She claims it's good for the skin. Doesn't stop her from looking five years older every time I see her, though."

A long period of silence ensued. Then Richard, as if he had suddenly remembered, said, "Shame that we left our locator thingummys in our backpacks."

"I've got mine in my pocket," said Robert. "I didn't want to risk using it before. It beeps every time you press a button or when a message comes in. That's a compromising design issue that Laoban needs to know about."

"To be honest, I was very surprised they didn't search us," said Richard.

"They probably will, Humphry."

More silence.

"Why don't you send a message now while we're here, then?"

"Because, Humphry, I'd have to press all those keys in the correct order, and I can't see which one is which. Don't want to send the wrong message."

Silence resumed.

"Pascal and I still have our CB radios," said Jimbo after a while.

"Mine's no good, Jimbo. The battery is flat."

"What is it about you and flat batteries, Pascal? It wouldn't work, anyway. All I can hear on mine is static. Probably because this container is steel."

Back to silence. For a few minutes, at least.

"You can turn off the beeping, you know," offered Beatrix. "Press buttons 1 and 4 together."

"Oh. Maria never said a thing about that." Robert wondered why Beatrix hadn't said this when he was talking about the issue mere moments before. Let him just carry on talking like an idiot about needing to get the things modified.

"I only found out by accident when I was experimenting with it," she explained. "You should be able to do it in the dark. They're the buttons to the left and right."

Robert pulled out his locator, turned it toward the crack of light, and pressed the two buttons. "OK. There's no sound when I do that."

"Exactly. You've just silenced it. Now press the button you want."

"And which one is that? SOS?"

"No!" Humphry exclaimed. "If the police or army come out here, we'll probably not even know about it if we're still locked in here. And then we'll be left to rot. Or just done away with and left out for the animals to feed on."

Beatrix audibly shuddered. "I think we're finished, anyway."

"Thanks for the optimism, Bea. But we can always drink the gin to anaesthetise ourselves as we go," suggested Richard.

"Be serious, Richard. Robert, I think you should press button 3. Unexpected delay to mission."

"Nothing happens when I do that."

"Boys who don't know how to use toys," muttered Beatrix. "You've forgotten already. You're supposed to be professionals with extraordinary powers of memory. Press four ones and then the number. 11113."

"Of course."

Silence once more. The heat growing ever more oppressive. Struggling to breathe now. Humphry broke the uneasy quiet. "No answer yet?"

"Nada."

"We really are done for," repeated Beatrix for a second time.

# Off into the Sunset

Time dragged by. An hour. Or two. Maybe six. No, not six, as there was still daylight showing through the crack, and they knew it got dark by seven. Then, all of a sudden, they heard noises. Unfamiliar noises. Men talking Spanish. Shouting at each other. Too far away to understand what they were saying. Banging, like other metal doors being opened. A truck's engine being turned over, eventually agreeing to start and spluttering into life. And, most interestingly, a sound they were starting to get used to: the low drone of an aeroplane, gradually getting louder.

At last, with a rattle of chains, the door opened, flooding the container with light and momentarily blinding its prisoners. "You had a good time in there?" chuckled Sancho, waving his gun at them. "Out!"

The team needed no second bidding. Staggering, disorientated, they emerged into the clearing outside the container. There stood a large and ancient-looking safari truck, much bigger than the Land Cruiser they had been driven in at the other lodge. This one could easily carry twenty tourists. Or prisoners. At the wheel was the self-proclaimed Reverend, still in his carmine garb but now sporting a wide-brimmed leather hat.

"I apologise for keeping you waiting, my children," he intoned. "I trust you were not too uncomfortable and have kept yourselves hydrated. I have had some chilled water bottles put into our transport for your further refreshment. And I bring good news. You will not have to endure the four or five-hour drive to the town. You will travel in our aircraft instead." He stopped and regarded the team. Nobody said a word. "Perhaps you were not brought up to be God-fearing children. I was expecting your gratitude."

"Thank you, Father," said Beatrix. "The plane will certainly be quicker and more comfortable than the truck."

Murmurs of false appreciation echoed all round.

"That's better. Now, climb aboard, my children. The runway is just a five-minute drive away."

"Our rucksacks?" asked Robert. "We need to take them."

"We have them here, in the trunk. They will be put on the plane at the airstrip."

Realising that they had no choice but to do as they were told and abandon the mission and the Mission, the team of six climbed aboard the truck, which crawled slowly away. The Land Cruiser might have felt like a bouncy castle, but this vehicle had no bounce at all. The bench seats were made of wooden slats with no cushioning, hence every rut, every boulder on the track, instantly and painfully transmitted shockwaves up each passenger's spine. Five minutes? It felt much longer. But, at last, they emerged through an opening in the thicket to the airstrip. There stood a plane, still with a single engine but much larger than the one they had travelled in before. Two heavily muscled African men wearing nothing but shorts were busy unloading metal drums from the plane. No markings to give away the drums' contents, but yellow hazard stickers were on each one. Seeing Robert staring, the Reverend spoke. "Cooking oil."

"There's a lot of it."

"Our disciples enjoy fried food."

Robert was fairly certain that the drums contained something rather more noxious than cooking oil, but nodded to show he accepted the explanation and kept quiet.

"When they finish unloading our supplies, you can get aboard."

After the drums came boxes and wooden packing cases, so the unloading took some time. Finished, the workers came over to the truck and opened doors at the back, from where they pulled out the team's backpacks and carried three each, throwing them into the back of the plane.

"Board now," said the Reverend, "and may God be with you." Then, almost as an afterthought, "I would ask you to repay our hospitality by not telling others about our mission here. There are many non-believers who could make our evangelical work difficult, and as you have seen for yourselves, we have no capacity for entertaining visitors."

With Sancho and his colleague toting their guns at them, the team clambered down from the truck and boarded the aircraft. The pilot, resembling a once-not-very-many-times-removed cousin of the Reverend — though attired differently, of course — busied himself with the controls, not even bothering to turn to see his passengers seated behind him. The door was closed from outside, and he started to taxi. No safety briefing this time. Just a cry of "seat belts" shouted over the din of the engine.

All but one complied. Robert, however, got out of his seat and made his way forward, even while the plane was moving. "Can I sit in the co-pilot's seat?" he asked. "I've always wanted to experience being at the front." The pilot nodded and grunted, gesturing at the seat belts he was wearing, a more complex affair than on the passenger seats behind. Two shoulder straps and a centre buckle. Robert made a performance of manoeuvring his way into the belt as if he was unfamiliar with the procedure, fastening it just before the plane finished taxiing to the other end of the airstrip.

And then they were off, into the setting sun. West. Not a direction they wanted to go in. The pilot levelled off at five thousand feet. Robert reached over his shoulder and pulled a set of headphones off a hook behind him, untangled the cable and plugged it into the socket in front of him. Now the pilot did take notice. Initially surprised, then he relaxed. Well, perhaps anyone knew how to plug in a headset.

Robert pressed the button for pilot-to-pilot communication. "Where are we heading?"

"I can't tell you."

"Never mind. I can see the navigation panel. We don't want to go to Windhoek."

"Well, that's where we're going."

"I don't think so." With that, Robert lunged left, pushing the pilot forward and locking his left arm around his neck, his left hand stretched out to clutch the pilot's right. The plane lurched downwards. Beatrix screamed. Somewhere, something electronic started hooting like a siren.

"What's that noise?" shouted Humphry.

"Stall alarm," replied Robert, taking hold of the control stick on his side with his right hand and pulling it towards him. The alarm stopped, and the plane levelled off again. "Sorry about that."

"You haven't killed him, have you?"

"No, Humphry. Should be out cold for an hour, though. Hopefully, he won't remember much when he comes round."

"Impressive. Smart move," said Richard. "Never seen that one before."

"Rear choke hold. Brazilian jiu jitsu."

"Where did you learn the Brazilian version?"

"Give you one guess."

"Stop congratulating yourself and tell me how we are going to land!" wailed Beatrix. "I know I shouldn't be, but I'm totally bloody scared."

"You're in safe hands. I'm a licenced pilot," replied Robert, shouting over his shoulder, to everyone's incredulity. "Been flying since I was fifteen. Richard, Pascal, since you're in the back row, go and check the backpacks."

"What for?"

"In case they put trackers in there or took ours out. Don't want them following us. At least the transponder on the plane isn't switched on."

Richard and Pascal got out of their seats and opened and delved into the backpacks. For a few minutes, there was just the sound of rummaging. Pascal broke the silence, holding up an aluminium cylinder, the size of a refillable water bottle. "What do you reckon this could be? It's not a water bottle. It's got a little plastic box glued to the side."

"Whatever it is, we don't want it on board. Bring it to me at the front. Very carefully!"

"I'll try." It wasn't easy for a six-foot six man like Pascal to move in the little plane. Bea solved the problem by gingerly taking the cylinder from him and passing it to Humphry, who passed it on to Robert.

"Hold on to your hair. I'm opening the window." Now the passing-the-parcel exercise made sense. The pilot's window was the only one that opened. Robert tossed the device out.

Humphry, looking down through the side windows, watched it fall, reach the ground, and explode. "What the f***?" he shouted.

"The plastic box was an impact switch," replied Robert. "Activated as soon as it hit something. Might even have gone off inflight if the plane was shaken by turbulence. Certainly would have upon landing. Wherever we were going, they didn't want us to arrive. Go on, look for more. It might not be the only one."

"Nothing else," Richard reported from the back of the plane. "The satellite locators are here, too. I would have thought they'd have taken those out."

"That wouldn't have been wise," observed Beatrix. "Assuming they knew what they were doing, they would realise that if they kept them, the devices would tell others we were still there. Better that they send them with us and blow us all to smithereens."

"Right," said Robert. "Now hold tight everyone, I'm turning and descending." With that, he banked the plane. No longer heading west into the sun, now roughly south. "Is that our river, Jimbo?" he shouted out to the back.

"Sure is, boss."

"Didn't come very far in the end, did we?" The river looked so close. "What I propose is to fly back to our lodge now. I can land this little baby there on the strip, I'm confident. We can debrief, get a proper night's sleep, and decide what to do next."

"And eat a proper meal," added Humphry.

"You've forgotten what the catering is like," Richard replied. "But the bar selection is excellent!"

"Won't they track and follow us?" asked Beatrix, ever the practical one.

"Let's hope there's nothing onboard that sends our location to them," replied Robert. "We've flown quite a way west. I've now descended to eight hundred feet, which should be too low to get picked up on radar. I'll fly round to the south before coming back east to the lodge."

"What about this plane? And him?" Humphry pointed to the unconscious pilot.

"Let's see what he knows and can tell us when he comes round. Maybe we'll let him take his plane back. Not that he's likely to get a very warm reception. They expect him to be dead — along with the rest of us."

As they flew south, the landscape below changed. It was now very different. More water than land. Jimbo pointed down. "Okavango Delta. Best not to go much further in this direction. There are many lodges. Busy ones. This time of day, everyone will be outside having their sundowners. We'll be bound to be seen."

"Ah, sundowners," sighed Richard.

Robert turned the plane eastwards and climbed. "Why ascend?" asked Humphry. "I thought you wanted to fly low."

"Yes, but if there's anyone around, they might read the registration painted under the wing. At two thousand feet that's much less likely. Even with binoculars. It'll be quieter too. Can't cover every eventuality."

They were now following the river, around ten kilometres inland. "Jimbo and Pascal, tell me when you see the lodge landing strip. Are your CB radios working at this altitude?"

"Battery's flat. I told you," replied Pascal.

Jimbo regarded him critically. "Mine's nearly flat, but I'll try."

"See if Joshua can pick us up. If not, how far is it to walk?"

"An hour. Only ten minutes with the Land Cruiser."

Jimbo fiddled with his radio. "Might be a problem?" he queried. "If I call from here, the guys at Dreamtime will hear. It's the same frequency."

"Can you tell him there's a supply plane coming in? If the other lodge doesn't know we've gone, they probably won't think anything of it."

"Good idea. No signal yet."

They flew on for another ten minutes before Pascal shouted out, "Ten o'clock!"

"Got it, thanks," replied Robert. "Lady and gentlemen, we will be landing in five minutes. Fasten your seatbelts and return your seat backs to their upright position."

"Joker," replied Richard, nevertheless doing what he was told.

"Joshua is on his way, Rob," said Jimbo. "Wants to know if the plane is carrying the fresh fish he ordered."

"Tell him no, but we've got a killer whale on board. Second thoughts, don't tell him anything."

Just as the landing strip came into view ahead of them, the engine stuttered to a halt, the propellor now just pushed by the headwind, and they glided down to the ground. They hit with a big bump and came to a halt.

"That's unusual, isn't it? Cutting the engine before landing?" enquired Humphry.

"Ran out of fuel," smiled Robert.

# The Debrief

Joshua seemed less than overjoyed to see the team, though the only reason that Humphry could wring out of him, at least until they got back to the lodge, was that they had returned before he could restock Richard's favourite brand of gin. On his instruction, the men pushed the plane to park it underneath an ancient and heavily rusted corrugated iron roof. "The hangar is best, so it can't be spotted from the air," he explained. Hangar was a hyperbole for something with no walls or doors, only a decrepit roof supported precariously on four rusty pillars that looked likely to cave in on the plane underneath it at any time.

Jimbo and Joshua dragged the still unconscious pilot from his seat and into the waiting Land Cruiser. "He's alive, right?" asked Joshua.

"He'll probably come to any time now," said Robert. The victim let out a groan in confirmation. "Keep him between you on the front bench seat, and if he shows any signs of stirring, restrain him until we get there."

"What are you going to do with him?"

"Don't know yet. We'll start by interrogating him. See what he knows about the operation at the so-called Mission."

"And then?"

"Depends on what he knows or what he'll tell us. We might let him go. Or maybe we'll feed him to a hungry croc." Robert grinned. Joshua didn't look as if he found it amusing, but helped Jimbo push the pilot onto the seat, climbed in next to him, and started the motor.

"There's a surprise for you back at the lodge," Joshua announced.

"Something edible for dinner for a change? I keep remembering the barbecued hartebeest I had in the Carnivore restaurant when I stopped in Nairobi on my way over. Delicious. Don't know why you don't serve it here." Richard was as fond of his food as his drink.

"They lied to you. You probably ate imported venison. They took all the wild animals off the menu over twenty years ago. Anyway, hartebeest is tough as old boots, even after Hilda has stewed it for eight hours. You wouldn't like it."

"So, what's the surprise, then?"

"You'll see in a minute. Or less."

Joshua pulled up in front of the lodge. Waiting for them was a diminished welcoming committee of Glenda, in a housecoat that had probably been pink before she entered the kitchen, and a slim and rather shapely boy scout. Or, rather, girl scout, dressed in a khaki shirt and a pair of shorts and a baseball cap, all in pristine condition — a designer version of lodge uniform.

"What on earth are you doing here?" shrieked Beatrix, as if the new arrival might be her friend. Then she remembered. "Sorry, Laoban."

Humphry and Richard looked mystified. "Laoban? Is that you?"

Robert jumped in. "Back when we were working together on another project, the guy we were looking after called her Chameleon. Because you never know where or when she's going to pop up or what she's going to look like when you see her. Very appropriate, I thought."

"Then stop thinking." Laoban didn't want people to call her that. Or reference the past. Though, in truth, she had grown quite fond of the moniker. She was proud of her abilities to appear unexpectedly in different places and perform quick changes of dress, appearance, and role (the coiled poisonous tongue stayed the same in all situations) and was glad to have those talents recognised. Even if it was only by Ronald Jones. That filthy dirty man. And now by Robert.

Meanwhile, Robert was recalling how Ronald Jones used to call him Pilot, even though he saw him at least as often in other guises. Jones might have been despicable in other ways, but at least he got the Pilot bit. Recognition. Shame that Laoban didn't. Anyway, nice to have names now, even if none of them were real. He yanked his mind back to the present.

"Why are you here, anyway?" asked Beatrix. "Nice to see you, of course."

"One of you pressed the problem key on the satellite tracker. I thought I would come myself. I only flew in an hour ago."

"We were going to set up a search party for you tomorrow," added Joshua.

"Just as well we are back, then, Ma'am," said Jimbo. "Joshua is a hopeless guide. Scaredy-puss, aren't you, Josh?" Joshua cuffed Jimbo around his ear.

"Enough of this. Debrief. Now. On the deck."

"Can I grab a drink first?"

"No, Richard, I need you to have a clear head. Or as clear as realistically possible, anyway."

"I meant water, Laoban. We're all thirsty."

"Water is on the table. Drink as we talk. Now, sit and tell me exactly what happened. One at a time. You!" pointing at Robert.

"Just a moment. What about our prisoner?"

"Hmmm. Men!" she shouted out to Jimbo and Pascal, who were gossiping in the bar area. "Lock the pilot up in the manager's office. Tie him up first. Oh, and search him for phone, pager, anything like that. I'll see to him later."

The team debrief took over an hour.

"So," said Humphry, summing up, "they're nasty pieces of work out there at the Mission, and something dodgy is going on, but it's obviously not the place we're looking for. Tomorrow we'll go in a different direction, see if we have success that way."

"How do you know it's not what we're looking for?" asked Laoban. "You didn't see the whole place, so you can't be sure. And even if it isn't what our client is interested in, something underhand and secretive is certainly going on there, and I'm sure I can find another new client who would value the information. So, you must go back. You'll be better prepared this time."

"When?"

"I think tomorrow at first light. But let's see what we can learn from your pilot. I'll interview him. Robert, sit beside me in case there are any technical questions. The rest of you can go to your rooms." The two of them went to the manager's office.

The others looked disappointed, but went on their way as instructed, Richard first sneaking across to the bar and pilfering the first bottle that came to his hand. 'Don't go looking, just go taking' was a motto he'd followed for many years.

# The Namibian Pilot

"What happened?" The pilot might have been a tall, well-built, heavy-looking African, but at that moment, in the tiny office, lashed with rope to a rickety wooden chair facing his inquisitors, Laoban and Robert, he was the picture of fragility. Scared out of his skin.

"You fainted at the controls," said Laoban. "You were lucky that this man here knows how to fly." The pilot nodded humbly.

"What's your name?"

"Samuel. Sam. Where am I? Are we back at the lodge?"

"Not the one you came from, no. Here, you're safe."

"I can never be safe. They will be looking for me. They will come here. They will kill us all." He looked to be on the verge of a panic attack.

"They very nearly did. But why? They're a Christian mission, aren't they?" The pilot threw his eyes skywards, then spat on the ground.

"You need to tell us all you know."

"I can't. They will kill me."

"If you don't tell us, you won't live here either. Lots of hungry carnivores around here," said Robert. He looked at Laoban. Had she registered his joke? Sam was neither amused nor more scared.

"Can I have something to eat?" Sam was fidgeting in his seat, looking as if he was trying to make up his mind whether he could wriggle out of his restraints and get up and go.

"Sit still! You can eat later. After you talk," said Laoban.

"I need to drink. Now." Probably true. He definitely wasn't looking any better. Laoban told Robert to bring him a bottle of water from the bar.

"Feeling better now?" Laoban asked. Samuel nodded. "We will keep you safe here if you tell us everything you know. You need to trust us."

Robert thought that if it was him being addressed by Laoban in such an aggressive tone of voice, he wouldn't have trusted her an inch, but Samuel didn't seem flustered anymore. He nodded.

"So who are they? What do they do?"

"I don't know. I just fly in and out. Supplies."

"What supplies?"

"You saw them." He moved his head, looking towards Robert. "Boxes, metal drums, things."

"What's inside them?"

"I don't know. They don't tell me. It's not my business. I just fly the plane."

"And people?"

"Not often. Sometimes."

"What people? Local people?"

"Sometimes. Not many."

"Foreigners?"

"Sometimes. Not many."

"*Makwerekwere*?" Sam looked surprised to hear Laoban use the offensive slang term for Africans from other countries.

"No."

"Oriental? Chinese?"

"No."

"So where do the foreigners come from?"

"I don't know. You saw them," he said, addressing Robert. "People like them. Don't know where they come from."

"How long do the people stay?"

"I don't know. Perhaps they don't leave. You're the first people I have ever flown out of there."

Sam, getting ever more nervous, was now fidgeting so much that the chair fell sideways to the floor with a crash, with him still tied to it.

Robert, hauling him back to vertical, asked, "Where were you going to fly us to today?"

"Windhoek."

"You didn't have enough fuel. Try again."

"There was plenty. I'd only used half the tank in one wing coming out."

"The other tank was empty. So, what was your destination?"

"Windhoek. Honestly." Samuel was sweating now. "That tank was full when we took off. I checked. Pilots always have to go through a check routine before taking off."

"Yes, I know. OK, suppose we made it there. What did they say was going to happen to us when we landed?"

"Nothing. They told me nothing. They just said that you'd be looked after."

"What were you supposed to do after landing?"

"The usual." Seeing Laoban and Robert raising their eyebrows questioningly, he added, "Park the plane. Go home. Wait for instructions. That's all I know, boss."

"She's the boss, not me."

Laoban went back to asking the questions. "How often did you fly there?"

"Four, five times a month?"

"Is it only you who flies there, or are there other pilots, other planes?"

"I never heard any of the other guys say they went there. But I'm sworn to secrecy. So, I never told any of them I go there. I suppose if others fly, it would be the same thing. They wouldn't tell me."

"What do you do the rest of the month?"

"Fly tourists to lodges. Down south in the dunes. That's what the company does."

"The company at the lodge?"

"No, the guys who own the planes."

"They tell you to go to the lodge?"

Samuel explained that he'd get instructions to do a charter flight to carry boxes of supplies to a mining concession that was on the way to the Mission, if that's what it was. He'd then have to wait a while to see if he got a WhatsApp message from another number wishing him 'god speed.' Code for 'go to the mission instead.' If he got the code, he still flew towards the official destination but didn't land, at that point descending to a thousand feet and turning off his transponder. He then carried on to another disused airstrip that lay beside a road. There would be a truck parked there with more supplies, like the drums that Robert had seen earlier. Guarded by men with guns. He'd load the supplies on to the plane, then fly on to the Mission strip. After unloading, he'd then turn round and fly back as soon as possible, turning his transponder back on again as he overflew the official destination.

"Have you been inside the lodge?"

"No, no, never. Just the airstrip."

"I don't believe you."

"Honest, boss." Samuel looked down, clearly nervous, avoiding her gaze.

"Yes, you have. What do they do there, Sam?" Laoban was now seriously angry, hitting the table with her fist.

"I don't know, boss," he wailed.

"I'm going to send you back there tomorrow to find out, then."

Now Samuel really did look terrified. "No, don't, I beg you. I can never go there again."

"Why? What do you know?"

"I know nothing. I've told you everything. Honest."

"You keep saying that, but I don't think you are being honest. I think you know more." She fixed him with a stare, willing him to continue.

"I'm scared. There's nothing else I can tell you. Can I eat now? I'm so hungry."

"Later. I'm sure you know more."

Robert cut in. "Did you know they were going to kill us all today? You and us?"

"No!" Sam would have gone white if he could have.

"We found a bomb on the aircraft. Put into one of our bags. And if what you told us about thinking you had enough fuel is true, they also punctured the fuel tank. So, we'd have run out of fuel, and the impact switch on the bomb would have exploded it when the plane reached the ground. Either way, we'd have gone up in flames somewhere in the middle of nowhere. Probably where nobody would ever find us. All of us would be dead. You too."

Samuel listened, wide-eyed with incredulity.

"So, you see, we saved you. You fainted, we found the bomb, I got the plane down here safely. You're alive. Thanks to us. Now you need to tell us everything you know."

"Where are we?"

"In another lodge. A safe one."

"They will come for us, I am sure of it."

"Why? I told you, they think we're all dead. They'll assume the plane came down somewhere in the bush when it ran out of fuel. Exploded on impact. Possibly, the wreckage would never be found. They won't be expecting to see anything about it on the news bulletins."

Samuel didn't seem reassured by that.

"What about my boss? The owner of the aircraft?"

"He'll call his customer, the Mission. They'll say that you left, and they know nothing, and he'll assume you've crashed somewhere. The transponder was off all the time we were flying here," added Robert. "No way of tracking us."

"Why are you looking so worried?" shouted Laoban, irritated at having her interrogation taken over by Robert. "We're the good people. You're a lucky man." Then, after a few moments' consideration, she said, "You can go and eat now. We'll talk again later." More threat than a promise — as was her way.

Robert untied Samuel from the chair he was sitting on and opened the door to find Pascal standing outside. Listening in? "I was just coming to call you for dinner." An excuse? He was overheard by Laoban.

"No dinner or drinks yet for my team! That is an order! Robert, go and tell Joshua to come in here. And make certain that Richard doesn't go anywhere near the bar until I say so."

Joshua looked more like an errant schoolboy sent for by the head teacher than a man entering his own office. "You wanted to see me, Ma'am?"

"Call me Laoban or nothing. Never Ma'am, understood?"

"Of course, Laoban."

"Take Samuel the pilot and feed and water him. Or, rather, give him a few beers. Try to loosen his tongue. See what else he can tell us."

"Can Pascal do that?"

"You, not Pascal. Just you. You and Samuel, the two of you make friends, understood, Joshua?"

He raised his eyebrows. "Not Pascal. Beers for the pilot. Sure, Laoban. I understand."

"Now send my team in here. I'll brief you, Jimbo, and Pascal later. This room's too small for all of us at once."

# Planning the Return

Truth be told, Joshua's office was too small for two, never mind five people, so they were all standing up. Humphry was surprised to find that Laoban was as tall as him. He'd never noticed that before. Was she standing on something? Some politicians do. Not something he could check; there was no way of seeing to the other side of the desk.

"You need to go back to that Mission tomorrow."

Humphry protested. "But why? Whatever it is, it's not what we're supposed to be searching for. It's not a mine."

"Not yet, it's not. But you heard them drilling. They could be testing samples."

Robert chimed in. "But there are no Chinese. You heard Samuel."

"We don't know that. Anyway, wherever they're from, however many of them there are, whatever they're doing, we need to find out. There's not likely to be more than one clandestine operation in that area. They didn't want you there. In fact, they tried to make sure you could never tell anyone anything about the place. I don't imagine they're going to tolerate any other business activity near them. Whatever it is they're doing. Even if they really are a religious mission." She looked around. Beatrix held her hand up like a schoolgirl.

"How do you propose we go about it, then, Laoban?"

Tetchily, she asked, "Robert, will that aircraft fly?"

"So long as only one of the tanks is punctured and there's fuel here, then yes, sure. But we can hardly fly straight back there. They'd probably try to shoot the plane down first. Or, if we manage to land, just shoot us."

"Is there another airstrip that at least gets you near? So you don't have to trek all the way through the bush again? Does Joshua know?"

"That's something to ask Sam. See if he'll give us a straight answer. The maps here are old and only cover Botswana."

"Maria gave me some better maps to bring here. She forgot to give them to you. She said you already know about them?" The way that she was looking at him gave Robert the definite impression that Laoban suspected something had been going on between them.

"I know I took her a package from a map shop, but I didn't open it. She didn't tell me what was inside." Changing the subject quickly, he said, "There's another problem. The punctured tank. One gives me enough fuel to get there, but not to get back again."

"Can you fix the hole? Stick something in it or tape it over?"

"It's an aircraft, Laoban, not a toy model. I'll take a look in the morning. Is there any fuel here at the lodge, do you know? The tank that doesn't leak is empty now."

"Talk to Joshua. Let's look at the map I brought here."

They laid it out on the desk. Better than the one in the lodge, but it still wasn't very clear. It looked as if the cartographer had started with a black and white aerial photo and simply inked in the roads and some of the tracks. They could see the river, but none of them could identify the lodge they were in.

"It's rather an old map," Richard pointed out. "From 1998. This lodge might not have been built then. Nor the one that has been taken over by the Mission."

Humphry, who was nearest the door, left at this moment and returned seconds later with Joshua. Now the room was definitely too small. Claustrophobic. Placing two hands on the top of the filing cabinet, Beatrix pulled herself up, twisted her body, and sat to attention, all in one smooth action. "Remarkable. How on earth did you manage that?" asked Richard.

"Used to be a gymnast, didn't I?" Twinkling her eyes, she refused to let on any more than that tantaliser. A lady doesn't tell which year she competed in the Olympics.

Joshua confirmed the lodge had opened in 2002 and pointed to its location on the map, working it out by reference to the river channels nearby. He moved his finger north into Namibian territory. "This could be where you went," he said. "It's called 'Greensword Camp' here. There are no tracks between it and the river, which makes sense, and it's got an airstrip."

"But it wasn't a camp," objected Humphry. "It was definitely a lodge."

"Lots of lodges are called camps. Ones that used to be tented, but then they built proper lodges. With rondavels. Tourists like their comforts, don't they?" Joshua poked Richard, who was next to him, and chortled at his own joke. "Anyway, what do you think, Robert?"

"It's the only thing that's in the right area. Is that another airstrip just to the left?"

"Yes. Strange that there's nothing else there, though. No tracks leading there either. There must have been a plan to build a camp or lodge. Perhaps there is one there by now."

"We'd have flown over it when we left the Mission, and I didn't see anything."

"Well, this map is over twenty years old. If the airstrip isn't in use and hasn't been cleared regularly, it must be overgrown by now. The jungle reclaims land quickly," explained Joshua.

"If the vegetation hasn't grown too high or too dense, it might still be usable. If we go west and then come back in a big loop, we won't overfly the mission. I think the strip is far enough away for them not to hear the plane."

"How far?" asked Laoban.

"Looks to be about two kilometres. Could be more. Richard, you're the navigator. What do you reckon?

"There's a stream in the way. Can't tell how wide it is from this map. Assuming the scale is accurate, and based on what we walked yesterday, I'd say three kilometres. Need to allow half a day at least, as we know it's not open country."

"So, how do you want us to go about this, Laoban?"

"Joshua, do you have fuel for the plane? Enough to fill both tanks? If they're not leaking, of course."

"We should have a couple of drums, but I need to check if they're full. We're given a small stock to hold, but it's only for emergencies. I don't think we've needed to fuel a plane for years. Certainly not since I started working here. That fuel will be stale. Does that matter?" Robert shook his head.

"Go and check it now," commanded Laoban. Joshua stood there, hesitant. "Please." She scrunched up her face in a futile attempt to look like she meant it, but merely made herself look more sour and angry.

"It's out by the airstrip, and it's night now. Can it wait until morning?"

"Hmmm. Well, since the plane needs to be checked over too, I suppose it can and will have to. Robert and Joshua, go out to the airstrip at first light and assess the situation. Everyone, back here for a morning briefing at eight." The team nodded, but hesitated. "Now you can go and eat." It sounded more like an order; it wasn't in Laoban's psyche to make generous gestures. This was as good as they would get from her. The team manoeuvred their way out of the office one by one. Just as he got to the door, a final arrow was released. "Richard! One glass of wine, no more. Understood?"

"Yes, Laoban."

"Oh, and Joshua? Tell Sam I'll talk to him again in the morning."

Dinner was another sorry affair. Congealed pasta once again, this time glued together with what was probably tomato ketchup. Glenda no doubt got the idea from watching the team on a previous evening, but whatever it was, it certainly didn't deserve the accolade of 'sauce,' at least in Bea's opinion. It smelt revolting. The dish was made even less attractive by being served somewhere between tepid and cold, despite the metal serving tray having a few candles flickering underneath it. All they seemed to be doing was illuminating the underside of the tray without adding any effective heating. But in the absence of any other sustenance, the team held their noses and ate.

"The energy bars that we had in the bush were tastier than this gloop," Bea remarked to Humphry. "More nourishing, too." They refilled their wine glasses. If they were going adventuring again, they needed energy. Had to get their calories from somewhere. Except for Richard, that is. He rose from his chair to follow the others, saw Laoban sitting in the shadows on the far side of the deck, thought better of it, and sat down once more.

Also lurking in a far corner was Pascal, concentrating on something under the table. Presumably looking at pictures on his phone again. Intending to be discreet, but under observation. Beatrix wandered towards the bar, then made a last-minute turn and stood still, some distance behind him but near enough to see that his screen was displaying some kind of messaging app. Time to give him a fright. "Let me see your pictures, Pascal."

Pascal's immediate response was to press the 'off' key. "Sorry, they're private. Family pictures. You wouldn't want to see them."

Laoban had moved to stand beside Beatrix. She had obviously seen the screen too. "Who were you messaging, Pascal?"

Not used even to mild confrontation, he was now a gibbering wreck. "My wife. Back in my village."

"How? There is no signal here."

"In this corner, you can sometimes get a signal from Namibia. Very weak."

"You told us you had never been to Namibia. But you have a Namibian phone."

"I never went there before. A guide from another group sold it to me. Long ago."

"You also told us the other day that you didn't have a wife," said Beatrix.

Pascal hunted for words to say. "Not my wife yet. We will marry next year." Even a child would have thought he was lying.

Laoban left Beatrix standing with Pascal and went over to Joshua. "Did Samuel have a phone on him?"

Joshua looked sheepish. "Sorry, I forgot to look."

"You didn't search him?" Joshua hung his head. "Where's Samuel now?"

"We put him in a staff bedroom, Laoban. He's probably sleeping."

"Go and fetch him. Yourself. Now." Joshua scuttled away.

Robert and Humphry had joined them, but Richard was nowhere to be seen. They decided he must have gone to bed. Hopefully not clutching a bottle. In less than a minute Joshua hurried back, looking alarmed. "He's gone!"

"Then go after him!" shouted Laoban. "He can't have gone far, surely?" Seeing Jimbo sitting looking unconcerned, she added, "This is your fault! You were supposed to be guarding him. Get up! Join the search party!"

At that moment, they heard an engine being started, and all of them raced outside. Just in time to see a Land Cruiser drive off. "How did he get hold of the keys?" asked Beatrix.

"We leave them in the ignition. No need to put them away, as it's only us here."

Laoban gave Joshua one of her most viciously withering looks. "Jimbo, take Humphry and go after him. You know the tracks and he doesn't, so it shouldn't be difficult to find him."

"What about Pascal?" asked Jimbo. "He's the expert tracker."

"He stays here. In fact, Joshua, do you have a room you can lock him up in?"

Pascal interrupted. "You're not my boss. You can't lock me up. I've done nothing."

"Exactly. You've done nothing when you should have done something. Like guarding Samuel. Give me your phone."

"No. I said, you're not my boss."

Robert, who had moved behind Pascal while this exchange was happening, grasped both his hands and pulled them behind his back. Beatrix pulled the phone from his pocket and gave it to Laoban.

"Today, I'm everyone's boss. Those people are dangerous. They tried to kill my team. If you don't do as I say, we're all in danger. I don't trust you very much right now, Pascal."

"There's a store cupboard. I think that will do for a cell," said Joshua. "It's got a padlock on the outside. Nothing much on the inside, though."

"Good. Take him there. Robert, supervise. Humphry, Jimbo, what are you still doing here? Go! Find Samuel."

"Please," Humphry muttered under his breath.

"Bea, with me," said Laoban.

# Bea Takes the Initiative

The men having left, Laoban invited Beatrix to sit with her on a sofa in the corner of the deck. This was unusual. And uncomfortable in every sense. "You're the brains of the team, Bea, and you've been to this so-called mission in the jungle. What are your thoughts about going back?"

Bea pondered for a while, then chose her words carefully, suppressing her surprise that Laoban was actually allowing someone else to have an opinion, equally certain that whatever she proposed would be rejected.

"Well, do we assume the plane is repairable and there's enough fuel? And that airstrip is usable?"

"For now, yes."

"We should carry camping equipment and supplies for a week on the plane. That way, even if there's no fuel to fly back, or some other emergency, we have what we need to survive."

Laoban nodded.

"From what I saw flying back here, it's mostly woodland around the mission, so it's probably not too hard to creep up and get close undetected. They won't be expecting us to come back, as they believe we were blown up with the plane. At least, they will unless Sam gets some sort of message to them. But, even so, they're probably more on their guard than before, in case we somehow managed to alert others before we went down. They know we had those devices." Laoban sat quietly, allowing Bea to continue.

"The reason we're going back is to find out what's actually happening in that place. To spy. Gather information. Not to disrupt whatever they're doing. The problem is that, as they say, the natives aren't friendly."

Laoban nodded, and Bea continued.

"I don't think it's wise to go in mob-handed like before. Six of us is just way too many. It was a good idea when we were pretending to be a group of tourists, but we can't do that again. I think you want us to leave Pascal behind?"

"Yes. I don't trust him."

"Nor do I. Right. So, the five of us go, and set up camp somewhere we think is safe enough, as near as we can to the runway."

"Four of you. Richard stays here."

Bea raised her eyebrows. "OK. In fact, that's probably better. So just the four of us. Humphry and I then go alone to the mission, leaving Robert and Jimbo at the camp."

"Why you and Humphry?" Had anyone told Laoban about the other night? Bea sensed not, and hoped it was a straight question. It would be the same answer, anyway.

"Of the four of us, we're the best at moving quietly, so I think we have the best chance of getting close before anyone notices us. We'll find somewhere hidden, where we can watch what's going on for as long as we can. When we're sure we can do so without getting stopped or shot, we'll literally walk up to the front door, posing as doctor and nurse, saying we've had a call that there are injured and sick people there."

"Surely that's not credible? They've seen you already."

"Well, Humphry really is a doctor, and I'm sure I can pass as a nurse. Sort of Médecins Sans Frontiers."

"They'll recognise you."

"Not if Humphry shaves off his beard and I disguise both of us. Remember, I used to be a makeup artist."

"They'll ask how you got there."

"If you look at the map, you'll see that there's a road about eight kilometres north of there. Not as far away as the guys here told us before. We'll say that we were dropped at the junction with the track and walked the rest of the way."

"Why not take Jimbo? He's your muscle."

"Rob's the most important asset because he's the only one who can pilot a plane. First option of escape. If the plane won't fly for any reason, or something should happen to Rob, heaven forbid, Jimbo is the only one who can get us out of the bush safely on foot. Second option of escape. So, assuming Humph and I complete our bit of the mission safely, they can wait there, ready to get us out and back here as quickly as possible."

"And if you can't complete the mission, they come and try to rescue you?"

"No. They come back here and raise the alarm. Better you lose two assets than four."

Laoban looked sceptical. "I don't want to lose any of you. Do you think your lives are in danger?"

"Well, if the Reverend had had his way, we would already all be dead. So yes, of course. But I'm confident we'll manage. That's another reason for me to go instead of Robert. They're less likely to be rough with a woman."

"Even one who's a black belt in karate?"

"It's always good to have a trick or two up the sleeve of one's uwagi, don't you agree?"

"Good. I like that plan," said Laoban, actually smiling. "So, Plan B? If the plane doesn't work, Jimbo guides you to the Mission?"

"Yes. If we have to go overland it should be quicker than last time, since we know roughly what we're facing and can probably take a more direct route, but it's still going to take us about two days. It'll be much more difficult to achieve any element of surprise, as the last part will be open country. Unless we take a day longer and keep to the forest."

"Let's hope there's fuel and the men can fix the tank, then. We will convene at eight. Get some rest."

"Do you mind my asking why you're keeping Richard here?"

"He's the tech guru. I need him to find out what's on Pascal's and Sam's phones. And guard them until I decide what to do with them."

"Hmm. Better keep him away from the drink, then."

"Yes. I have a plan for that. Good night."

# In Hot Pursuit

Without waiting for Laoban and Beatrix to go back into the lodge, Jimbo and Humphry jumped into the other Land Cruiser, as instructed. Jimbo started the engine, then said, “Forgot something,” and went back in, returning moments later clutching two rifles.

“I don’t think Laoban wants us to shoot him,” said Humphry.

“No, but we might come across night hunters. Wild dogs, for example. Or he might shoot us, of course.” Seeing Humphry looking quizzical, he added, “Looks like Sam took one of our guns. A box of ammo, too. We’re lucky he left us these.”

“You don’t trust him?”

“Pah. His tribe? Liars and thieves, the lot of them.” He put the vehicle into gear and accelerated away.

“Which way are you going? There are so many tracks he could have taken.”

“Let’s start with the airstrip. He doesn’t know the plane is out of fuel, does he?”

“Not unless Laoban or Robert told him. But he was unconscious when we got to the lodge. He wouldn’t remember the way.”

“He was faking it. Remember, he was sitting next to me. He had his eyes half open.”

“Still, difficult to find the way in the dark when he’s never been here before, surely?”

“You have a better idea where to go, then?”

They fell silent for the rest of the few minutes it took to reach the strip. Jimbo turned off the headlights. There was no need. The white sand appeared to fluoresce in the moonlight and stretch much further than its five hundred metre length. They drove slowly, keeping to the edge, passing the so-called hangar sheltering the plane, but saw no sign of Samuel.

"Where next, then?" asked Humphry.

"Let's follow the supply road west. He's seen the river from the air, so he'll know there's no place to cross going eastwards."

"I thought you said that there was no vehicle crossing nearby."

"There's an old ford about twenty K after the concession boundary. No idea what condition it's in, but the river's low at the moment. Impassable for sure after the rains come."

"But how would he know that? He doesn't even know where we took him."

"Don't you believe it. Before we took him into Josh's office, he was staring at that huge map on the wall of the dining room. Our lodge is marked with a big red star, remember? Even if he's never been here, he must have flown over in the past, so he'll have a good idea of the geography."

Now they were bumping down a very narrow track, pushing their way through a thicket, brushing the vehicle on both sides. "This is the supply road?" asked Humphry.

"No, a short cut. Keep your body in and clear of the trees." Easier said than done, thought Humphry. The combination of the deeply rutted track and the speed that Jimbo was going made the ride even bumpier than usual, but at last they emerged into open country.

Suddenly, Jimbo stopped and turned off the engine. "Listen! Elephants!" The sound of distant trumpeting broke the silence of the night. "They're angry. That's probably where Samuel is." Jimbo drove off again at high speed, Humphry grasping the rail in front of him with both hands, hanging on for dear life. Jimbo stopped to listen a few times, once changing direction. Then suddenly, he cried out, "There he is!" A stationary Land Cruiser, glinting in the moonlight, surrounded by a troupe of elephants. Now they approached slowly, stopping fifty metres away.

"Are elephants really dangerous?" asked Humphry. "I assumed they would just walk away."

"Depends. That one in front of Samuel is an alpha male. He'll be aggressive if he's in musht."

"Musht?"

"Randy."

"Oh. Surely, he can tell the difference between a female elephant and a Land Cruiser?"

"If he thinks Sam is stopping him from getting to his woman, he'll attack. Let's scare him." Jimbo picked up a rifle and shot into the air. That certainly scared the elephants; the one who had been confronting Samuel literally ran away into the bush, the others scattering too at a slow lumber. Samuel took the opportunity to start his engine and move forward. Not bothering to look for a track, Jimbo drove over the open ground in an attempt to cut him off. Which might have been fine, had they not forgotten that Samuel had a gun. Which was now trained on them.

"Out of my way!" he shouted.

"Where do you think you're going?" asked Humphry.

"To safety. Now, out of my way."

"Sorry, not going to happen. Get out of the truck and get in here. We're taking you back. You want safety, you'll have it there with us."

Samuel's reply was to shoot over their heads. "Next time, it will be one of you. Now get going."

Jimbo now shouted something that Humphry found incomprehensible. "What was that you said?" he asked.

"Surrender. In Bantu."

"Doesn't look like he's planning to do that. Reverse about twenty metres."

"What? Let him go?"

"Trust me."

"OK." While Jimbo reversed, Humphry raised the gun, pointed it at the rear of the truck that Samuel was driving, and shot. "What did you do that for?" asked Jimbo.

"To puncture his fuel tank. Got the idea from the plane. He won't get far now."

"You could have set fire to the truck."

"I doubt it. It's diesel."

Robert must have scored a direct hit, as Samuel made it hardly any distance before coming to a stop. He was making repeated and futile efforts to restart the Land Cruiser. Humphry leapt out, keeping his rifle trained. Samuel stopped what he was doing and reached for his gun, but in his struggle to restart the vehicle, it had got snagged under his seat, so he couldn't lift it before Humphry was right in front of him, the muzzle of his rifle inches only from his temple. Jimbo, having now moved his vehicle closer, was holding a length of rope that he'd extracted from somewhere in the depths of the truck and quickly moved to wrap it around Samuel, binding his arms behind him. Not up to police arrest standards, but adequate in the circumstances. Good enough to stop him from escaping into the bush.

Jimbo and Humphry made to drag him out of the driver's seat, but that proved unnecessary; Samuel, admitting defeat, walked to the other vehicle. Having him in the front row was too risky, as he might loosen the rope and jump out or grab at the wheel. Hoisting a large, well-built man up three steps and into the back of a safari truck, with his hands tied and therefore unable to hold on to the grab rails, proved a challenge, solved by Jimbo giving his butt an almighty push, projecting Samuel headfirst onto the floor with a scream of pain. Humphry climbed in behind him, deciding that with Samuel in a supine position, the best and safest thing to do was to sit in the middle of the bench seat with his feet firmly planted on the prisoner's back. By keeping the rifle in hand, he could also nudge Samuel's head from time to time should he attempt to move.

Jimbo must have been following an extraordinarily long shortcut before, as it took him less than ten minutes to make it back to the lodge by the direct route. Helped by Robert and Joshua, they lifted Samuel out and onto the lodge deck, where Laoban and Beatrix had just finished their discussion.

Three of the men restrained Samuel while Jimbo retied the rope, this time securing Sam to the chair with his arms behind him, and the chair to a central pole in the hut. "Won't get out of that in a hurry," he said with a satisfied grin.

Humphry handed a phone and wallet to Laoban. "Didn't even have to search him. He had these on the seat beside him."

"Why did you leave, Samuel?" she asked.

"I'm injured. These guys hurt me. I'm not talking to you."

"I think you will. And believe me on this, I can hurt you a lot more than these men did."

He didn't doubt it, but was still not going to cooperate. "I've got nothing to say. I just fly the plane."

"So why escape from here? Here, where you're safe?"

"No comment."

"Your customers tried to kill you. We saved you. So where were you going?"

"No comment."

"Don't 'no comment' me. You've been watching too many TV police programmes. And it won't work. Here, there are no rules."

"Joshua, Humphry, Robert, move Samuel into the office. Cut his clothes and strip him to his underwear. Take turns guarding him! If he talks, let me know. Then, Jimbo, take everyone to their room. Everyone needs to be at their brightest in the morning."

As they filed off the deck, leaving her on her own, Laoban strolled over to the bar and set about methodically emptying the contents of every bottle down the sink.

# Intrigue in Angola

In Luanda, Ronald Jones lay still in his hospital bed, pretending to sleep. Four weeks of rest and feeding had restored his strength, and now he yearned to get out, to return to the real world. The doctor, though, was insisting on at least another week of recuperation. Ronald suspected that had more to do with milking what were no doubt extortionate 'foreign patient' fees for as long as possible as any actual medical necessity.

Ronald had two compelling motivations for getting out of the hospital. One was the food. He had no doubt that rice and beans were nutritious and had enabled his recovery, but three identical plates of them a day, every day, was simply too much. For anyone, let alone a gourmet like him. Tasteless and boring. So much so, he even found himself craving the daily tuna that he had been fed in his former prison apartment.

The other reason was to get away from his roommate, a gargantuan black man. His snoring sounded like an elephant's trumpeting. His body odour permeated the room, and probably the corridor outside, too. Ronald chuckled to himself, thinking what Chameleon would say were she to visit.

That patient was definitely not there to be fed up to restore his strength; more likely, he was there to have a tummy tuck. Though there was no way of knowing. It seemed strange that no doctor ever attended to him, and the nurses didn't bother with taking his temperature or blood pressure. Almost like he was there just to hide out. Except that he obviously wasn't hiding; every day, a different man, but always dressed in a dark blue suit with a white shirt and burgundy tie, would arrive, bringing papers to sign and a package wrapped in silver foil. Meat to eat. Steak, chicken drumsticks, ribs. Lucky him. Ronald hadn't minded too much until now. At first, it was that he couldn't stomach solid foods, and more recently, he just appreciated that the enticing smells emanating from the big man's dinner temporarily smothered the smell of his sweat.

Ronald was pretending to sleep because he was listening in on a phone call that the big man was making. He had a loud, booming voice, so it required no effort to overhear, even with his head under the sheets. Evidently, the man didn't think it necessary to be discreet. He almost certainly assumed that Ronald didn't understand Portuguese, since the doctor and nurses only ever spoke to him in English. He certainly wouldn't be aware that he was sharing a hospital room with a gifted linguist. And occasional spy.

The big man had made a lot of calls over the last week, so, whilst Ronald still hadn't determined exactly what line of business the big man was in, since he could only hear one side of the conversations, he knew it involved importing some valuable commodity from over the border in Namibia where his brother had a business, then exporting it to Europe, that somehow it involved both Latinos and Chinese, and that whatever it was, it was all most definitely illegal. A mineral of some kind? Possibly diamonds, since whenever the big man talked about money, it was in terms of millions of dollars.

Today's call had, for the first time, provided him with new information that the big man's activities were in competition with some organisation based there in Luanda, and that the brother in Namibia had a factory that was referred to as 'underground.' Presumably more hidden off-radar than actually under the ground, but Ronald couldn't be sure.

Making a mental link to some translations he had made for the Smiths months earlier, while in the apartment, the outline of a plan began to take shape in his head. Worth making a point of memorising any names that he overheard.

Since he'd first had the strength to climb out of his bed, two or three days earlier, and walk the length of the corridor, he'd negotiated the use of a computer in one of the doctors' offices 'to catch up with the news.' Which he did on the BBC website, where, down near the foot of a screen, he found an update on a legal case. Something about corruption, industrial espionage, and politicians. Not a topic that would normally have interested him, and he would have overlooked it had he not been drawn to the pictures of the defendants. Mug shots. Surely the man in the middle was Smith? Except it said underneath that his name was Arbuthnot. He was the spitting image of Smith. A nurse had told him that his hospital fees were being paid by a Smith, so presumably it couldn't be him? Ah, but then he read the article again. The company was called Smith. So, no effort to conclude that the man who had called himself Smith was really Arbuthnot. He'd never told Jones that was his real name, after all. But if Smith-alias-Arbuthnot was in jail, how come he was paying hospital bills? A mystery, but not something to worry about. There was an actual Smith as well, though. The left-hand picture. He was on remand too. He didn't recognise the others; obviously Smith's — or was it Arbuthnot's — assistant and his acolytes in Latin America had not been arrested.

A short time spent searching the web revealed rather more detailed articles about the nefarious activities of Smith, Smith, and Associates. Some of them Ronald could easily relate to, recognising his own involvement. It had certainly never occurred to him at the time that what he was asked to do might be illegal. He was relieved that he hadn't been implicated and that he could watch from the sidelines. It didn't seem to be a clear-cut case, however, and according to the *Guardian*, legal arguments looked set to delay the trial for many months.

What Ronald Jones found most interesting were the details of the eye-watering fees that the Smiths were alleged to have charged their clients. Big corporations and small governments paying millions for unlawfully obtained information. With all that money coming in, surely they could have afforded to feed him better in all those months trapped in that apartment? Or bought him some more comfortable furniture, not least a decent bed?

No sooner had the big man in the other bed finished his phone call than the nurse came into the room and, also deceived into thinking Ronald was sleeping, shook his shoulder roughly. "Wake up, Mr Jones. There's somebody here to see you."

This was a surprise. He wasn't expecting anyone. He didn't know anyone here. And the only people who ever came to see him back home in Slough were the meter readers. He sat up in bed to see a young, white-skinned woman standing behind the nurse, clutching a briefcase in one hand. She offered the other to shake. "Good afternoon, Mr Jones, my name is Trisha Cooke. I'm from the consulate."

"The British consulate?"

"Yes, of course. The hospital administrator called us. He told us you have no papers and asked us to confirm your identity."

"Oh. That's right. I lost my passport." Jones wondered what the woman had been told. He probably ought to tread carefully. Fortunately, she seemed to know as much as him. Or as little.

"I understand you were trapped in an apartment without food and brought to the hospital to recover?"

"That's right."

"Do you know the people who sent you here?"

"No, they were strangers." That was honest, at least.

"The administrator says your bills are being paid by solicitors in London. The name on the transfer is Smith. Do you know Mr Smith? Maybe he is the solicitor?"

"Honestly, I have no idea. I'm just glad that somebody rescued me and brought me here. And that they're paying the bills, of course. If you find out who they are, please tell me so I can write and thank them."

"How did you enter Angola?"

"On a plane, I suppose. I don't know. I wasn't conscious at the time. I'm very tired, sorry."

"Of course, I don't mean to distress you. Are you well enough just to tell me your personal details so that I can confirm them with London?"

Jones reeled off his address in Slough and his date of birth and answered Trisha's other simple questions.

"Let me get in touch with our people in London. Once it's all checked out, we can get you a new passport so you can go home just as soon as you are well enough."

"Very good. Thank you." Then, as if an afterthought, he asked, "Can you contact my bank for me too? And get them to send me a new card? I have no money."

"I'll try, of course. Now I need to take your photograph, please."

"Why?"

"For your new passport, of course. Are you able to walk? It's just that your picture has to be taken against a white wall. Perhaps in the corridor?"

Photograph taken and notes tucked into her briefcase, Trisha Cooke departed, promising to return in a day or two as soon as she had got the confirmation she needed from London. Jones breathed a sigh of relief, surprised that she hadn't been more inquisitive about where he had been or how he had got there. A junior functionary, just performing the job she had been tasked with and no more. Very likely, when she came back, it would be with someone more senior. An interrogator, to grill him with the troublesome questions. At least that gave him a little time to prepare and think of answers. He was pre-warned.

True to her word, Trisha did return two days later. On her own. No companion interrogator. What a relief. "I have a letter for you here confirming your identity. You can show the hospital, but don't let them keep the original," she told him. "You may have to show it when you leave the country, as you have no entry stamp in your passport. You will need to come to the consulate to collect your new one. When do you think you will be well enough to leave?"

"Tomorrow, if the doctors allow me. But I have no clothes to go out in, only this hospital gown."

"Do you not know anyone here in Luanda?"

"No, and I've never been here before, either."

Trisha looked surprised, then thought for a minute. "There is a charity that brings clothes from England to the townships. I know the woman who runs it. I'll call and ask her if she can give you some clothes to get you started."

"Thank you. What about the bank?"

"A colleague in London said she would call them. I've heard nothing yet. I'll try to find out before you visit the consulate. I have two hundred thousand *kwanga* for you here to keep you going." Ronald looked flabbergasted. Trisha laughed. "That's only about two hundred pounds sterling. Think one thousand *kwanga* equals one pound. You need to sign this form to agree that you will pay us back for this facility."

A few hours later, Ronald had a second visitor. A tall middle-aged woman, eccentrically dressed in brilliant red and blue with an emerald-green cloth wrapped around her head, struggling with a battered suitcase. "Jasmine," she announced. "Welfare worker. Your embassy sent me. These are for you." She opened the case and tipped its contents onto the bed. "I hope some of them fit." Not waiting to find out, she turned and left as suddenly as she had arrived.

If Ronald thought Jasmine's costume was outlandish, it was nothing compared to the mix of clothes she had brought him. He tried on shirts and trousers, ones that looked about the right size to him, thereby discovering how much weight he must have lost. He remembered once being described, when Chameleon was being relatively polite, as 'portly.' Now, 'stick insect' would be a more accurate description of his physique.

It wasn't just that the clothes hung off him; no two items matched. Time was, he wouldn't have cared or even noticed. But that was before Chameleon. Two nurses coming into the room on their evening round took one look at him and collapsed in shrieks of laughter. He supposed that he must resemble something like a cross between a mad professor and a circus clown.

Recovering their calm, the nurses decided that dressing up Ronald would be much more entertaining than collecting bedpans and taking body temperatures. After strewing all the clothes over the bed and floor, and much discussion between themselves, they picked out the items they thought were best, made him put them on, and then busied themselves with making them fit better, which entailed emptying most of a box of hospital safety pins. Ronald regarded himself in the mirror. He would pass muster. He had never been into fashion, and from his point of view, he looked as good or bad as he ever had before. He'd just have to buy some clothes that fitted properly before he next had to go through a metal detector. He undressed again, careful not to dislodge any of the safety pins.

# Returning to a Sort of Normality – Ronald

As I had anticipated, the doctor was more than happy to be able to go on charging whoever was paying for a few more nights' lodging, and readily agreed that whilst I was fit enough to make tentative forays into the city, I should come back each evening to be monitored and take my tablets. Thus, the following morning, I walked out of the hospital, and, now considering it safe to start talking Portuguese, asked one of the guards on the door to negotiate the fare with the first taxi in line to take me to the embassy. It seemed extortionate, but since it was rather less than half what the driver had initially asked for, I supposed it must be reasonable. And it certainly proved to be quite a long journey. Thinking back to some of my previous experiences, I confess I was somewhat nervous that the driver might abduct me, but after engaging him in conversation about the traffic, his family, his children, the corrupt politicians, and other favourite taxi-driver chatter, I relaxed. Once again, it struck me how only a year or so before, I had been a hermit — isolated and shirking any contact with other humans. Now not only was I talking to strangers in a strange city, but I was initiating conversations!

Luanda wasn't at all how I had expected an African city to look. Not that I had ever thought about this very much, but the generalisation I had in my mind was of somewhere dusty and run-down. Not a city that made Santiago de Chile look dowdy. Tower blocks lined the sky, and the roads we drove along were six-lane highways.

Leaving the modern buildings behind, the driver pulled up beside a long and high, dirty, cream-coloured wall lined with dozens of young Africans, all of whom seemed to be clutching brightly coloured plastic folders. The driver pointed to the doorway at the top of the queue. "Consulate entrance," he said. I paid the agreed fare. "I'll wait for you just around the next corner."

"I don't know how long I'll be."

"It doesn't matter. I'll be there." Heavens, either the driver must have inflated the fare massively or the taxi trade in Luanda was really slack.

I assumed that having an appointment meant I wouldn't need to wait in line, so I walked past the queue, and, feeling rather self-important, announced my business to the heavily armed soldier — or was he just a security guard? — standing outside the gate. It seemed I was expected, as the guard checked my name off a list, swung the gate open, and motioned for me to go into the guardhouse.

The metal detector test came sooner than I had expected at the entrance to the consulate. I didn't actually notice it until I approached, instantly setting off an alarm and a flashing beacon. Not that the security guard took the least notice, simply flicking a switch on the side of the arch and muttering the equivalent of "it happens all the time." I wondered whether I should tell Trisha or her colleagues that anyone could walk in with a gun or a bomb or some other weapon? Be a responsible citizen? I decided against it.

Once the front desk flunky had established that I was a genuine British citizen and, unlike those queued up along the wall, not some foreigner trying his luck to snag a visa, I was ushered into an empty waiting room. There, after spending nearly ten minutes exhausting the reading material provided — a pamphlet extolling and probably exaggerating the amazing benefits of British investment in African farming, and a dog-eared copy of a book commemorating the Queen's Diamond Jubilee more than a decade previously — I was left to sit and fidget for nearly an hour. Through the window I could see the embassy building, which housed the consulate. It looked impressive, perhaps historic. The sort of building that architects reverently describe as '*grande dame.*'

At last, a smiling and breathless Trisha breezed in. "Here's your new passport!" she said excitedly. "Look, they're blue now, not like your last one!" As if the colour was important. Well, perhaps it was to some.

"I rather liked burgundy. I liked being in the European Union even more. Not that I ever visited it." I shouldn't have said it, but couldn't help myself.

Trisha, initially embarrassed, adopted a chirpy tone. "We're all supporting Brexit now," she said. "It's going to give us lots of benefits." I couldn't help looking sceptical, but I kept quiet this time and simply thanked her for her efforts and the passport.

"Did your colleague get through to my bank?"

"Oh, yes, I'm sorry, I nearly forgot. You'll need to go to their office here." She looked at her watch. "Tomorrow. They'll be closed now." She scrolled through some emails on her phone, picked up one of the pamphlets on the windowsill, and scribbled a name and address in a blank space on the back.

"This is not my bank," I told her.

"I know. Your bank doesn't have an office here. They have an arrangement with this bank instead. They will be able to help you."

I didn't feel very confident that she knew that for a fact, let alone that my branch in Slough would have an arrangement with any bank in Angola, but it was a start. On my way to the embassy, I had considered whether I should tell Trisha about what I had learned from the big man in the bed next to me. I decided against it. I'm not sure why, but her attitude discouraged me. Also, seeing all the impressive buildings *en route* had prompted me to think of another idea. This was a wealthy city.

Leaving the embassy, I found the queue of visa hopefuls still lined up against the wall, and my taxi driver deep in a heated conversation with the security guard. "Football," he said. "This man likes Arsenal. Would you believe it? They're rubbish. Everyone likes Manchester United, don't they? You support Manchester United, of course?" I nodded. I didn't support any team or even understand the basic rules of soccer, but now wasn't the time to say so. We walked around the corner to the cab.

"Where to now?" asked the driver. "Back to the hospital?"

"Not yet, I think. Do you know somewhere I can get a good lunch? Cheaply?"

"How cheap?"

"Twenty thousand *kwanga*?" Surely twenty pounds would be enough to dine like a king in Africa?

"Hmm. This is a very expensive city. But if you don't mind a backstreet family place, then I know one that does a great lunch. You might find it a little rough, mind, but the food's very good."

"Perfect. I hope. As long as they do something better than beans and rice."

"You have to try the *moamba a galinha*. Chicken stew. Their speciality."

We left the freeway and the modern towers behind us, first driving through a poorer neighbourhood of single-storey buildings, then arriving in a shanty town.

The restaurant the driver took me to was indeed rough and ready, more a lean-to than a building, and had probably never entertained a white Englishman.

The taxi driver hugged me by the shoulder and told the matron in charge that I was his new best friend, and within minutes we were both seated face to face on picnic chairs at a rickety table over large bowls of aromatic chicken stew. The driver, correctly guessing that I was thinking I would now have to pay for two dinners, said, "Don't worry. I bring a customer to the restaurant, I get a free lunch." I snorted. They might not charge the driver, but I had little doubt they'd pad my bill to cover the costs. Not that I minded. The company was pleasant, and the food was worth it. The glass they had given me with a beer hadn't seen a dishcloth since it was manufactured, so I drank from the bottle. No doubt the absence of attention to hygiene extended to the plate I was eating off. Never mind, I could always ask the hospital for some antibiotics. Just in case.

Lunch finished, we returned to the car. "How far is it to Talatona?" I asked.

"Quite a way. About half an hour. Why do you want to go there?"

"Business. Never mind, it's better we go tomorrow. After the bank." By now, both of us were acting as if the driver was my personal chauffeur. "Let's go to a clothes shop where I can get something that looks more professional than these clothes. A cheap one."

I was enjoying myself enormously. Finally released from over a year's confinement, my more recent dice-with-death starvation almost forgotten, and a liberating drive around a strange city.

Alfonso the driver — we were now on first name terms — delivered me to a vast store, the sign over the door proclaiming it to be a Chinese hypermarket. Fifteen months previously, I'm sure I would have had a panic attack before even entering; now I strode in purposefully, demanding of the first assistant I met to lead me to where the men's clothing section was located. Twenty minutes later, I left with a carrier bag bulging with two white shirts, a pair of black trousers and a grey jacket — clothes that I thought Chameleon would approve of. New underwear too, all for a little over fifty pounds. I'd have bought a tie as well, but they didn't sell any — they seemed to sell everything else under the sun, including kitchen sinks. And anyway, the temperature outside was nearly forty degrees, and I hadn't seen any other men wearing them. Except for the big man's visitors, that is. The taxi driver drove me back to the hospital for a well-earned nap.

# Preparing to Return to the Mission

Well before eight, the whole team was assembled around the lodge dining table, Laoban taking pride of place at the head. The last to arrive were Robert and Jimbo, both looking as cheerful as if they had just won the lottery. They sat on the two vacant chairs at the foot of the table.

"I assume from your expression that the plane is fixed?"

"Yes, Laoban. They'd simply taken off the rubber seal around the drain plug under the wing. Easy enough to fix."

"Good. I'm surprised there are any rubber rings around here, though."

"Chewing gum. Makes a great gasket."

"If you say so. And fuel?"

"I'd say we have enough if I go light on the throttle. One drum was almost empty, but the other was nearly full. We've put it all in the tanks."

"Good work, men." The team looked at each other. The first time any of them had heard Laoban making a compliment. "Beatrix, tell everyone the plan for today."

Everyone seemed to be on board, except for Richard. "Why do I have to stay here? I didn't come all this way to be sidelined. I suppose you're expecting me to stand guard over Sam twenty-four hours a day?"

"No," replied Laoban. "I need you here to manage communications. I understood that was what you were good at."

"What communications? There are no phones, and those satellite bleepers just send simple messages."

"I've brought something better." She reached behind her and pulled out two silver devices from her bag. "This one is the base station for the tracking devices. The same as the one that Maria is monitoring. This other one is a satellite phone. It makes and receives calls."

Laoban explained her thinking. If the team got into trouble, Maria was too far away to provide practical help. They would now split into three teams. Beatrix and Humphry going into the Mission. Robert and Jimbo staying by the plane but available as close backup. And finally, Richard and Joshua in the lodge, able to reach the Mission in an emergency or arrange reinforcements or security services there.

Richard was somewhat mollified, but not entirely happy. "Surely it would be better that I stay with Robert and Jimbo? If it's satellite comms, it will work as well there as here."

"You and the equipment need to be here. This is Botswana. They will be in Namibia. Here the equipment is legal. There, maybe it isn't. Also, the phones and base station have to be kept fully charged. There's no electricity in the bush, in case you hadn't noticed."

Richard still didn't seem convinced. Laoban continued. "There is also a risk that the people at the mission will hear or see the plane and attack Robert and Jimbo. Or there may be another problem with the plane and they can't get back. No, we need you here."

"Are you going to stay here as well?"

"No, I am leaving this morning. In two hours." She checked her watch. "Team, if you are ready, you need to leave right now."

As they stood up, the sound of an aircraft engine became noticeable. "Your flight out must be arriving early, Laoban," said Richard.

"It's not one of ours," said Joshua, looking worried.

"Can you tell the difference? They all sound the same to me."

"Definitely. When they come every day, you learn the sounds. All ours are Cessnas. That sounds like a Piper Cherokee to me. It could be the one that came to look at us the other day."

"Can they see your plane from the air, Robert?" asked Laoban.

"Nope. It's still under that roof. It seemed best to leave it there until we were ready."

"Indeed. So, we all stay still here, under cover, until it's gone." They all sat down again, and meanwhile the engine noise intensified, then changed tone.

Robert looked worried. "I don't think it's going away, Laoban. I think it's going to land."

"Joshua and Jimbo, you'd better get out to the airstrip, then. If they land, I suppose they'll see the plane?"

"Maybe, maybe not," replied Robert. "Depends which direction they land in. If we're lucky, they'll stop at the other end of the strip. That's the way the wind was blowing when we were out there half an hour ago."

"Joshua, give me the key for the room you locked Pascal up in before you go." He rooted in his pockets and tossed the key to her.

"What should the rest of us do?" asked Beatrix. "Hide?"

Laoban nodded and looked inquiringly at Joshua. "Everyone go to Rondavel Twelve," he said. "You'll have to climb over a fence to reach it. It's about two hundred metres after Rondavel Eleven. You won't see it until you're nearly there."

They all hurried towards the steps to the path, but Laoban stopped them. "Beatrix, Humphry, go to Rondavel One instead. Take everything you need for the operation with you."

"What about you, Laoban?" inquired Beatrix.

"I want to see who's coming here and find out why. And then get rid of them." If Laoban was going to put on her most obnoxious attitude, Richard thought the visitors, whoever they were, would probably wish they'd never come and scarper without delay. "I will send for you when the coast is clear. Richard!" she called after him. "You've forgotten the comms equipment."

# More Unwelcome Visitors

Jimbo and Joshua turned the last corner on the track to the airstrip and pulled up sharply. Standing in front of them were Sancho and Benny, the two Latinos from the Mission, who had decided to walk towards the lodge rather than wait to see if transport materialised. What looked like machine guns and ammo belts were slung around their necks. They were an image straight out of a Spaghetti Western — had they not been in the African bush. Jimbo gulped and hoped that they didn't recognise him. Joshua did his best to command the situation, putting on his widest grin and performing his tourist greeting patter.

"Welcome to the Paradise Lodge," he announced. "Did you want a room? I'm afraid we're closed for the rest of the season."

"We've come for our pilot."

"I'm sorry? What pilot? Surely you just flew here?"

"Stop being stupid. Where is he? And the gringos." The two had by now pulled pistols from their belts and were training them on Joshua and Jimbo. They walked towards them and, one on each side, leapt into the first passenger row of the Land Cruiser. As they did so, they changed the focus of their pistols to the back of the head of the man in front of them. "Drive! Take us to them!"

"To who? We came from the lodge because we heard the plane. But we're closed. There's nobody there. Just us."

"We'll see for ourselves. Drive!"

The lodge was indeed deserted. Not a soul on the deck. Nobody in the kitchen. Nobody in the staff quarters. Not even anyone in the office where they'd been keeping the pilot. Likewise, the storeroom where Pascal had been held overnight was empty, and the door was wide open. A nasty stench emanated from it, but the Latinos made no effort to investigate. Joshua and Jimbo wondered where the men had gone. They couldn't have escaped. No doubt Laoban had them under control somewhere.

"Guest rooms!" Their visitors had now put their pistols back in their belts, but unholstered their AK-47s, increasing the menace. Still keeping them trained on Joshua and Jimbo, they moved along the path to the left, Joshua unlocking each rondavel in turn, Benny going inside to inspect, Sancho keeping guard over the two Africans. Rondavel Six. Five. Four. Every one of them empty. As they followed the path towards Rondavel Three, the sound of a piston engine starting up shattered the quiet. "Runway! Now!" screamed Sancho, yanking the arm of Jimbo, who was in front.

Once again, they boarded the Land Cruiser, retracing the track towards the airfield. "Faster!" cried Sancho. Jimbo complied, the combined effect of acceleration and the deep rut in the track ahead of them catapulting Benny upwards, banging his head on the metal bar supporting the roof above, whereupon the gun fell out of his hands, and he collapsed unconscious on the seat.

Sancho fared little better but managed to hold on to a bar in front of him to avoid the same fate. That created the opportunity Richard needed to jump up from where he had been lurking under a tarpaulin on the floor of the row behind and seize Sancho around his neck in a headlock. A good trick that he'd learnt from Rob on that flight the day before, he thought, except he hadn't got it quite right, as the man was obviously still conscious and struggling. Richard twisted his arm harder. Joshua risked a glance behind him, then reached over towards Jimbo and pulled the steering wheel sharply towards him, forcing a ninety-degree turn. Now they were off the track, careering over rough ground, in doing so disturbing a herd of zebras and wildebeest who, until then, had been enjoying a peaceful lunch. Seeing Richard hanging on to a still-struggling Sancho, and fearing he might lose the battle, Joshua told Jimbo to slow down, then turned and punched Sancho in the face. That seemed to do the job; at least the Latino stopped struggling, giving Joshua the opportunity to wrest his AK-47 from him. He tossed it out of the Land Cruiser, hoping he could find it if he came back later. It might come in handy.

Now that he could let go of the headlock, Richard jumped over the partition into the row in front between the two groggy Latinos, removed their pistols from their belts and gave them to Joshua and Jimbo. From the footwell, he retrieved the AK-47 that Benny had dropped when stunned. "Keep driving," he told Jimbo. "But not too fast or bumpy!"

"What are we going to do with those two?" asked Joshua.

"Do you have any rope here in the vehicle?"

Jimbo nodded. "In the box on the floor in the back row. Can you reach it without me stopping?"

Holding on to the roof bars, Richard climbed two rows back, extracted the rope, then climbed forwards again. Both Latinos were now stirring. Richard hit them both on the head with the butt of the AK-47. Unconsciousness resumed. Now he had rope, but it was futile trying to tie them up while the Land Cruiser was bumping up and down.

"Look!" shouted Jimbo, pointing up and ahead of him to where a small red plane was climbing above them. "That's the plane they came in."

"Did they have a pilot with them as well, then?"

"They must have had. We didn't get close. They were already walking towards us up the track."

"So, no doubt he'll soon be back with reinforcements. Let's go to the airstrip, anyway. Just in case it's a different plane."

They reached the end of the air strip a few minutes later. No sign of a red plane, so it had been the same one. But much to their surprise, they found Pascal standing there on his own.

"What are you doing here?" asked Joshua.

"They made me guide them here from the lodge. Then they left me here. And they took my phone!" He gave the impression that had been the worst thing ever to befall him.

"Who did?"

"That woman you call Laoban. And the white people."

"Where are they now?"

"The woman and two others went in the red plane. The woman and the man who shaved his beard off."

"You mean Beatrix and Humphry?" Pascal nodded.

"Was there a pilot?"

"The boss woman. The Chinese one. She said she was a pilot."

"What about Robert and Samuel?" asked Richard.

"They went to the other plane down there." He pointed to the end of the runway.

"We'll find out about them later. The priority is these guys in the back of the truck. Let's tie them up here. Help me to get them out, fellas," said Richard.

Not such an easy task from a vehicle with no doors, where getting in and out meant clambering up or down metal ladders on the side. The three Africans made it look like it was something they did every day, though, lifting the Latinos one by one and dropping them unceremoniously over the edge of the Land Cruiser onto the ground. While they were still unconscious, Richard got to work tying the men to a convenient tree. Checking their pockets, he pulled out knives and a satellite phone. "Didn't they have backpacks?" he asked Joshua.

"Yes, small ones. They must have left them at the lodge." Changing the subject, Joshua said, "Are you going to leave them down there? There's shade now, but they'll be in full sunlight in the afternoon. They'll die of exposure. If a predator doesn't get them first."

"Do you care?"

"Well, no, to be honest. They're not the friendly sort. But I don't want to find rotting skeletons here next time real tourists come in."

Whatever Joshua said after that was drowned out by the noise of Samuel's plane taxiing down the runway and coming to a stop in front of them. Robert, at the controls, turned off the engine and opened his door. "Jimbo, open up the back hatch. Get Sam out of there. I've restrained him with some cable ties I found in the plane. Laoban says he's to go back to the lodge with Joshua. And stay there."

"Why didn't you just leave him there?"

"Laoban told us we had to leave the lodge empty. She's gone ahead with Humph and Bea. Jimbo, you and I are to follow them. After you've got Sam out, load up the supplies."

"We haven't brought any supplies. All our time has been taken up getting these two under control." He nodded to the tree under which the two Latinos, now conscious but groggy, were sat and bound.

"Joshua, give that gun to Richard. Go back and get supplies. Food, water, anything that looks useful. And all our backpacks. Get back here as quick as you can. Jimbo, Pascal, go and stand guard over those two. Richard, we need to talk."

What Robert wanted to discuss was what to do with Sancho and Benny. He didn't like the idea of leaving them tied to a tree any more than Joshua did, but for different reasons. First, they might escape. Richard doubted that was possible until Robert reminded him that, in their Tuesday evening group, they had recently read a thriller where hostages were tied up but, against all odds, managed to free themselves. Secondly, if their organisation, whatever it was, sent reinforcements, and they arrived soon enough, they'd just untie them and have two additions to their team.

Robert's idea was to put them in the back of the plane and kick them out somewhere remote. "I don't like killing people any more than you do, Richard, even nasty ones," he told him, "so what I'll do is look for somewhere remote with no obvious wildlife, descend, skim the ground, and have Jimbo drop them out of the back from about twenty or thirty feet. They'll get a nasty bump, but they'll survive. Unless the lions get them, anyway. Maybe throw them a few bottles of water to keep them going."

"Sounds like a plan. Shouldn't we try interrogating them first?"

"Let's have Jimbo do that when we're up in the air. They'll probably find the prospect of being thrown out without a parachute more terrifying than simply being threatened with a gun down here."

"But you'll still drop them out, anyway?"

"Oh yes. Even if they offer to lead us to the crown jewels."

# Arbuthnot

"Before anything more is said, I'm only here as your friend, not as your attorney." Jasper Evans, KC, looked Arbuthnot in the eyes, both leaning towards each other across a bare table topped in dirty blue Formica. The only thing of colour in the small, plain room. Off-white walls. Grey flooring. A small window with a view on to a corridor. A single door with a prison officer standing immobile beside it.

"I need to get out of here. It's been nine months now, and nothing's happening. I need you to represent me."

"I'm sorry. Even small straightforward cases are taking an age to come to court these days, and this one's big and complex. Anyway, I can't represent you. I'm sorry. You can't afford me any longer. Your assets have all been frozen. If you're convicted, they'll be seized as proceeds of crime. If you're acquitted, they'll be frozen again since the tax man is after you in the civil courts. You'll just have to hope that whoever's been assigned to you on legal aid is competent."

"She's not. Completely hopeless. Wet behind the ears. Determined to get me sent down, I think."

"I'm sure that's not the case. All defence barristers sign an oath to defend their clients. To be determined to do their best to get them acquitted."

"Hmm. I don't think this one's got the message. Anyway, the money angle is not a problem, really. There's a trust that will pay your fees."

"Seriously? If you haven't declared an offshore trust to the police, you're just going to be in even deeper trouble than you are now."

"Calm down. It's a blind trust. There's no link back to me. Go and talk to the administrator. I'll give you his office address. I'm sure he'll be willing to pay."

"Why would he, if he or the trust are not related to you?"

"Call it me claiming on an insurance policy."

"Does this go for Smith too?"

"No, no. He's best left on his own. Let him rot. He'll just say he was a sleeping partner. An investor. All he wanted from the business was money. He neither knew nor cared about what we were doing. I'm sure he'll be fine with his legal aid chappy or chappess, ha ha! Anyway, his wife's loaded; she can pay."

"There are a lot of charges against you. Procuring protected information is the least of them." Evans pulled a folder from his briefcase and consulted it. "Extortion. Racketeering. Impersonation. False Imprisonment. It's not just in this country, either. The States want you, even Panama wants you. Other countries are considering their options."

Arbuthnot interrupted. "There's no extradition treaty with Panama."

"Not the point. What sort of defence do you propose to make?"

"I'm not expecting to have to defend anything. I'm expecting you to get them to shelve the case and let me out."

Jasper laughed. "I'm not a miracle worker, you know. Just a jobbing attorney. Rather a good one, if I say so myself. But the CPS isn't going to shelve the case, as you put it. What makes you think they would?"

"It's obvious. Because of what I know, and who I know. One doesn't spend one's life cultivating relationships to be left in this situation, does one?"

"Which relationships are you referring to?"

"The PM for one."

"Have you been in touch with him?"

"No, of course not. I can't call the Prime Minister from Belmarsh. They've taken my phone away so I can't just send him a WhatsApp or make a call."

"You can write a letter."

"It would never get through. They read and censor everything. Even if they did let it go from here and it reached Number Ten, it would just get treated as a prank by some junior dogsbody. No, I need you to see him and tell him I'm expecting his help."

"How do you expect me to meet him? I don't move in the same exalted circles as you do. Or did. I'll have no more success asking for a meeting than you will."

"You're a member of Boodles, aren't you?"

"No, actually. My club's the Athaeneum."

"Of course it is. Well, you'll have to go and see Gideon first to arrange your payment. Get him to sort out your access to the PM. Tell him he has to get you an invitation to Boodles. The PM's usually there on Wednesday evenings when the House is sitting. One place he can escape to for an hour or two without his minders. Getting in a few snifters to get over PMQs, ha ha!"

"You seriously expect me just to walk up to him unannounced?"

Arbuthnot looked pensive. "No, no, of course you can't do that. Tell Gideon he needs to leave a message a day or two before with the doorman — his name's Charles, by the way, first class chap — saying that you'll be in the snug and would like a discreet word. Write something like 'I have a message from Arbuthnot about Buenos Aires.' That'll get his attention."

Evans raised his eyebrows. "And what is that message, exactly?"

"That I have a complete dossier of the Buenos Aires project in a safe deposit box. Incriminating pictures and all. Not here in London. In another country. In the hands of a guardian who has irrevocable instructions to release it to the press one month from today if the case against me is still outstanding."

"This sounds rather like blackmail. That could equally be understood as an invitation to make you disappear, don't you think?"

"Ha ha! Thought of that. If I die or disappear before the month is out, the guardian will release it to the press immediately."

"And you believe he'll go for that? And you'll succeed in this ploy? The Crown Prosecution Service doesn't react well to pressure from politicians. Even the PM."

"In this case, I think they will."

"So, just let me get this straight. You're asking to have all the cases against you dropped. Or maybe put on file in the absence of sufficient evidence?"

"Either will do. As long as I get out of here. I'm sure Naismith at the CPS can be creative if he needs to be."

"The Buenos Aires dossier reflects on him, too?" Arbuthnot nodded. "Anything else?"

"Yes, a one-way ticket to a country with no extradition treaty with the UK on a commercial airline. Somewhere warm. Africa, perhaps? Oh, and business class, of course."

"So, who is this man Gideon I need to go and see?"

"Gideon Caesar. You'll find him at his office on Brook Street. Zansusu Investments. He's the CEO."

"Never heard of them. What do they do?"

"Let's call it international multi-disciplinary services, ha ha!"

# The Business of Espionage

Ronald Jones felt quite squiffy. He hadn't touched a drop of alcohol in at least three months. Since that last glass of drugged wine, in fact. Or, rather, since the one before that, since the very last one had tasted so repulsive that he'd tipped it down the washbasin and opted for water instead. Thereby never fully understanding how his captors intended to end his days. If he'd known he had a choice between starving to death and descending into a drugged sleep of no return, he might have chosen the wine. But, blissfully ignorant of all that, Ronald was now quite content. Happy, in fact. And squiffy.

He'd only had a couple of bottles of the local beer. Mind you, the bottles were the size of wine bottles, and whilst it might not have been the best beer in the world, it was definitely alcoholic. He had been out for lunch with his new best friend, Moses the bank manager. Moses was celebrating opening the tenth new expatriate account that month, thereby securing himself a valuable bonus, and Ronald was celebrating having a new debit card and access to his money, no longer languishing unloved in another bank in Slough. Ronald's funds were miserly compared to many expatriates in Luanda, but not insignificant, and Ronald only needed to tell Moses of his intention to 'do business' locally for him to be upgraded instantly to the bank's platinum status.

Moses had opened accounts for many Englishmen, but few who spoke Portuguese fluently. And none who could chat in the local dialect. While they sat in the bank manager's office and waited for myriad minions to perform the various tasks of African bureaucracy necessary for account opening and international funds transfers, the two men chatted happily. Ronald wanted to learn more of the local slang and get tips on approaching local businesspeople, and Moses was happy to oblige on both fronts. Indeed, they got on so well that going out to lunch together seemed just a natural extension of their meeting.

Moses was suitably impressed that Ronald already had his own driver and leapt in and gave quick-fire instructions to Alfonso. The driver didn't seem too happy, having just had a contretemps with the front door security guard who thought the bank's image was being sullied by having an elderly battered Toyota hovering outside for two hours. Ronald hoped that the restaurant would feed him, and he would cheer up as a result.

And what a restaurant! He'd found out during the drive around town the day before that Luanda was on the coast, but he hadn't been expecting a beach, nor what was clearly a very posh restaurant with a terrace overlooking the ocean and, further improving the view, a pool surrounded with well-heeled, bikini-clad young women on sun loungers, dripping jewellery and sweat. He was relieved when Moses assured him that he was invited on his expenses, his guest. He wouldn't have to test out his new bank card.

Away from the bank and comfortably seated at a terrace table overlooking the ocean, Ronald felt confident that their conversation would neither be overheard nor recorded. He hoped that Moses would let down his guard and be willing to allow himself to be pumped for information. He need not have worried. After a delicious starter of *camaroes termidor* and a plate of tender octopus tentacles, accompanied by two bottles of beer and much insignificant chatter about Brazil, a country that Moses craved to visit and believed Ronald to be an expert on, it was easy to steer the conversation to business. Far from being reticent, Moses was exuberantly enthusiastic about sharing whatever knowledge he had. Having covered the trivia of Angolan business meeting etiquette — there didn't seem to be any, though they spent a long time talking about it — the repurposed spy decided to ask point blank about Industrias Farmaceuticas do Angola. The company that the fat man in the next bed was out to hoodwink.

By good fortune, the company had its accounts with the same bank, and by better fortune still, Moses claimed to be a personal friend of the Chief Operating Officer. To prove it, he put down the menu even before ordering dessert, took his phone from his pocket, and two minutes later, Ronald had an appointment arranged for ten the following morning. Moses didn't enquire what Ronald's business was. Perhaps he divined that the commercial activities of a man who had only recently arrived in Luanda and who listed his address as the local hospital were unlikely to be conventional.

Having dropped Moses back at the bank, Alfonso turned to Ronald. "Are we going to Talatona now?"

"No. My appointment is for ten tomorrow morning." It was just as well, Ronald thought, after all that beer. A good nap was justified and necessary.

"Bad time. Lots of traffic then. We will have to leave before nine. Oh, and don't go to that restaurant again."

"Why? It's a beautiful restaurant, and the food is excellent."

"Not for me, though. They don't welcome drivers. I had to go to Burger World." He turned his head and made the impression of spitting on the floor.

The burger must have had truffles and caviar on it, Ronald thought, when Alfonso told him what he expected to be paid for the day. Apparently, that wasn't the reason. "You've got money now," he explained. "You have to pay regular rates. See you tomorrow at 8.30." He drove off. Ronald wondered whether he should look for another driver, but decided he had now had enough excitement for one day, and that was a decision that could wait until after his meeting.

After as long and luxurious a sleep as one could ever hope to get in a hospital bed, he woke early. He promptly installed himself in front of the computer in the doctor's office, intending to search for all he could find about the pharmaceutical company he was visiting and Joao Amaral, its Chief Operating Officer. He only got as far as his LinkedIn profile before being kicked out by the doctor himself. It was his office, after all. "Why don't you go down to the canteen and get breakfast? You can come back afterwards. I'll be done then."

Breakfast? In the canteen? Might they offer something different from rice and beans? Such riches had never occurred to him. Realising that he would have to pay, he returned to the ward just to pick up his new bank-branded souvenir wallet. Not a place he wanted to extend his stay while the big man was still snoring and stinking out the room.

It wasn't gourmet cuisine, but they did have bread and ham and cheese and cake. Better still, real coffee. Nourished for the morning ahead, he returned to his research, dressed in his finest new suit, and was outside the hospital waiting for Alfonso by the appointed time. Five minutes went past, then ten. Finally, at ten to nine, just as Ronald was thinking of hailing another passing taxi, Alfonso arrived. "I told you how bad the traffic is this time of day, didn't I?"

Senhor Amaral was courtesy itself, delighted to make the acquaintance of such a close associate of his friend the bank manager. Though he was mystified as to the reason for the meeting. Social niceties completed and coffees served, Ronald explained.

"A few months ago, you were interested in the activities of the Sonora Cartel, were you not?"

The COO's eyelids twitched. "I don't know what you are talking about."

"Well, if not you, you have colleagues who will. I have new information that the cartel is seeking to damage your company. Alternative sources of supply, that sort of thing. I thought you would like to know."

"How did you get this information? And why do you believe it has anything to do with us?"

"A competitor of yours was using a London based consultancy to do some covert research. It revealed a link between you and the cartel." Ronald congratulated himself on having such an excellent memory. He had been sent dozens of documents to translate and comment on. In fact, none of them had mentioned Sr Amaral's company. But they had referenced a company in Luanda, and, judging from the expression on the COO's face, Ronald had arrived at the correct conclusion.

"Which of our products do you believe are compromised?"

"Ones that are not on your standard price list. The ones you obtain from a third party, repackage, and export to other countries."

"You are mistaken. Our company only sells the medicines we manufacture ourselves." Senhor Amaral spoke the words but didn't look as if he as if he was expecting them to be believed.

"I think you are the one who is mistaken," a new, confident Ronald spoke. A Ronald who surprised himself with every new utterance he made, every new thing that he did. Not the self-effacing shrinking violet of old.

"The research showed that it's your company's most lucrative activity. Your suppliers aren't interested in renegotiating their contract with you. They're instead planning to take over another company to do the job. So that they own the entire process, end to end. Manufacture. Sales. Export." Was this too much information? What if the takeover had already happened, or if the competitor's plans had been ditched? How long ago had he worked on those documents? It felt like it was recently, but the last few months were a blur.

"Is this other company you talk about here in Angola?"

"It's in Africa, not Angola. Another country. Nearer the source of supply."

"This has nothing to do with us."

Ronald raised his eyebrows, while Senhor Amaral hesitated. "But if you were to be right, what would you be proposing?"

"My company provides tailored ultra-discreet professional research and business surveillance services to exemplary organisations worldwide." He'd read that a million times, printed as a footer on every page he had translated for the Smiths. Words etched into his brain, but never spoken by him before.

"I'm sure I've heard that before. What did you say your company was called?"

"Jones, Jones, and Associates."

"Hmmm. That wasn't the name, though. Something similar."

"So, may I ask what you think?"

"I think I should talk to some colleagues. You should come back tomorrow. Same time."

# Rendezvous at a Disused Airstrip – Robert

"There it is," I shouted, pointing to a tiny speck of red in the green and brown forest below.

"Doesn't look like an airstrip to me," said Jimbo, who had moved forward to the co-pilot's seat once he'd disposed of our unwanted passengers.

"Well, Laoban managed to land there, so I'm sure we can," I replied, dropping a few hundred feet and circling the disused airstrip to check it out.

From above, the only evidence that there had once been a functioning runway was the rectangular shape and the fact that the vegetation wasn't quite as high as on the surrounding land and was somewhat flattened at one end where the red plane had come down, demolishing bushes along the way. But it seemed to still be in one piece.

"Hold tight, Jimbo. I'm going to land in the opposite direction, so we'll park up at the other end."

"Why? Surely it's better to be close?"

I explained I didn't want to risk a collision, and my somewhat crazy theory was that if I could skim really low without damaging the wings, it would help demolish a few bushes. Save us a bit of effort going back the other way. We were going to have to clear the runway before we could take off again, and that was clearly going to be a heck of a job to do by hand.

"OK. I just hope that the Mission people haven't heard us. We're closer than I thought we were going to be." I wondered how he had worked that out. His next comment explained it.

"Look. That must be their airstrip over there. Nine o'clock."

Jimbo was right. I had been concentrating so hard on getting to the overgrown airstrip undetected that I hadn't noticed it before. We could see the mission-lodge just beyond it. The tin roofs had been covered with branches and greenery. No wonder it couldn't be spotted from aerial photos. "If we can see them, they can see us," I told Jimbo. "Better get down fast." I banked the plane hard to the right and twisted back towards the runway, descending now as quickly as felt safe. Within seconds, we had skimmed the top of the red plane and were ploughing into bushes, coming to a halt in less than fifty metres. I collapsed with laughter. Jimbo looked like he thought I had gone mad. "I was nervous about that!" I told him. "But it's just like an emergency landing on foam. Bushes probably damaged the wings, though. Let's get out."

No sooner had we opened the doors than we heard a shout of "over here!"

"You took your time," said Laoban, almost unrecognisable from before, dressed now in military camouflage but proving again she could be just as unpleasant whatever she was wearing.

"Nice to see you, too. First, we had to solve a problem with some unwanted guests and then wait for supplies. But we're here now. Where are Bea and Humph?"

"Already on their way to the mission lodge."

"How long have they been gone?" asked Jimbo.

"Twenty, thirty minutes?"

"I'm going after them then. I should catch up before they get there."

"You need to stay here, Jimbo."

"No, Laoban. They'll need their backpacks. And before we dropped them off, I got info from the Latinos that could be useful."

"Dropped them off? After they pointed guns at you, you decided you would be nice and give them a lift home?" Laoban said with peak sarcasm.

"Not exactly. We chucked them out of the plane about fifteen kilometres south of here. Alive, but trussed up like chickens."

"You should have terminated them. But we can talk about that later. What information?"

"Well, assuming it's true, there are about twenty men there. There's a big assembly hut. They dug under the floor to make some sort of laboratory. Something to do with the plants that they get from the forest. If anybody comes, they can put the floor back down and then sit there praising the Lord."

"So, it's a drugs factory. Not a mine."

"That's what it sounds like, Laoban."

"I suppose that might explain why there are Latinos there. Skilled at making and moving drugs. Never heard of it being done in Africa, though."

I decided I had better say something. "Jimbo's theory is that they're working on scaling up some of the old tribal drugs. Witch doctor stuff turned into big business."

Jimbo interrupted. "Some of the pharma companies are now making drugs from the forest here. Well, not here. Down in the capital. Oh, and the Latinos aren't Mexicans. They said they're Colombian."

"Interesting. That ties in with some information we uncovered. Off you go then, Jimbo. As quick and quiet as you can. Come back as soon as you've explained to them. We need you here."

"All right, Laoban. Keep an eye out for snakes." He turned and disappeared into the shrubbery.

"Quite an asset, don't you think?" I said. "He moves so silently for such a big man."

"I agree. One hundred percent." Laoban saying something positive about someone? It was only yesterday that she had complimented someone else. Another mutation for the chameleon in her.

"Well, back to business. Talking of which, I really need to be in Johannesburg for a meeting in two days' time. So, let's hope we can get this project closed down quickly."

"We had better start clearing the runway, then, or none of us will ever get out of here."

"Where do we begin, Robert?" This was a new Laoban. Transformed. First agreeing to Bea's plan of attack. And now asking for my advice too? Had she been substituted with a lookalike? What had happened?

I told her our first job should be to cover the planes, especially the red one. We didn't want anyone flying over and spotting us, and, as I had seen for myself, the red plane stood out like a sore thumb.

"But if we clear the runway, it'll be obvious," objected Laoban.

"I think we can get around that," I replied. My plan was to pull up the bushes, but leave them lying on the ground, so the view from the air would be more or less the same. Then, when we needed to go, it would be quick to throw the branches and everything we had pulled up to the side to clear the runway. There'd be others to help then, too. But first we needed some foliage that we could use to cover the wings of the planes. "Let's start with that giant fern over there," I said.

Pulling up jungle plants was easier said than done, especially since we first had to make sure that we weren't antagonising any wildlife lurking near the roots. The two of us struggled for five or ten minutes before I remembered Joshua had loaded two pairs of garden shears into the plane. At the time, that had seemed a silly idea. Now, brilliant. Whilst the shears looked ancient, they were well-oiled and made quick work of the thinner stems. We'd just finished covering the red plane when a new loud mechanical noise approached. A helicopter. We hid as best we could and watched as the aircraft first closed in on us, then swerved and flew away to the west.

"Do you think they saw us?" asked Laoban.

"My guess is no," I replied. "If they had seen the other plane, surely they would at least have flown lower and hung around to take a better look. Better hurry up and cover it before they come back."

We walked down the runway towards the other plane, clearing a path as we went, to find Jimbo had almost already finished the job of covering it. "Back already? Did you find Bea and Humphry?" asked Laoban.

"Sure. It's pretty easy going from here. They're going to camp out somewhere safe, in sight of the Mission, then head in early tomorrow morning. Unless they get sussed out first, of course."

"Good work, Jimbo," I said. "And tell me how you pulled up all those bushes without any tools."

Jimbo grinned broadly. "Technique and experience, Mr Robert. And these!" He flexed his enormous biceps.

# Putting the Plan into Action – Beatrix

I was never attracted to any of the men in the reading group when we were meeting for 'reading,' which is hardly surprising, I suppose. Sitting in a draughty library in one's winter coat and thermals, trawling over passages from spy novels, isn't conducive to getting the juices flowing. Not mine, anyway. And, of all the men there, the last one I would have considered a liaison with was Humphry. But put him in a warm climate, take away the coat and scarf and bobble hat, reduce the beard to designer stubble, and hey presto, a much younger, handsome, and athletic man is revealed. Our newly discovered attraction is plainly mutual, and I can't wait to discover him in more intimate detail. Our initial fumbling the other evening had been interrupted even before I could get beyond taking his shirt off.

But romantic matters will have to wait for another day. Our return to the mission would require us to be at our most professional, though neither of us complained about being cramped together at the back of that tiny red aeroplane. Laoban had proved herself to be a most competent pilot. I thought I could sense that she really wanted to be dressed in the right uniform, though, rather than in military fatigues. Perhaps that was because I remembered Rob telling us that someone else had called her Chameleon. The landing was hairy, though. We'd been flying perfectly smoothly up until then, but then the plane started rocking left and right, and we hit a lot of bushes and trees. I audibly sighed with relief when we came to a halt, which caused Humph to laugh and Laoban to turn around and glare at me.

The original plan was to wait for Rob to arrive with the other plane, since it would be bringing our supplies. We expected it would be right behind us, but when half an hour had passed, Laoban got visibly impatient.

Meanwhile, Humph had found a canvas bag with bottles of water and some food in the back of the red plane. Not wanting to hang around with Laoban in an increasingly tetchy mood, we decided that would be enough to sustain us for a day or two and got on our way to the Mission.

We got the shock of our lives when Jimbo crept up on us. Talk about strong and silent. A very salutary lesson in the risks of not staying completely on your guard at all times. We hadn't got very far, and were considering going back and waiting for Rob as we realised we needed stuff from our backpacks, not least a knife or something similar to deal with the vegetation we had to walk through. So, Jimbo bringing them to us saved us a lot of time.

His information about the people at the mission was interesting, but there was nothing there to change our approach. He gave us a pistol that he said he had taken off one of the Latinos. "Just in case." The best thing, though, was that he brought us energy bars. I'd taken just one bite of one of the tamales in the Latinos' bag and the residue was still stuck around my teeth. Like eating a massive glue stick. I hadn't been looking forward to subsisting on those for a day or two.

Duly reminded of the need for stealth, we crept on towards the mission, not able to match Jimbo's silent moves, but, in our opinion, anyway, doing pretty well. There was surprisingly little wildlife. All we came across was a family of baboons sitting in a small clearing and doing what baboons do, until we disturbed them, at which time they made a lot of noisy chattering as they clambered upwards into the canopy over us. We kept our eyes on the ground for snakes but saw none. Fortunately. Just armies of ants marching single file across fallen twigs towards their nest, each one proudly parading the triangle of leaf it had cut from some innocent plant above its head.

When we reached a thicket of acacia trees where we could get a line of sight to the front of the mission lodge, we stopped to camp overnight. The sun was already low in the sky, and we didn't want to risk being caught in the lodge at night. We had approached on the opposite side to our first visit but couldn't make up our minds whether this could be described as the front or the back. We guessed the front, as there was a track leading up to the entrance. Since that was how I had planned we would arrive, we had to hope it was the one that led to the nearest road. Between where we were lying down and the lodge entrance, we had a clear view of the shipping container we'd been trapped inside for those few hours the previous afternoon. I couldn't believe it was only twenty-four hours since we'd left here.

There was nowhere to pitch a tent, but we cleared a space of fallen branches and sharp twigs and laid everything flat. It was more comfortable for us to sit and lie down on. We just had to hope that we'd find nothing nasty underneath it when we came to roll it up again.

For the first hour, nothing happened. The lodge appeared to be deserted. Then we heard the sound of an engine, and a few minutes later, the big truck that had taken us to the airstrip lumbered into view and stopped in front of the lodge. The driver, who looked like one of the men who had been unloading the plane the day before, climbed down from his cab, opened the doors of the container, and started slowly carrying boxes into it from the truck. The ones that he had unloaded from the plane the day before? We counted ten before he shut the back of the truck and went into the lodge.

"He's left the container open," Humph said. "I'm going to try my luck. See if I can sneak a look inside."

It didn't seem like a smart idea to me, but Humph was confident he could get there unobserved, so I stayed behind and watched. It wouldn't have made sense to risk having both of us caught. I'd have expected some heavies to monitor the delivery, even if they didn't plan for visitors. But there was no one around. Maybe the Latinos were the only security they had? I watched Humph make his way around the back of the container. Just moments later, the driver came back out of the lodge carrying more boxes. My heart was in my mouth. I just had to hope that he didn't see Humph, or, worse still, lock him into the container. But the man just loaded the boxes into the truck, got in, and drove off, presumably forgetting that he hadn't shut the container. Nobody else followed, and all was quiet for a long five minutes.

I didn't see Humph come back until he was almost on top of me, panting breathlessly — interrupted by bad thoughts as I write this…

"Those boxes contain bottles of a chemical called acetic anhydride," he told me. I knew that acetic acid was vinegar, but this was something very different. Humph wasn't sure, but thought he had learnt in medical school that acetic anhydride was used to make drugs. Both good and bad ones. So, was that what they were doing? Humph was reading my thoughts.

"I don't know much about the manufacture, but it could be crystal meth, it could be something else they're making. I suppose they're doing it here because they can't get the ingredients in the Americas anymore. And they need to stay hidden, obviously. They'd need other nasty dangerous ingredients too. The big drums we saw unloaded yesterday, for example. They're already in the container. From the symbol on the side, I think that it's some sort of acid." Then, changing the subject, he said, "Oh, and I brought these. Might be useful."

Hand scythes? Machetes? These tools were a sort of cross between the two. Razor sharp and much better than the knives we had purloined from the lodge kitchen. Those had probably never met a tougher challenge than carving through Hilda's lasagne. These machetes would be useful for slicing our way through the bush on our return journey. If we didn't need them for self-defence first, of course.

While we were examining them, we saw three men come out of the lodge, walk towards the container, and start to carry boxes and drums back into the lodge. All as if in slow motion. We counted four round-trip journeys by each man. The Reverend — if that's what he was — then emerged, no longer dressed as a cleric. Sporting a t-shirt several sizes too small for him and bright red shorts. He collected another box from the container and closed and padlocked the door behind him. He carried the box back to the lodge, but tripped over as he climbed the steps. Humph and I heard a heavy thud and the sound of breaking glass, so we supposed there must have been bottles in the box. We saw two men come to help the big man get up, and the three of them disappeared inside.

The days are hot, and I'd found it surprising how chilly it begins to feel in the bush once night falls. Humph and I managed a few cuddles to help stay warm, but with one of us having to stay awake and alert at all times, that was the limit of our romantic entanglement. We decided to take guard duty in three-hour shifts. I took the first, during which absolutely nothing happened. Just the rustling of leaves above us and the jungle sounds we were now used to.

Thankfully, we didn't need our torches. With a clear star-studded sky and an almost-full moon, there was plenty of light filtering through the trees. Every so often there would be sudden movement in the trees. Nothing that concerned us. I supposed it was just some birds moving around to get comfortable, or perhaps a monkey turning over in its sleep. Do monkeys sleep like we do? Nothing worth reporting, anyway.

Humph took over, and I climbed into my sleeping bag and fell asleep within minutes. But I had probably only managed less than an hour's shut-eye when he shook me awake. "Something's coming towards us," he whispered. Sure enough, there was movement close by. A bit more than rustling twigs. Humph drew the pistol, and I grasped one of the machetes, prepared to hold our ground. We probably looked a bit ridiculous to the inquisitive mongoose that poked its nose out of the undergrowth a few minutes later. We relaxed by laughing and hugging.

The rest of the night passed without incident. It just got colder and colder. I couldn't stop wishing we could get together in the sleeping bag, but duty comes first. At daybreak, we ate some of the rock biscuits. We had no hot drink to dunk them in but found that holding them unchewed in the mouth for a minute or two achieved the same result. Sweet, pure carbohydrate energy for the day ahead. We were going to need it.

Still no sign of life at the mission lodge. To decide on a credible time to go and knock on the front door, we attempted a rough calculation of how long it would take to get from the nearest town. The trouble was that we didn't know where that was. So, we guessed at an hour in a vehicle from the town to the junction with the track, then an hour and a half to hike the eight kilometres to the lodge. Total, two hours thirty minutes starting from where we were. We'd go in at nine a.m., barring any earlier emergency. Plenty of time to get ready.

I dug out my makeup kit from the bottom of my rucksack, wishing that I'd not had to leave some of the items behind in Pingu. I hoped Maria was taking good care of him. Nail scissors aren't made for hairstyling, but they did a good enough job trimming Humph's curls. Back home, he'd grown his hair almost as long as his beard. With his beard shaved off and hair cut short, he looked like a different man. Transformed from a vagrant to an Adonis. He only needed a few light touches of makeup for me to be confident that nobody who saw him yesterday would recognise him as the same man today.

My metamorphosis took a little longer. I didn't want to cut my own hair, especially now I had seen how the scissors tended to jam and yank at the scalp. I put up my hair into a bun, a style I would normally never have dreamt of wearing. Hoping it made me look like a modern Florence Nightingale. Using a different shade of foundation and pencilling in some discreet lines with mascara succeeded in adding at least ten, perhaps twenty years to my age.

We were ready for action; the young dashing doctor and the late middle-aged spinster nurse. Well, those were the roles we were about to act out. It was just a shame we didn't have hospital scrubs to dress up in. All we could do was change out of camouflage gear into jeans and t-shirts and hope nobody would question our casual appearance.

Now we had to wait. It had taken us over an hour to change our clothes and appearances, but we still had nearly half an hour to go. It felt like forever.

# Medical Attention – Humphry

Whatever was going on in the mission lodge was happening on the other side. There certainly wasn't any sign of life on the side we were watching from. There was definitely human activity somewhere, as, ever since daybreak, the noise of machinery of one kind or another was incessant. The constant rumble of a generator, the augur — at least, that's what Richard had told us it was — intermittently boring holes, another sound we decided was a chainsaw, and one that I thought was an air compressor. None of the sounds were especially loud but were quite enough to shatter the calm where we were camped out and to scare off any birds or monkeys perching in the trees above us.

Finally, on the stroke of nine, we picked up the first aid kits we had filched from the lodge — at least they had a red cross on the outside, and the best we could do in the circumstances to look medically competent — walked from our camp to a place on the track that wasn't in line of sight of the lodge and approached from there. It proved to be an unnecessary diversion, as nobody saw us coming. In fact, nobody noticed us at all until we had walked up the steps and onto the mission lodge deck.

Three men, quite possibly the same ones as had been carrying the boxes the night before, were engaged in some desultory cleaning. Well, they had a big waste bin, and each had a broom, but all they were doing when we walked in was leaning on them and chatting. They didn't seem bothered by our arrival. "Who are you?" one of them asked.

We explained we were from an international medical team and, lying through our teeth, told them that the crew on a truck on the main road had told us we were needed urgently to attend to someone sick at this lodge. We'd expected a reaction somewhere between doubt and hostility. What we hadn't anticipated was an enthusiastic welcome. "Thank God, thank God!" the man exclaimed. "We thought it would be days before you got here. Come, come." He led us towards some double doors at one end of the deck.

So, the good news was that we were welcome, and nobody was getting ready to shoot us, at least not yet. The potentially bad news was that they had actually sent for medical help. We might not be able to help whoever it was who was sick or injured. And there was the additional risk that a genuine medical team might roll up at any moment while we were there, revealing us to be imposters. Risks we would have to accept. We probably had a comfortable hour or so given the distance to the nearest civilisation.

The room we entered was arranged as a combined office and bedroom, and the injured party, lying on the bed, turned out to be the Reverend himself. Luckily, he didn't recognise us, though that might have had something to do with him writhing in pain. His left arm, his hands, and the lower parts of both his legs were scarred with chemical burns from where he had fallen on to the broken bottles of acetic anhydride. Had he been wearing his priest's outfit, his legs would have been covered. It might have saved him… just an amusing thought that occurred at the time.

At least this was something that I knew how to handle. From questioning, we learnt that neither the man who had led us in nor the others had done anything for him except put him straight to bed. It hadn't occurred to them to wash off the chemical. They didn't think they had a first aid kit in the lodge. It was weird thinking that we were now there, trying to save the life of someone who had tried to kill us the day before.

Bea sent the men to fetch water to wash the Reverend's skin while I rooted around in the first aid kits to find anything useful. I passed Bea a tube of antiseptic cream and went on searching. Instead of the action of smoothing the cream over his damaged skin relaxing him, however, it had the opposite effect. He screamed in agony while Bea was administering it. It didn't stop her — she enjoyed it, I think!

I delved further and made a far more interesting discovery in the other first aid kit. Flunitrazepam. About the last drug I'd expect to find in a kit like this. "This'll make him feel better," I remarked, crumbling a few tablets into a glass, adding some water, and forcing the Reverend to drink it. The effect wasn't instantaneous, but it was remarkably quick. The patient stopped moaning, stopped struggling, and fell fast asleep.

"What is that drug?" Bea asked, examining the label on the bottle. "I've never heard of it."

"You might have. It's usually called Rohypnol. One of the date rape drugs. One pill makes a girl do anything and not remember, three makes a fraudulent priest dead to the world. For a few hours at least. I hope."

Adopting the most professional bedside manner I could manage in the circumstances, I instructed the two men, who were standing watching, apparently overawed by the treatment, to watch over the Reverend and tell us if he moved. I put the first aid kits back together again and motioned to Bea to stand up and leave.

"Where are you going?" asked one of the men.

"I want to check out all the other people you have here." The man looked doubtful, moving as if to stop us. "It's our policy and a government requirement," I added. "When we visit a lodge to attend to the sick, we must not leave without confirming that all the residents are healthy or have appropriate treatment. We have to follow the procedures of the Communicable Diseases Register." I suppose it sounded a bit formal, but it had the desired effect of impressing the guy, who now acquiesced.

"Bill will show you," he said, opening the door and explaining in some incomprehensible local language to the third man, who had been hovering outside. "My name is Junior, by the way."

Bill was not of the communicative sort, ignoring whatever we said and responding with animal grunts. He led us to the end of the deck and through an entrance to the kitchen. Two men were there, one peeling, the other chopping a big pile of some root vegetables. They looked like oversized white carrots. Turnips? They were working at an island in the middle of the kitchen, surrounded by piles of dirty crockery, jars, bottles, pans… chaos. Insects buzzed all around. I was surprised everyone who ate here wasn't suffering from dysentery or worse. Now that I'd said we were going to check everyone, we had to play our parts.

Seriously, while wearing a stethoscope would have usefully added to my disguise, I could have put one to good use. In the circumstances, I had to resort to tapping chests and backs and telling them to say "aaaaah." We had to demonstrate, as they obviously didn't understand English. Initially, they were suspicious, but waving the first aid kits in front of them proved as effective as a white coat, and they submitted willingly. Just as well there didn't seem much wrong with them. We didn't want to spend all day attending to the sick; we were on our mission at the Mission.

My cursory examination of them finished, Bea tried explaining — again through demonstration since Bill didn't understand us either — that they needed to do some serious washing up. The two kitchen staff nodded and gave thumbs-up signs, but went straight back to their vegetable chopping.

Back out on to the deck, Bill led us back towards the Reverend's room. We stopped him and asked where the others were, to which he just shook his head. I decided to ignore him and returned to a pair of double doors that we had just passed. Luckily for us, just as we got there, we heard a crash on the other side. I went for the door handle and Bill moved quickly to try to stop me, but he was too late. I entered a much larger room, dimly illuminated only by high-level openings in the walls, an altar at one end, covered with a white satin cloth bordered in purple with a large gold metal dish on it. There were benches to sit on. Well, pews, I suppose. So, this must be the assembly room that Jimbo had told us about.

Standing against the end wall opposite the altar were two terrified-looking men holding the two sides of a huge trapdoor lifted from the floor. I waved the first aid kit at them. "Health check!" I called out. "I'm a doctor, and this lady is a nurse."

Those men looked Latino, their skin swarthy like the thugs we'd encountered the day before but with a totally different physique. Skinny, almost to the point of skeletal.

"They're fasting," said a voice from behind me. Junior. I hadn't noticed him come into the room.

"These men are ill. They need food," I told him.

"They cannot eat. It is a penance. The Reverend Father has ordained it. It is their pathway to heaven."

Heaven or hell, they were going to get there very soon if they had no food, or, more importantly, treatment. In any case, they'd probably passed the point of no return. Tuberculosis as a complication of HIV? I knew that was relatively common in Africa, but there were other diseases that could cause wasting, too. My medical speciality was as a trauma surgeon fixing broken bones, and although I had all the requisite training, I was no expert on infectious diseases.

At least we had masks, but to get close and be safe from whatever virus or bacterium they were infected with, we probably required full kit respirators. I needed to be selfish; protecting our own safety was paramount, so I took two surgical masks out of the kit, gave one to Bea and put one on myself. Better late than never.

I went through the motions of checking out the men. They definitely had a respiratory disease and almost certainly a fever. Could be SARS. Could be MERS. Could be Covid. Heaven help us, don't let it be Ebola. I couldn't find a thermometer in the medical kits, and had nothing suitable to treat them, if they weren't already beyond help. We still had to go further, find the others at the mission lodge, find out what was really going on. To get past these sorry individuals, I needed to demonstrate that I was delivering medical treatment.

In the box, tucked behind some bandages, I found two foil-wrapped Ibuprofen tablets. 'Use by November 2007.' Only about fifteen years out of date then. They couldn't do them any harm, and if there was still any active ingredient in them, it might at least calm their fever. They certainly wouldn't do anything else.

When I offered the tablets, the men looked even more scared. Perhaps they thought the pills were poison. I asked Junior to explain to them that it was medicine to make them better, to which he replied, "They understand English." Hmmm. They didn't seem to understand mine.

There was a water dispenser in the corner, and I pointed to it and the tablets. Reluctantly, they took them, dropping the trap door as they moved away.

"What's down there?" I asked Junior. "More people?"

"You cannot go there," he replied. "It is forbidden."

"Are there people down there?"

"I do not know. I have never been. We are forbidden."

I leant down to take hold of one of the rings in the floor, and Junior moved quickly to stop me, standing on top of the trapdoor. "I said it is forbidden."

It wasn't until then that I realised Bea was no longer there.

# Uunderground – Beatrix

While Humph was attending to the two skeletal men and Bill and Junior's attention was directed at them, I took the opportunity to look through the open hatch. I couldn't see anything down there, but a wooden stairway beckoned me to go down and take a look. I wasn't expecting the hatch to slam shut above me no sooner than I had reached the bottom. The hatch was big and of thick timber. It must be very heavy if it took two men to open it from the other side. I had to trust that they would soon open it again and Humph would come down and join me, or at least that I could push it up from the inside to get out again. Well, that would be later. First, I would explore.

The dimly illuminated room I was in was a plain cellar with a tiled floor but unfinished earth walls on three sides. Piles of cardboard boxes were stacked against one of them. Probably the stuff we'd seen them carrying the day before. There were two big drums with yellow diamond danger warnings stuck on them. Nothing else was present except a steel door in the fourth wall, the one under the stairs. It wasn't visible from above. Just plain steel painted black, no handle, no lock. No entry.

Then, suddenly, the light went out. I couldn't see a thing. I could find the stairs. Should I climb up and try to open the hatch? No, that would defeat the object of our mission. I had to find out what was on the other side of that door. I could knock on it, but instinct told me that wouldn't be wise. Whoever usually went that way would know how to open it, so anyone on the other side would suspect danger. No, this cellar was intended to just look like a storeroom should any unauthorised person, like me, get a glimpse of what was under the hatch.

Even though I wasn't planning on trying to leave, I climbed the stairs. As I reached the halfway point, the light came on again. Good, at least I now knew how that was controlled. I went back down, walked under the stairs, and looked back up. Well camouflaged, recessed into the side of one tread, was a black button. I pressed it. Success!

The metal door swung open to reveal a laboratory. An ultra-modern one, certainly not something one would expect to find underground in the middle of the African bush. Glossy white walls and ceiling, gleaming stainless steel counter tops covered with an array of glass and stainless steel apparatus. Standing right in front of me were two men in white Tyvek suits. They were concentrating on something in a glass-fronted cabinet, their hands and arms hidden inside tubes that ran inside it. They froze on seeing me.

"Who are you? What are you doing here?" asked one of them. From what I could see of their faces through the hoods they wore, the men could have been Chinese, but whatever this place was, it was no mine of praseodymium or any other mineral.

I realised that I'd left my First Aid Kit upstairs, but decided I'd better stick to the plan, despite my lack of ID. "I'm part of the medical team. Come to do a health check on you all. My colleague, the doctor, will be here soon."

"Nobody is allowed here. How did you get in?"

"I walked through the door, of course," I said, trying to sound as nonchalant as possible. "Is it convenient to check your health now?" The two men looked at each other, neither knowing how to respond to such an unexpected request. They hadn't moved, though, and still had their arms up to their sleeves inside the clean cabinet. Excellent. An opportunity to explore further. "I can see you're busy. I'll come back later," I said and then hurried past them, between the workbenches, and turned the corner at the end, ignoring their shouts to stop.

The sight that greeted me was not so much a laboratory as a factory. An electrifying spectacle. A production line, all gleaming stainless steel, occupied a long corridor. Not noisy, just gentle whirring, the factory vibrating, the rhythm resonating in my bones. Too long to see what was happening at the furthest point. At the end where I was standing, pills were popping out of an orifice in the machine. As they popped, they were deftly collected in bottles by two operators. I could see at least another ten men sitting or standing along the length of the line, all dressed head to foot in white Tyvek.

It was a fascinating sight, but I couldn't linger. I wasn't going to be allowed to perform relaxed medical examinations while studying the operation in more detail, as by now the men I had passed earlier had pulled their arms out from their clean cabinet, crept up behind me and were grasping me roughly by the shoulders, one each side. As they held on to me, other men were approaching from the far end of the line. All were clearly unsure how to handle the unexpected situation, and none of them looked friendly.

I couldn't afford to wait for them to decide what to do. If I didn't make an instant decision to fight, they would inevitably move to incapacitate me and take me to their leader. They wouldn't know, of course, that he was sleeping soundly upstairs. Heaven knows what they would do when they discovered that. Being locked up again in that container was the gentlest treatment I could hope for. It was obvious Humph wasn't coming, so I was on my own. And at that instant, someone must have pressed the alarm button. Lights started flashing, and a siren sounded in the distance. I had to take the initiative.

My rush of adrenaline was exhilarating. It was incredibly satisfying to find I had forgotten none of my judo moves. I wasn't as fit and lithe as I had been in my twenties, of course, and I hadn't had to use them in anger for at least ten years. None of the men working here were skilled in martial arts, though, so none were a match for me. They were just technicians.

In that moment, I thought of myself as a modern-day female incarnation of Jackie Chan, creating a whirlwind of chaos. I imagined a film crew there to record me tossing one man over the top of the production line while kicking a second to make him collide directly with a third, the domino effect tipping them over machinery and smashing glassware. I worked my way along the line until all those who hadn't escaped to cower under the line were lying unconscious on the floor. There was no praseodymium mine here. But we did now know what went on in this fake Mission. Accomplished.

This was not a place to hang around, and I couldn't go back the way I came. The 'factory' was filling with acidic fumes that were already hurting my throat and lungs, and I needed to get to fresh air. I grabbed a bottle of the pills that were spilling out all over the shop and stuffed it in a pocket. I videoed the scene on my camera phone and then legged it swiftly to a steel spiral staircase helpfully labelled 'Emergency Exit.' This situation probably wasn't what it was intended for, but it was definitely an emergency for me to exit before I collapsed from the fumes, or any of the men came round.

Amongst the supplies piled up by the side of the staircase were three one-gallon containers of engine oil. Fighting the fumes, I lifted them up to the third tread, climbed onto the first, and opened and emptied all the lubricant onto the floor below me. I didn't know how slippery that would make it, but I trusted it would be enough to delay anyone trying to come after me. I could see a steel trap door at the top of the staircase. I briefly wondered where it would lead. I had no choice but to find out.

For a few long moments, I thought I would never escape. I pulled aside the bolts holding it shut, but pushing up against the hatch had no effect, however hard I tried. Taking a last gulp of contaminated air, I summonsed all my might for one final herculean heave. Suddenly, there was movement and fresh air accompanied by a cascade of soil and leaves that I thought would never end. A camouflaged hatch, set into the forest floor. Couldn't have been opened for ages.

Taking gulps of air, I pushed harder until there was enough space to poke my head out to look around. I was at the back of the lodge, as I could see the lawn, and between two of the huts built for accommodation. Nobody in sight.

I levered myself out of the hatch, closed it again, and searched around for anything heavy to cover it. Heavy enough to stop anyone following. I laid down a couple of logs that were lying nearby. They probably wouldn't resist a really hard push, but the effort would at least delay them a bit more. Having wasted precious moments moving the logs, I realised that they could all simply leave up the stairs by which I had entered, and no doubt that was what they would do.

The siren was loud now, but I could also hear raised voices. Tense, I crept commando-style back to the lodge. Humphry emerged from the assembly room — or chapel, or whatever it was — followed by.... OMG. The two Latinos, Sancho and Benny. How had they got back here? Or were they different ones? They certainly looked the same. And they had guns. Not the

AK-47s they'd had before. Just ordinary rifles, like the ones that Jimbo and Pascal were carrying to defend us. The butts pushed into Humphry's back. They hadn't seen me. Yet. I knew I needed to do something, and quickly. Time for some more aggressive judo moves while I was psyched up for it.

Fuelled by raw determination, I surprised not only myself but them by grasping the banister that ran the length of the deck with my right hand, lifting my body and vaulting over it. I landed on the back of the taller of the two Latinos, my right leg striking my quarry's gun arm while snaking my left leg across to disarm his partner.

Humph, quick-witted, lost no time in grabbing both guns, kicking at the legs of the man I wasn't holding on to, and rifle-butting him. While we performed our theatrical moves, Bill, Junior, and the other African who had been on the deck when we arrived just stood watching. As the second man fell, they actually applauded.

"Quick, let's get out of here," said Humph. We moved as speedily as we could to the main entrance, where he hesitated. "You go. Run. I'm coming in just a moment." I didn't wait for further encouragement and hared off towards the spot where we had camped overnight. As I ran, echoes of shattering glass rang in my ears and, just as I reached the tent, I was engulfed by sudden intense heat. I stopped running and looked behind me. The silhouette of Humph sprinted towards me, flames bursting from the lodge behind him. As he arrived, he collapsed on top of the tent.

"How did you manage that?" I asked.

"Never mind that. Wash my eyes and face with water like a good nurse," he replied. "That stuff is horrible."

Once treated, Humph explained that he'd seen the rest of the bottles of acetic whatever-it-is from last night's accident just left piled up by the door. The box had fire hazard stickers on it, so it occurred to him to smash the bottles and try setting fire to it. He'd almost been overcome by the fumes in the process.

"How did you set fire to it, though?" I didn't think he'd been carrying matches.

"Remember how Pascal showed us how to light a fire with two sticks?" A glimmer of mischief flashed in his eyes. Yeah sure, Humph! But you're still my Tarzan.

# Not the Kind of Pickup I'm Used to – Latviana

Thank goodness Laoban finally invested in a satellite phone. It was one thing marking the path of electronic blips onto a completely useless map and quite another actually being able to talk to somebody. The map that Rob had brought from London was better than those I could find online, though really the only additional detail was a road and a few tracks, all miles away from where our team of lion-hearted safari spies actually were. Like the online map I'd first looked at back in Rotterdam, all it showed of where the team was going was green nothingness. So, until the satellite phone, I just had to sit in the little room I'd rented in the airport admin building and wait for something to happen. Presumably all was well, as the only time one of the paging devices had been triggered was with the 11113 project delay code. That had been Rob. At least he remembered how to use the locator. The other spies might simply have forgotten. They were all useless.

Laoban hadn't told me she'd bought the phone. Probably slipped her mind. The first I knew of it was when Richard called me out of the blue. Or should that be out of the green? I was not surprised to hear that she had gone to the lodge as soon as I had told her about the alert from Rob. It's the sort of thing she does. She didn't tell me she was going, she just said "OK" and told me to stay where I was.

I didn't, though. Kasane was boring, the wi-fi was terrible, and I felt isolated, a long way from the action. I guessed that at some point I'd be needed, so I decided to move. To Windhoek. The team was in Namibia, so it made sense for me to be there too. And Windhoek was a much bigger place, a capital city, from where it would be easier to organise and get things done. If anything needed to be done.

It was a spur-of-the-moment decision. There were no regular flights from Kasane to Windhoek. In fact, there were hardly any regular flights going anywhere. But that morning when I went into the terminal, just to get a drink from the only functioning coffee machine, a flight was showing on the departure board. One of the check-in agents I'd made friends with told me it was a private charter, so I had no hope of getting a seat. He hadn't reckoned with my inventiveness.

I dressed up in my travel agent uniform from the other day when I'd greeted the team. I wasn't expecting to use it again. Just as well I'd hung it up, so it wasn't creased. I crammed everything else I'd brought into that rather cute penguin case Beatrix had brought with her. It hadn't been in my heart to get rid of it. We girls have to stick together. Draping a sweater over the Antarctic bird so that nobody would see and remark on it, I simply walked round the back of the terminal on to the apron and up the steps of the waiting Gulfstream jet.

The pilot, hearing movement, opened his door to the cabin. "Who are you? What are you doing here?"

I smiled sweetly, stroking down a crease in his shirt and flicking some dandruff off his tie. Skills I'd acquired from Laoban. "Your passengers asked for a flight attendant. Has the catering been loaded?"

"They told me they'd help themselves. Must have changed their minds. We loaded champagne and some snacks in Joburg. If they didn't finish them all getting here, you'll find them in the usual place." He went back to the flight deck and paused. "Board in five. Off stand in ten. Flying time fifty-five minutes at twenty-nine thousand feet. And if there's any champers left, I'll have a glass." With which he moved inside the cabin and closed the door.

The flight was unremarkable except for the passengers. Four looked Chinese, two South American. Drunk as sailors, all of them, even before we took off. Plus one Brit, tall, neatly trimmed beard, shaven head, sober and refusing a drink. Unpleasant looking guy. He seemed to be in charge of the other six. None remarked on my being there; having a stewardess was quite normal. I emptied out a water bottle, refilled it with the sparkling wine that was masquerading as champagne, and gave it to a grateful pilot. I trusted that he'd still be able to land safely after half a litre of wine.

At Windhoek, the plane parked well away from the passenger terminal. A dark minivan with blacked-out windows awaited the party that descended, one practically falling down the steps, all of them having to be pushed on board the van by the Brit. I'd neither seen nor heard anything to indicate as to why they were there or where they were going, but I couldn't help suspecting that they were connected in some way to our mission.

As soon as the passengers were down the steps, I squeezed into the tiny lavatory at the back of the plane and changed into jeans and a t-shirt. The pilot was just finishing his paperwork and looked surprised to see me out of uniform. He was even more taken aback when I planted a lingering kiss on his lips and asked his name and where he stayed when he was in town. No harm in having another tame pilot to call on. Just in case, mind. Not that I'm not faithful to Rob, of course. Most of the time.

I looked around the tarmac. Windhoek might be a capital city, but the airport was quiet. Just a few small jets and prop planes parked up. No big planes. I strolled towards the terminal. The only people I saw on the way were ground handling guys loitering around their tugs, waiting for a plane to attend to. The few that noticed me waved. One gave me a wolf whistle, which was nice. It's always reassuring to know that someone fancies you, even if it's a juvenile baggage handler.

I was wondering how I would manage to enter the country without raising suspicions, but my concerns evaporated when a big Lufthansa plane came in to land. I lurked in a corridor until the passengers started to disembark, then joined the throng for passport control. With a Latvian passport, it was logical that I would come via Frankfurt. Not that the immigration officer cared.

I took a room at a place almost opposite the airport. It was unprepossessing as a hotel. More like a lodge, but without any wildlife anywhere nearby. Imagine a farmyard with seven or eight prefabricated bungalows arranged around a pool. Not a place that many people chose to stay, evidently.

"Are you heading for the dunes?" The young man at reception was trying to be friendly. I shook my head, not knowing anything about dunes. "That's where most tourists go." Seeing that I still looked mystified, he continued. "Like a desert. All sand. Very high dunes. Very impressive. People come from all over the world to see them. About three hours south of here. I can arrange a tour for you?" He looked hopeful.

"No, well, not yet anyway. I have work to do." I realised he was about to ask who I worked for and where the office was. "I'm a journalist. I have a lot of writing to do. In my room."

Either the clerk hadn't heard of remote working, or he simply couldn't believe that anyone would choose to do it from his hotel in Windhoek. He was curious that I insisted on checking the wi-fi signal in the room before signing the register and shook his head as if he was just witnessing another weird European habit.

As soon as I got inside my room, worried that I had been out of contact for nearly three hours, I powered up the base station for the locators and turned on my phone. It rang immediately. "Maria, where have you been?" asked a male voice. "I've been trying to call you for an hour."

"Who is this?" I asked.

"Richard. On the team. Remember me?"

Richard told me about the satellite phone and updated me on everything that had been going on. It was good to catch up, even with someone I had already concluded from my brief previous experience to be incompetent. Laoban knows best, I suppose. Given the latest news, I couldn't help feeling worried about my Pilot, Rob. Flying a plane that might run out of fuel to a remote and overgrown airstrip that he might never be able to leave again. A project intended just to identify, observe, and determine what was going on in the jungle turning into an unexpectedly deadly dangerous mission. And now Laoban had put Richard in charge of comms? What was I expected to do?

In a perfect coincidence, the sounds that were making it impossible to hear anything else Richard was saying provided me with the answer to my question. Throbbing. Loud throbbing. The walls of the room were thin, and the roof was corrugated metal. Not so much soundproofing as amplification. Was this sound and vibration going to go on all night? I opened the door to see a helicopter hovering low over the hotel swimming pool, making waves worthy of a tropical storm. Then, as quickly as it had arrived, it ascended and flew off in the direction of the airport. "What was that all about?" I asked the receptionist.

"Pilot training," he explained. "This is the nearest place they can practice without upsetting air traffic control. They finish around now."

I went back quickly to my room, noted down the coordinates of what I presumed to be the overgrown airfield since there were three blips coming from the same place, locked the base station in the room safe, and jogged back across the road to the airport. It wasn't hard to find the office of the helicopter people. Or person. One helicopter, one rather dishy pilot, name of Theo. All he did was training. No, I couldn't charter him to fly me anywhere. Oh, you have dollars. Lots of dollars. Of course, where would you like to go? Shall we leave now?

It took a little over half an hour to reach the airfield. At first, it just looked like all the surrounding vegetation, an invisible runway, but Theo suddenly pointed down and I could see the white wing of a plane. Just one wing, but as we flew low, the turbulence disturbed the camouflage as big leaves flew away, revealing a bit of the other wing. No sign of human life, though. I just had to hope they were all right. At least I'd now seen with my own eyes where they'd touched down.

As we ascended and turned to return to Windhoek, a lodge came into view only a little distance away, with a white and apparently serviceable landing strip. I assumed that was our target. I hadn't expected it to be so close and hoped that we hadn't been spotted. Laoban would kill me if my little reccy compromised the mission.

Back in the hotel, my first thought was to call Richard. I had a base station, but if Laoban had put him in charge of comms, it was up to him to tell the others about my helicopter surveillance. No answer. I kept trying. Still no answer.

I got out the map and marked the overgrown airstrip and the target lodge with a pen. I compared the blips from the locator base station. It would have been nice if they'd shown positions on a map, but all it would give me was coordinates. Updated once a minute. I had to mark my own map. So Rob and Laoban were at the airstrip. Humphry and Beatrix were somewhere near the lodge they called the Mission. I thought it very confusing having a mission to a Mission, but never mind. I supposed Brits would find it amusing. None of the four appeared to be moving, but since it was nightfall, that was to be expected. Richard was at the lodge in Botswana. He wasn't moving either.

I slept fitfully, waking every twenty minutes or so, trying to call Richard, getting no answer, and checking the coordinates of the team, nobody moving.

Soon after dawn, Laoban and Rob started moving, but slowly and not very far. I speculated they were trying to clear the runway. From what I'd seen on my helicopter ride, that was going to take a long time. Humphry and Beatrix were static until nine, when they moved slowly in a long arc towards the mission-lodge. The mission was on. I watched the coordinates change with bated breath.

Rob and Laoban continued to move gradually along the airstrip. If what they were doing was clearing it, as I supposed, it was going to take a week at the rate they were going. I was more interested in Humphry and Beatrix. For nearly an hour, the coordinates stayed the same. They were in the mission-lodge, but were they succeeding in whatever they were doing? Or were they prisoners? I had no way of knowing. At least there were no alarm signals sent to the base station. Then, ominously, Beatrix disappeared. Or her coordinates did. Flat battery? Unlikely; the charge was supposed to last for fifteen days. Some communications fault? Surely not, Humphry was still beeping away, once a minute, not moving.

I tried calling Richard again. Nothing. What on earth was he doing? His coordinates were still showing at the Botswana lodge.

Then, eight minutes later, Beatrix reappeared. Or her coordinates did. Thank heaven. Interestingly, she had moved quite a distance from where she was before. But then she was moving back towards Humphry. One minute, two. After three minutes, Beatrix had moved over a hundred metres, a minute more and she was back where she and Humphry had spent the night. But Humphry was still at the mission-lodge. Was he safe? Trapped? But then there was sudden movement, and within another minute he had rejoined Beatrix. Two blips together. After a minute, they moved again. And again. They were hurrying now, back towards the airstrip. I might have only had bleeping coordinates, but it was pretty obvious they thought they needed to get out of there fast.

My call to action. Stopping only to grab a handful of hundred-dollar bills from the room safe, I sprinted to the helicopter office. I caught Theo the owner-pilot on his way out of the door with a young man. "I'm just going to give a lesson. I'll be back in an hour," he told me.

"The lesson is cancelled," I panted. The young man looked surprised, but Theo wasn't. He simply told his pupil to come back in the afternoon. It hadn't taken him long to realise that rescuing spies from the bush in the company of a devastatingly beautiful woman pays better than giving flying lessons to hopeful young men.

I thought it possible that we'd get to the airstrip before Beatrix and Humphry got back there, but I needn't have worried. It had taken them four hours the day before, trekking from the plane to the mission-lodge, but only a little over an hour to get back. Amazing how fast you can move with a fire behind you, as Beatrix later put it. No, the actual problem I faced was that the team didn't know I was coming and would almost certainly think we were the baddies come to attack. Theo, my pilot, who was quite excited at performing a rescue mission but less so at the prospect of being shot at, suggested waving a white flag — or the equivalent. He had quite a pile of junk stashed in the back of his machine, amongst which I found a towel. Not exactly white, more cream with yellow stripes, but it would have to do.

From above, it didn't look like they had done any clearing of the airstrip. It was still covered with vegetation. Theo hovered at six hundred feet, which he figured was just out of the range of any gunshots, and I opened the side door. While Theo kept the copter under control with one hand, he reached back to hold on to one of my ankles with the other, so I could reach out and tie the sheet to one of the bars underneath. Let me tell you, it's not easy doing that when the rotor blades are kicking up a storm.

Surrender flag attached, we now descended to a hundred feet and swept along the runway. Bushes and leaves beneath us were now flying away, revealing that they had cleared part of the runway and simply covered it again with the plants they pulled up. Clever. It had us fooled, anyway. Theo landed in a cleared area. I opened the side door fully, stood there and shouted to the jungle, "It's me, Maria!"

Nothing stirred. Where had they all gone?

Then a big African materialised in front of me, who appeared as if out of nowhere. "I'm Jimbo," he said. "Are you on your own?" It hadn't occurred to me they might think I was being held hostage and used as bait to get the others to reveal themselves and be captured. I jumped out and told Jimbo to check the helicopter for himself. He greeted Theo like a long-lost friend. "You know each other, then?" I asked them, incredulously.

"No, but we are of the same tribe. Always brothers," Jimbo replied.

By now, the others had emerged from wherever they were hiding. I rushed towards my Pilot and gave him an enormous hug before I remembered about Laoban. "Sorry, it's just that we've worked together for a long time," I told the others, giving a rather more perfunctory hug to each of them. Not Laoban, of course. She's not the hugging kind. But she did give me an approving almost-smile as she made sure she was the first to board the helicopter.

Theo was taking a head count. "I've only got five seats, and there are six of you." Not a question, but clearly expecting an answer.

"That's OK," said Jimbo. "I'll walk." And with a wave and "see you guys," he evaporated into the undergrowth as mysteriously as he had appeared.

# Friends that Open Doors

"Do you see the warehouse over there?" Latviana asked Laoban, pointing out of the window of the helicopter as they approached Windhoek.

"What about it?"

"The name painted on the roof. Nabmines. It's the email address where most of Caesar's messages come from."

"So he is in the mining business, after all."

"Except that none of his emails specifically mention it. I suppose the commodity they keep referring to is praseodymium. Don't know why he has to be so cloak-and-dagger about it in that case."

"Let's take a closer look." Laoban tapped the pilot on the shoulder. "Can you fly low over that building?"

"Sure. They are friends of mine. Sometimes they need a helicopter, and they always come to me."

"Find out more," Laoban whispered to Latviana.

"Already planned to, Laoban. I'm going out on the town with him tonight."

Closer aerial inspection revealed a modern warehouse with a yard full of heavy equipment and a two-storey office block fronting a busy road at one end. Three open-top tipper trucks were backed up to the warehouse, disgorging their cargo of what looked like black rocks, three more trucks queued up and waiting their turn. Nothing suspicious there. An active and highly visible mining business. Presumably completely legal.

Theo knew something about it. "That black stuff is pressed-something. They mine it about a hundred kilometres north of here."

"Praseodymium?" asked Laoban.

"That's the stuff."

Theo swung the machine back around and headed for the airport. At that moment, Latviana's phone rang. "It's Richard. Where have you been? I've been trying to reach you for hours."

"There's no coverage in the jungle. You know that. You're the one with the satellite phone. I've only got a normal one. And I was calling you all day yesterday. No answer."

"Sorry. I wasn't very well. Anyway. Where are you? It's terribly noisy."

"Never mind, get on with it."

"You have a message from someone called Toshio? He says he texted you something about a meeting that he says sounds important."

"I'll take a look and call you back."

When Latviana left Kasane, she had asked Toshio to keep an eye on the emails Mariana had been sending and receiving, but in the heat of recent excitement had forgotten to check if he'd found anything and go back to looking again herself. The email exchange in question had come in the day before. Somebody at the Nabmines' end saying that they had an unexpected supply issue. A reply from Mariana, on behalf of Gideon Caesar, insisting on a meeting to discuss the matter. Thursday at ten local time. So tomorrow. Online meeting link conveniently included. Toshio, their digital wizard, could get them linked in without their presence being obvious to the other participants.

The little party took all the available rooms at the airport hotel. In fact, they were one room short, but Humphry volunteered to share with Rob. Bea secretly hoped that Rob would be discreet and that Humph could creep into her room later, but she gave up on the idea when she found that he'd have to pass Laoban's room on the way. Knowing her propensity to pop up unexpectedly, it wouldn't be worth the risk. There'd be lots of opportunity when they all got home to London. She left the door off the latch, anyway, just in case.

The team, minus Latviana, congregated in the little hotel's restaurant for dinner. Such as it was. They all quickly realised that the other guests staying there, presumably not exhausted after an exciting day's espionage, were dining elsewhere. Very wise of them, they thought. The multi-tasking receptionist mutated to waiter and then chef, if that title can be applied to someone who, admittedly competently, fried a dozen fish fingers and a few chicken nuggets, scrambled some eggs, and heated up a tin of baked beans. Well, better than Hilda's lasagne or camping food out in the savannah. And an awful lot better than ending up being trapped in a shipping container, or worse. There was a bottle of wine that made it more tolerable and would ensure all enjoyed a deep sleep.

Meanwhile, Latviana readied herself for a night out with Theo the helicopter pilot, doing what she could with the few clothes she had brought with her. She knew he wouldn't be too bothered and would be hoping to get her out of them pretty quickly. It was nice, though, that he gave her an appreciative look up and down when she came to meet him in the reception area and complimented her choice.

Plainly, the helicopter business wasn't doing too badly, as his car was a gleaming white Mercedes 4x4, the seats smelling of leather. Brand new? He looked sheepish when she commented on it. "It's not mine. Wish it was. I borrowed it from a friend, a car dealer. Demonstration model." They smiled at each other.

"Drinks then dinner?"

"Sounds like a good way to get the night started."

The drinks stop was an enormous and noisy bar packed with people, where Theo introduced Maria to a lot of his friends. All of them just met casually. It seemed that every man Theo bumped into was a friend of his. Builders, mechanics, car salesmen. All of them in the habit of doing favours for each other. Helicopter ride for a group of seven-year-old children exchanged for the loan of a posh motor for the night? No problem. And so on. Amongst the men, pilots, lots of pilots. There must be a big flying fraternity in Windhoek, Maria remarked.

"I've a really close friend who's a pilot. We went to school together," her date commented after doing the rounds. "Haven't seen him around for a few days." Then, grabbing at the sleeve of another pilot trapped close to them in the melée. "Have you seen Sam recently?"

"Bad news, man. I hear he went down somewhere in the bush. Couple of days ago. Nobody knows. He never came back. The plane must be down there in the jungle somewhere. The boss is furious."

"That's terrible. Are you sure? We haven't lost anyone for years, have we?" Theo was seriously upset. He hadn't connected the news to his observation of the partial white wing that they had seen near where they rescued the team. That gave Latviana the opportunity to find out more. In her alter ego, Maria aimed to be something between sympathetic and solicitous, asking a mix of serious and trivial questions. In this chatter, she learnt that the plane was a Piper M class, that it was on a charter with no passengers to take some supplies to one of the Nabmines concessions in the East of the country, and that on the return journey it had simply disappeared. They didn't know where. The transponder had stopped working soon after it left Windhoek.

"I suppose you know the boss of the plane company, too," she teased Theo.

"I do. Probably all his pilots, too."

"Does he have a lot of planes?"

"Six or seven. They fly tourists to lodges and do supply runs to remote places. Like that mine that Sam was flying to."

"I'd love to fly on one of those little planes. It was my first time on a helicopter yesterday, too." Lying was second nature.

"Joe would love to take you on a trip. I know he would. I'll take you over there to meet him tomorrow." Theo was getting to be a useful guy to know.

"Dinner, before it gets too late? I'm starving."

"Me too. I know a fantastic place."

"Of course you do!" she replied, twinkling her eyes at him.

Maria supposed it to be the tallest and most impressive hotel in the city. The valet opened the car door, and she practically leapt out, almost colliding as she went up the steps with a man clutching two cases who had arrived in a taxi just in front of them. She recovered her poise, linked her arm through Theo's, and they sauntered through the lobby to the lift. The last rays of the sun were disappearing over the horizon as they walked out onto the roof terrace. An illuminated pool at one end, but ahead of that tables laid for dinner, sparkling fairy lights festooned above, all along the terrace. Magical.

Either the waiting staff were even more deferential than one might expect in a five-star hotel, or Theo was a regular. Probably the latter. "I suppose the hotel manager is a friend of yours too," she teased. Theo smiled and nodded. "Has he arranged a suite for us?"

Theo didn't expect her to be so forward, but took it in his stride. "Only a king room, I'm afraid. Suites are reserved for friends with two helicopters." They both laughed.

"Shall we take the rest of the bottle to bed, then?"

A contented hour or two later, Theo came to, realising that he had drifted off to sleep, to see Maria dressed and on the point of leaving. "Where are you going? Stay with me. We have the room all night."

"It's been wonderful, but I have to go. I have a meeting in the morning. I'll see you later in the day." She reached down and kissed his forehead, opened the door, checked that the corridor was empty, and made her way out via the service exit. No cameras that way.

# Gatecrashing

"Sorry, I overslept. Not like me." The others were already there, even though it was only a quarter to seven in the morning.

"Never mind." Laoban eyed Maria critically. "Did you actually sleep? You don't look as fresh as you usually do." Was this another manifestation of the new, polite, caring Chameleon? Latviana doubted it. Probably a criticism in a less-sour-than-usual voice.

Without waiting for a reply, Laoban faced the team. Well, the three of them that were there plus Latviana. "Have your breakfast," she said, waving at a side table with assorted cereal packets and a jug of milk, "and then we will talk. I have arranged for us to have this room all morning. We can do the online meeting from here."

"No eggs? Toast?" asked Robert.

"Just what you see," replied Latviana. "I asked yesterday when I was the only one here. Oh, and the Weetabix box is empty. It's left just for show, I suppose."

The near silence as they slurped their cereal was broken by Latviana's phone ringing. Toshio. "That link for the online meeting doesn't work. They've either changed it or it was a deliberate fake. Perhaps they know that someone has hacked into their email."

Glum faces all round. "What do we do now, Laoban?" asked Humphry. Before she could answer, Latviana spoke up.

"Laoban, didn't you say that Gideon Caesar has curly ginger hair?" The boss nodded. "And is he about my height, quite slim, around forty years old, and with terrible dress sense?"

"Correct on all counts. Why?"

"I think he's here. In Windhoek. I saw a man who looked like that checking into the Hilton last night." Latviana wasn't normally the type to blush. But. "When I was out with the helicopter pilot."

Robert looked annoyed. "I suppose you spent the night with him." He and Latviana had always told each other they had an open relationship, but she was regularly much more open than he was. What's more, here they had to act simply as colleagues. Professional.

"Not the whole night, darling, no."

Now it was Laoban's turn to look irritated. "What's the 'darling' about, then?"

"Oh, nothing. Just a normal thing to say in English." Robert and Humphry nodded conspiratorially. "Anyway, don't complain. My methods get results. And we may need Theo's help again." Robert turned away so the others couldn't see his face.

Laoban looked around the team. "So, that means the meeting will be face to face. We need to get one of you in there. If the meeting is still at ten, we have two hours." Her gaze focused on Humphry.

"Why do we need to infiltrate the meeting? Surely we have fulfilled the project? You can meet him as the boss and tell him what we found."

"Two reasons. One, I don't trust him, and two, we didn't find a mine, which is what he specified. I want to make sure that he pays the rest of our fee."

"How will tapping into that meeting help?"

"If he knew there never was a mine, but he did suspect a drug factory and that's what he really wanted us to find, I can confront him and prove he lied to me. He won't be able to wriggle out of paying us our success fee."

"You mean blackmail him?" asked Humphry.

"Of course not," scolded Laoban. "I was thinking of telling him that I have a public interest obligation to alert the authorities to the information we have uncovered." Humphry smiled to himself.

Robert put his hand up. "We don't know where the meeting is going to be."

"I would say it will almost certainly be at Nabmines' offices."

"Or the hotel, perhaps?"

Laoban shrugged. "So we cover both. Robert, you go to the offices. Take your locator and press the emergency code if you hit problems. Use your phone to record everything you can. I'll go to the hotel myself. Humphry and Beatrix, with me."

"What's my cover story? I can't just walk into the office and say I want to sit in on a meeting which they're treating as top secret." Robert looked at Laoban, then at the rest of his colleagues to see if any had a suggestion. Latviana was the one who broke the silence. "I have an idea."

Prompt on 9.30, Rob, now wearing a black suit borrowed from the hotel receptionist ("I never wear it, it's too hot. Bring it back before the boss sees it's missing") and enormous dark glasses borrowed from Bea ("they're genuine Ray-Ban, don't break them") jumped down from Theo's helicopter on to the roof of the hotel, closely followed by Latviana in her 'Maria the Tour Guide' uniform. They hadn't even got as far as the door of the stairwell before two men burst out. Hotel staff. "You can't land here. This isn't a helipad!" one shouted over the din of the engines.

"We've come to collect Mr Caesar for his meeting. It's top security." Maria pushed hundred-dollar bills into each of the men's hands. It did the trick.

"Of course. Allow us to escort you to his suite." Suite, eh? Maria allowed a fleeting moment of envy. But then, she supposed he was paying full whack for it.

Gideon clearly didn't think the meeting merited getting dressed up for, considering he answered the door in tan chinos and a green t-shirt that had seen better days. "What's this about a helicopter? I have a car coming at 9.45. All arranged."

"Your hosts decided that this would be safer for you. More discreet." Maria smiled her best hostess smile.

"And who are you?"

"My name's Robert. Your personal security officer."

"I didn't ask for one. I don't need one."

"All of us hope you won't need to call on my services. Unfortunately, there are dangerous people out there. This city is not familiar to you." He didn't add that he'd never been there before either.

He'd said enough to convince Gideon. "OK, OK, let's go, then," he replied, pulling the door closed behind him. He followed Robert who was already striding down the corridor, flanked by the two hotel employees who had taken those comments on risk far more seriously than he had. Maria took up the rear, having difficulty keeping up in her tight skirt.

As usual, Rob wished it was him at the controls, but he had to admit to himself that Theo was a superb pilot, landing perfectly smoothly on the Nabmines yard in a space only slightly larger than the diameter of the rotor blades. This time it was men in boiler suits and hard hats that came out to challenge them. Or, rather, expecting the helicopter to do a supply run, harangue Theo for arriving early without warning. They were quite put out when Rob, in his security officer guise, insisted on patting them down.

The executives in the office building who were waiting for Gideon didn't find his aerial arrival in the least surprising, instead congratulating him on having organised not only his own transport but security and secretarial assistance too. Rob and Latviana were nervous that he was going to say something, or at the least express surprise, but no, Gideon just lapped up the praise. The man who had introduced himself as the CEO suggested they move into the conference room.

"If you'll excuse me, I just need to sweep it for bugs and check the security first," said Rob.

"Our own security officer did that just ten minutes ago," replied the CEO.

"I'm sure he did a thorough job. But do you mind if I do it again? To put Mr Caesar's mind at rest?"

"Sure, be my guest." There was an air of resignation in his voice. He waved Rob into the room, the men staying in the corridor.

The room looked as plain as any conference room could be. Rectangular table. Three chairs on each side, one at each end. A notepad, a pen, a glass, plus an individual bottle of water in front of each. No whiteboard. No flipchart. No projector. No microphones. Nothing on the walls. Nothing to see. Until he clambered under the table. He switched his mobile phone to silent and set an app to record voices, then stuck it under the table with some double-sided sticky pads he'd filched from the hotel stationery cupboard. Just as he was doing so, he noticed a tiny box stuck to one of the table legs. Definitely a listening device. He wished they had something as sophisticated as this with them rather than having to rely on a mobile phone. He removed it and strode back to the corridor, holding it aloft between finger and thumb.

"Just as well I checked. This was under the table," he said. "Your man must have missed it. I assume that if you wanted to record the meeting, you wouldn't do it using a device like this?"

The CEO looked embarrassed, though whether because Rob had discovered it or his security had missed it was uncertain. "No, of course not. This meeting has top security. No recording allowed. Don't you agree, Mr Caesar?"

Gideon certainly did. "Good job. Just as well you found it."

"I'll hold on to this for you until your meeting is over, then," said Robert, putting it in his pocket.

Gideon and the two men from Nabmines filed into the room, closing the door behind them.

Rob and Latviana hovered in the corridor outside. They'd have to find out what was said in the meeting later, after Rob retrieved the phone, but were aware of a heated exchange going on. Gideon was fond of his swear words, shouted loud enough for them to hear outside the door. The rest of the conversation was unintelligible muffled noises.

The meeting lasted less than half an hour. Gideon emerged looking thunderstruck, the other men trying to calm him and invite him for lunch. "I don't want f***ing lunch!" he shouted. "You have to solve this problem today! Customers are waiting!" Then, turning his back on them and addressing Rob, "Let's go."

"Just a moment, Sir," he replied. "I have to check that nothing has been left behind in the room."

Rob was expecting just to grab the phone quickly and leave. He hadn't planned on finding a big burly African man down on his knees under the table, clutching his phone. He reversed out, stood up, and grabbed Rob immediately by the lapels of his jacket. "What are you doing here?" he growled. "Looking for this? I'm taking you to the boss."

"I don't think so," replied Rob, taking advantage of the man having both hands holding him to land a punch on the side of his face. "Give me that!"

"Yes, give my man his phone," a voice came from the door. Gideon's. "Jake, get in here. That man there is your spy. Deal with him." So saying, he hauled Rob out by his jacket collar. "You see, I told you I didn't need security." Grinning. "Don't stand there, let's go!"

Rob needed no further bidding. He and Gideon ran down the corridor, following Latviana, who, helpfully, had remembered the way they had come. Theo started the rotors as soon as he saw them approaching across the yard. Less than a minute later, they were lifting back up into the air, returning to the hotel.

This time, three people stood on the roof waiting for them. The two hotel employees from before, and a third person. Laoban, back in her dark navy business suit. "It's so nice to see you again, Gideon," she greeted him.

"What the hell are you doing here? You're all I need after a morning like this one."

"Indeed I am. We have completed your project. I am here to present our report to you."

"It's not convenient. See me in London."

"But since we're both here, w should talk now. I think you'll find that what we've discovered is of urgent importance to you. And very relevant to the meeting you've just had."

"What do you know about that meeting? It was just with my regular suppliers."

"Who told you that their suppliers have contracted with another company and so they cannot deliver to you anymore." Gideon stood still, silent, slightly shaking, staring at her, as if he was searching for words that wouldn't come. "We'll meet in the lobby in twenty minutes. We'll find somewhere quiet to talk."

"We can talk in my suite."

"I don't think so. It might be compromised." Gideon nodded, then turned towards the lift and left with the two hotel men, followed by Rob and Latviana. Laoban herself went down two floors using the stairs and used a key card to let herself into the executive lounge.

# Close Encounters of the Covert Kind

Laoban had only gone to the lounge intending to make herself a relaxing cup of Lapsang Souchong, not to stay. However, as she stood waiting for the drinks machine to heat up and perform its magic, she became transfixed. A meeting was taking place in an adjoining conference room separated from the lounge only by a plate glass wall. Eight men. Four looked Asian, she thought probably Vietnamese, two Latin American, a youngish white man at the head of the table, and — no, it couldn't possibly be — a familiar older white man. A man she had seen so many times before. No longer overweight, and with a face that had aged, but it couldn't be anyone else. Ronald Jones. But how? She and Latviana had left him locked away in an apartment in Sal. Nearly a year ago now. Given him one last glass of wine to drink, lethally laced with barbiturates, and abandoned him to his eternal rest. Never to return to this mortal world.

Yet, here he was. Large as horrible life. He couldn't have escaped. Nobody knew where he was. If the wine hadn't got him, surely starvation would have? Did he have a twin? A confident, business-like, well-dressed twin? She could see this one engaged in a close discussion with the two Latin men, then turning and talking to the others. The Jones she knew would have done anything to avoid sitting in a room with others, and entered into conversation only from sheer necessity. This one was acting as an integral part of the meeting. She sipped her tea, hypnotised and appalled in equal measure.

The meeting must have come to an end, as the men all stood. It woke Laoban from her trance. How long had she been standing there? It must be time to go down and meet Gideon. Or past time. Putting down her cup and turning to leave, she brushed against one of the men who were entering the lounge to get coffees. He turned towards her. Not a twin at all. The minted original. Ronald Jones.

"Is it you? How wonderful to see you again! What are you doing here?" he asked her. A sardonic smile playing round his mouth.

"I could ask you the same question. I thought you were dead."

"Haha. Very much not so, as you can observe. I'm the translator for this group." He waved at the other men, all queuing up as the lounge receptionist made them coffees from the machine.

"How did you get here?"

"It's a long story. Maybe we could have dinner and I could tell you all about it?" Laoban shook inside. This was a very different Ronald Jones. Reborn as a human. He talked. He smelt only of aftershave — not one she would have chosen, but an improvement. He didn't even have specks of dandruff on his jacket or stains on his tie. "That scoundrel Smith locked me away and left me to starve. Did you know that? Dreadful man. He's in prison now. Good riddance, I say."

"You're here as a translator? I don't believe you."

"Well, that's a little bit of a lie, to be fair. I'm rather more than that," he whispered, leaning close to her ear and making her recoil. "Like before, but more… shall we say… freelance, now."

"Are you staying here?"

"Goodness no. Somewhere much more discreet. And cheaper. Have to watch the budget." He actually smiled at her. A horrible, sickly smile, like he had information that was not to her advantage. "Oh, I should have said. Thank you for getting me out of my shell. I think of you every day. And for all those fashion tips and grooming advice. So very kind." Not something anyone had ever said to Laoban. "Do you have a name, now that you're not a Smith?"

"Laoban."

"A Chinese boss, eh?" He tittered. "Not the name I was told long ago, but it's a good one. See you later, Laoban." He went to join the queue for coffee, she to the lift down to the lobby. She was actually sweating. A trickle ran down the course of her spine. This never happened. She was always in total control.

Gideon Caesar was waiting for her in the lobby, flanked by Rob and Latviana. "Where's the safe place to talk then?" he asked, addressing Rob rather than Laoban.

"Terrace café outside. Far end. I checked, there's no one around. No bugs, but even if there were, they wouldn't pick up much with all the traffic noise."

"It's too hot to be outside," Gideon grumbled.

"That's why the terrace is empty. Perfect for us."

Gideon and Laoban sat at the furthest table. The server seemed a little put out that they all only wanted sparkling mineral water and kept offering cocktails even as he delivered the drinks, no doubt hoping for a bigger tip than he would get from the cheapest drink on the list. They started their conversation as soon as they were on their own.

Rob and Latviana sat at the adjacent table, trying (and failing) to overhear the conversation, keeping their eyes trained on the hotel entrance. Latviana broke their silence. "You know, I convinced myself when I met them that those assets Laoban hired for this project were a waste of space. But they were quite good, really, weren't they?"

"Humphry and Beatrix were true pros. They delivered the goods. You were right about Richard. Though he had his moments."

"You're my hero, though, Rob. You know that, don't you?" she said, pouting.

"You'll have to prove it. It sounds to me like all you've been doing is leaping into bed with other men."

"Only the once, honestly. You agreed we'd have an open relationship, remember? Anyway, Theo got you all out of there, didn't he?"

"Yes. But I'd have been able to fly out. Might have taken another day to clear the runway."

"Stop being grumpy."

The two fell silent again for a minute or more, then Latviana suddenly jumped up in her seat, pointing to the hotel entrance. "Look, those men are the ones that I flew with from Kasane the other day."

The objects of her attention were piling out of the hotel and into the black minivan she had seen them take to leave the airport. The young, shaven-headed white man got in last, seated in the front. Another much older, bald white man stood at the top of the steps, watching the van drive away. Then he looked around him, prevaricating about whether to go back into the hotel. Instead, he made his way along the terrace towards them.

"I've seen a ghost," said Robert. "Oh my god, look who's coming."

"Latviana! Pilot! You're here too! How wonderful to meet with all of you again!" Without asking, Jones pulled a chair from the next table and sat down with them. "I just met — oh, what did she call herself this time? Laoban, yes — upstairs. We agreed to have dinner, but I forgot to ask for her number, then I saw her here." He pointed to the next table. "Who's that with her?"

"A customer. And call us Maria and Robert, like everyone else does. More to the point, what are you doing here? I thought you had disappeared." Latviana thought 'wasted away,' or 'we killed you,' might not be the best choice of words.

"That bastard Smith had me locked up for more than a year. I was lucky I eventually got out. It's wonderful to see you all again." Latviana realised that, although it was Pilot who had flown him to Sal, and she and Laoban who had been his jailers for over a year, Jones would have — should have — no knowledge of that. Well, since he was alive, that was just as well. "Did you see that Smith, or whatever his real name is, is in prison?"

"Not anymore, I think," whispered Rob. "Look over there." The black minivan had returned. This time, instead of the six men they had seen leave in it, just the shaven-headed escort and an older white man. Wearing a white suit with a white Panama hat.

The man, busy talking to his escort and checking that his luggage had all been collected, didn't look their way. But Rob wasn't the only one looking at him. Gideon Caesar stopped his conversation with Laoban and stood up. "I have to go," he said to her. "My business partner has arrived." Then, as he hurriedly negotiated his way around the tables and chairs on the outside terrace to get to the door, he cried out, "Arbuthnot!"

Arbuthnot?

Laoban had been looking the other way, so had not seen him arrive. "It's Smith," Rob told her. "It has to be."

"Definitely," added Latviana, as she hastily tapped away on her phone screen. "He's been let go," she said, reading from a news website. "It says here that he has 'no case to answer' and he is the innocent party. There's some other man who really is called Smith. It says here that he's the guilty one. There's a picture of him. Never seen him before in my life."

"What it is to have friends in high places," said Laoban, sighing in resignation. The team, all looking at each other or their phones, failed to notice Arbuthnot and Caesar approaching them from inside the restaurant, followed by Humphry, who had been marooned in the lobby for the last two hours. Caesar pulled open the glass door to the terrace.

"Ah, excellent, my team is all here," Arbuthnot told Caesar. "I'm glad that my project manager here has been looking after your interests while I was unavoidably detained elsewhere, ha ha."

"I'm not your project manager," hissed Laoban, radiating menace.

"We'll discuss that, my dear. Over dinner, I think. It was a long journey. I need a couple of hours' kip. Come!"

The instruction wasn't addressed to Laoban or the others but to the shaven-headed man who had materialised by their side while they had been focused on Arbuthnot. The two men walked away.

Now joined by Humphry, the group sat back down together on the terrace. "I knew I'd seen that bald chap before," said Robert. "He was the new guy who turned up to the reading group in November. Grew a beard, then turns up at the lodge down in Botswana. And now he's shaved his head, and he's here, chaperoning a very dodgy bunch of individuals and obviously linked in some way to Smith. Or Arbuthnot. Or whatever his real name is."

"He was chairing the meeting I was just sitting in on upstairs," said Jones. "I was petrified he'd recognise me, but obviously he didn't. They wouldn't have said what they did if he had."

"Where do you know him from, then?" asked Latviana.

"He's Smith's Executive Assistant. Or was. Went by the initials EA when I met him." The others looked at each other. How was it that none of them had ever seen him before, yet Jones had? "He had hair then. Anyway, he's another one who's freelancing now. Though perhaps he's now going to throw his oar back in with Smith. Sorry, Arbuthnot. Can't get used to that name."

"And now Arbuthnot is expecting us to go back to working with him. If he's friends with Gideon, I suppose we can forget getting paid our success fee." Rob shook his head.

"I refuse to go back to working for him," said Latviana. "I'll do anything other than that. The bastard."

"Me neither," said Rob. "I'll go and fly commercial jets. Won't be as much fun, mind, but at least I'll get regular pay."

"No. This project has proved we are good at what we do and that we don't need him. We'll stay independent, whatever it takes," affirmed Laoban.

"Can I come along too? I set up my own operation a few months ago, and I have a customer, which is why I'm here, but I'm finding it lonely and difficult on my own. Could we work together, perhaps?" Ronald Jones was making them a proposal. The others looked at each other.

"Looks like we're already doing just that, doesn't it?" said Robert.

"Oh good. In that case, I have an idea. Something that I think will help us. I need to call a friend. Excuse me." Jones got up and hurried back into the hotel.

"He has a friend now?" said Latviana. "Heavens above, can a man change so much?"

"I wonder what his idea is?" mused Humphry, stroking at his now absent beard.

# No Hiding Place

Considering the scene that was about to play out, perhaps it was just as well that the hotel was quiet and the lobby empty, other than for three bored receptionists.

First down were Laoban and her expanded team. Pilot AKA Robert, Latviana AKA Maria, Humphry and Beatrix. Now Ronald Jones too.

Humphry coughed. "Bea and I have been talking. We weren't there in the morning, of course, but we just wanted to say that we're on your side. This character Arbuthnot seems like a nasty piece of work. We certainly don't want to work for him. So, we've decided, together, if he's out of the picture, we want to continue with you. This team. Otherwise, we'll go back to our day jobs." Everyone nodded.

Bea took Humphry's hand. "Whatever happens, we wanted to thank you for introducing us." They looked at each other. Laoban looked from one to the other, incomprehension on her face. She was losing her touch.

Before the two lovers could fall into each other's arms, or anything else romantic could happen, the lift doors opened and Arbuthnot emerged, followed by EA and Gideon. In the mode of a senior politician trailed by his acolytes. The two groups approached each other to the background music of a crescendo of sirens in the street outside. As it reached its climax, the lobby doors burst open. Four police officers dressed head to toe in black rushed in, two in the front with peaked caps and braided epaulettes, the two behind armed and apparently ready for combat.

"James Arbuthnot?" queried one of the officers. The man in question nodded and stepped forward. "You are to come with us. I am arresting you on suspicion of manslaughter, money laundering…," he hesitated a moment, reading the paper he held in front of him, "and a number of other charges that will be detailed to you at the station."

"I don't think so," replied Arbuthnot, smoothly. "Your paperwork must be out of date. You see, there is no extradition treaty between Namibia and the UK. And all charges against me were dropped last week."

"This is nothing to do with the UK, Mr Arbuthnot. This warrant was issued by the High Court of the Republic of Angola. And, as I think you know, our countries are close friends."

From the corner of her eye, Laoban glimpsed EA furtively creeping away and disappearing around a corner. Before he could escape too, she grasped Gideon by his clammy right hand. "It will be a pleasure to complete our business together, Mr Caesar. Our other associate here," she waved a hand at Ronald Jones, "has collected a considerable quantity of additional information that you will find extremely valuable. We need to renegotiate our success fee…"

# Back in Kasane

"You're good, man, perfect touchdown."

"Thanks for letting me captain this flight, Joe," replied Rob, smiling as he taxied the aircraft towards the terminal. "Great plane, this Piper."

"Any time for a friend of Theo's, man."

Laoban reached forward and tapped Rob on the shoulder. "Stop congratulating each other and let us out of here."

Rob and Joe opened their doors, jumped down onto the apron, and opened the rear passenger door. Laoban, Latviana, Humphry, Beatrix and their new partner, Ronald, clambered out and filed into the terminal, to be greeted by Joshua and Jimbo, beaming all over their faces.

"Where's Richard?" asked Humphry.

"On his way to Victoria Falls with a ticket back to London," replied Jimbo. "The driver left with him an hour ago."

"So, how are we going to get there?" asked Bea.

"We're not. We're just here to meet these guys, then we're taking the Airlink flight to Joburg at two. In a real aeroplane," added Laoban, looking pointedly at Rob.

"Did you hand in your notice already, Joshua?" asked Latviana.

"Yes indeed, Miss Maria. And we already found an office we like, right here at the airport. Josh and Jimbo Tours start business today!"

"Congratulations, Joshua," said Laoban. "And Jimbo, of course."

"Pascal?" asked Bea.

"He's going to work out his notice at the lodge. He's getting married in February, moving to his village in Namibia."

"So what he told us was true."

"Yes, Miss Beatrix. He's just very shy. Makes people suspicious of him, but he's a good man."

"What happened to Samuel?" asked Robert.

"You just missed him. He flew down here with us from the lodge early this morning. He's heading back to Windhoek with Joe right now."

The team bid their farewells to Joshua and Jimbo, who were in a hurry to take possession of their new office.

"Since we have a couple of hours here," said Latviana to Laoban, "can you explain how all these threads tie together? I've got really confused in the last few days. Starting with Gideon Caesar. What exactly is his business?"

"It turns out that he really does represent Nabmines in the UK, but he's also a facilitator for lots of other organisations. Most of them are probably what you English call 'dodgy.' Like the drugs connection. I'm almost certain that he set that up himself, but of course he'll never admit it. The drugs are made in Namibia, delivered in boxes to Nabmines where they hide them in the back of their trucks covered with tons of praseodymium ore."

"There really are praseodymium mines, then?" asked Humphry.

"Only one, I think, and that belongs to Nabmines. The commodity isn't valuable enough for competitors to start digging for it."

"Which means we would never have found another mine?" asked Bea.

"No. Gideon Caesar knew it, but he wanted the drugs factory found. You discovered exactly what he really wanted you to."

"Why not tell us that in the first place?"

"He knew you'd find the factory but not find a mine. That way, he figured he could justify not paying our success fee."

"But he paid it in the end, right?" asked Latviana.

"Oh yes. I have my ways," replied Laoban. Everyone nodded. They'd all experienced some of her ways.

Robert was the next to speak. "Hang on. His drug supplies that go to Nabmines. Don't they come from the underground factory that we found? Is it just that he didn't know where it was?"

Latviana replied. "No. The supplies that have been going to Nabmines come from a different factory. Somewhere in Namibia, but we don't know where. I'm not sure that Gideon knows himself. What we do know is that it belongs to the brother of the fake priest you met – what did he call himself, Reverend Father?"

"I not only met the owner of that other drug factory, but shared a hospital room with him," interjected Ronald. "Big, fat, smelly man. Thought I was *feelthy*? You'd have hated him, Laoban."

She shuddered. "He was the one who contracted Arbuthnot's Executive Assistant. We call him EA, correct?" Everyone nodded. "I'm speculating that he had Arbuthnot's contact details, and EA received the message and took on the job for himself. Looking for new customers, ones that would pay better."

Latviana took over. "What we've established is that EA contacted the Asian-Colombian cartel and convinced them to come to Africa for meetings."

"The same cartel that I contacted, using the same information that I'd remembered from some work I'd been sent when I was confined," added Ronald. "I got in touch with them when my clients in Luanda told me that their source of supply was drying up, and asked me to help look for a new one."

Laoban resumed. "The drugs hidden in Nabmines trucks crossed the frontier into Angola, and were removed at the processing plant and taken to this pharmaceutical company in Luanda. The one that Ronald was working for. They packed them up as if they were painkillers and exported them to Europe mixed up with all their other products."

"But I suppose it was Gideon who told the Luanda company that the supply was ending. Surely he was responsible for solving the problem?" inquired Humphry.

"I don't think he ever spoke to the pharma company in Luanda," said Latviana.

"He didn't," interrupted Ronald. "They found out from Nabmines. They were trying to solve the problem themselves."

"Meanwhile, Gideon was contracting us to find the competing mine so he could cut a deal with them and maintain the flow through the machinery he had put in place," said Laoban.

"Is that what he is now going to do?" asked Beatrix.

"I doubt he'll succeed. The Asian-Colombian entrepreneurs are greedy and want to take the entire production of both factories. Well, if the one that you spectacularly set fire to is back in operation."

There was silence for a little time. Then Beatrix asked Laoban, "How did you find Gideon in the first place? Did he contact you or did you contact him?"

"Maria here obtained a copy of Smith's, sorry Arbuthnot's, address book. Don't ask how. She and I simply called the numbers to see who they were and if we could do business. Gideon was one of them. When I went to see him, I knew nothing about his business or how he was involved with Smith. Just his name and number. I imagine that, if Smith, sorry Arbuthnot, had still been operating, he'd have got him to organise this mission. I just happened to call him at the right time."

"So Arbuthnot has been arrested and will be extradited to Angola?" asked Humphrey. "Do you think we can rely on him being out of circulation for a while? From what you've told me, I don't fancy working for him."

Ronald Jones replied. "I don't know, but my guess would be that he will be locked away for ages. I provided the Angolan police with all the information they need to connect him to a massive corruption scandal involving high-ranking ministers and international oil companies. He'll make a wonderful scapegoat." After a hesitation, adding "ha ha!" Nervous titters from Rob and Maria, even a grin from Laoban.

"What about EA?" asked Latviana.

"He's no threat to us," said Laoban confidently. "You saw that the moment he saw Smith, he tagged on to him. He's what you call a desk jockey, no experience in the field, which is why we never met him before."

"But now we know he has Smith's confidential phone or email. He probably has all his documents too," said Latviana. "We need to stay alert."

Laoban nodded. "Let's not worry about him now. Gideon has not only paid us, but we have a new project, too."

Bea grinned. "If Richard was here, he'd be cracking open the champagne right now!"

**The story continues in**
**Spies on the Silk Road, coming in 2024!**

# Thank You

I hope you have enjoyed reading this book. If so, please consider leaving a review, however brief, on Amazon or Goodreads. Reviews are critical to the success of any author, especially those without a big publishing house behind them.

Spies on Safari is the second in a series. The award-winning first book, The Repurposed Spy, is available from all booksellers.

For a free e-book copy of the prequel, The Apprentice Spy, subscribe to my newsletter at https://oliverdowson.com. Only free books, occasional newsletters and No Spam! – you can unsubscribe at any time.

**Oliver Dowson**
November 2023

# About the Author

Oliver Dowson was born in Lowestoft, England. After studying mathematics, statistics and computer science at university, he spent a long career building a multi-national business from scratch, exploiting his love of foreign travel, cultures, languages and food. He has visited – so far - 149 countries for business and pleasure – and tries to add at least another new one every year!

Oliver is no stranger to writing, having been editor of both Imperial College and University of London Union newspapers in his youth, and writing many articles throughout his business career. Trapped by the pandemic, he wrote his first book, a travelogue "There's No Business Like International Business", published in 2022. Now, Oliver has now turned to fiction, publishing "The Repurposed Spy" to critical acclaim. It won the BookFest 2023 Gold Award in the Thriller-Espionage category. Oliver is also a podcast host and mentors and supports several new young ambitious entrepreneurs. When he's not away adding new experiences further afield, he lives in North London and Oviedo Spain.

For more details and to stay in touch, see his website https://oliverdowson.com

# Also by the Author

**The Repurposed Spies series**
The Repurposed Spy – book 1 in the series
Spies on Safari – book 2

Other books
There's No Business Like International Business – a travelogue

Printed in Great Britain
by Amazon